The
Kahl'Nar
Saga
❖
Book I

the Awakening *of* Leeowyn Blake

The
Kahl'Nar
Saga
❖
Book I

the Awakening of Leeowyn Blake

MARY PARKER

WordCrafts

The Awakening of Leeowyn Blake is a work of fiction. All References to persons, places or events are fictitious or used fictitiously.

The Awakening of Leeowyn Blake
Copyright © 2010
Mary Parker

Cover concept and design by Mary Parker

Published by WordCrafts
Tullahoma, TN 37388
www.wordcrafts.net

For Mike and Paula
For Peach
For Bethany

Chapter 1

Why is it that I only ever want to buy sunglasses when it's autumn and the skies are in a perpetual state of overcast?

I know what you're thinking.

Couldn't I just save them? Wear them in the spring and summer? It's not like sunglasses have an expiration date. At least not in anything but fashion. Not that fashion has ever been on my Top Ten list of things that matter. Or even my Top Twenty.

I'm getting sidetracked.

The thing is, I only ever buy sunglasses in the fall because I'm desperately clinging to that last bit of summer. In the summer I can be a normal teenager. I can spend my days on the beach, hanging out with my friends, staying up way too late and sleeping until noon if I want.

I'm a normal teenager. I have a normal teenage life with normal teenage problems. The summer is my heaven.

I live with my mom during the summer months. We stay in her tiny condo in Jacksonville, Florida.

My parents split up when I was little. I'm not sure why. My mom never talks about it.

Whatever it was, it was bad enough to make my mom pack me up in the middle of the night when I was four years old and run to my Gran's condo.

My mom got the condo after Gran died. It's not like it was this big, grand vacation home; more like a little cottage. But it was enough for us. The first couple years were shaky, and there were more than a few times when the money just wasn't there, but mom never backed down or asked for help.

It was tough, but we made it through, and from that time on all I had known my entire life was beach life.

Until four years ago.

Until my uncle found me.

Apparently my dad's family had not been doing anything for the last ten years other than trying to find me.

My mom may be a bit scatter-brained, but when she sets her mind to something, she does it.

My mom had set her mind on us disappearing.

It was mid-November, the night of my fourteenth birthday. Mom had splurged on this huge monstrosity of a cake. We were sharing it when we heard a knock on the door. Mom answered it as I continued working on my third slice.

At first I thought it was just some pushy salesman. There seems to be lots of them in Jacksonville these days. I could hear muffled, angry words.

That struck me as odd, because my mom was never the type to be rude to anyone. She would be more likely to invite the salesmen in for a cool glass of lemonade and whatever store-bought baked goods she had on hand, even though she never bought anything from them.

"Your Gran would turn over in her grave if she knew I wasn't showing these people some real Southern hospitality," she always said when I got annoyed with her for constantly letting strangers into our house.

I didn't inherit my mom's patience. Nor her sense of Southern hospitality.

When I heard my mom starting to raise her voice I knew something was wrong. I was up and out of my chair in an instant.

I grabbed the first blunt object my hands came in contact with as I rounded the corner into the living room, wielding my mom's umbrella like it was a broadsword.

Points for trying, right?

"Look, Bud, if my mom doesn't want to buy anything, then she doesn't..."

My voice died in my throat.

Mom was crying, and shaking.

I had never seen such a sight. I mean, ever.

My mom just doesn't cry.

As shocked as I was by the sight of my mother in tears, I was more shocked by the man standing in the doorway.

He was at least six feet tall. His red hair was mussed out of place and he was wearing a well-tailored, three-piece suit, which made him look out of place.

I mean, this is Jacksonville. No one wears a suit in Jacksonville. Not unless they plan on sweating to death.

I noticed all of that in a moment, but none of that mattered once I saw his eyes.

He had my eyes.

I don't have normal green, blue, brown or even violet eyes.

I have tawny eyes; almost yellow, really.

My mom's eyes are the color of a calm sea, so I knew without asking that I got my eyes from my father.

And this man had my eyes.

"Dad?" I whispered.

The man half-smiled as he stepped into the living room.

My mom tensed and glowered at him.

"No, Leeowyn," the man said. "I am not your father. I am your uncle; your father's brother."

That stopped me in my tracks. I never knew my dad even had a brother.

Truth be told, I didn't know much of anything about my dad. The only thing of my father's that my mom kept when she left was his last name - Blake.

My mom and I pretended he didn't exist. It was like an unspoken rule between us.

I had always been curious about my father, but the few times I got up the nerve to ask about him, my mom got the saddest, far-off look in her eyes. She wouldn't say another word the rest of the day. I learned fast that it was an off-limits topic.

I tightened my grip on the umbrella.

The curiosity that I had kept on a tight leash my entire life began to gnaw against the restraint of my better judgment. My mom was still shaking and sobbing silently. It ripped my heart out to see her like that.

The man in the doorway – my uncle; my father's brother - was the reason. If he had only been within reach of my umbrella I would have... but no such luck.

"Your father is dead," he said.

I cast a sideways glance at my mom.

Not even a flinch from her.

Not a flinch from me, either.

It's not that I'm a cold person, but hey, you can't miss someone you've never known, right?

"Oh," I said.

The man in the doorway - my uncle; my father's brother - continued staring at me with those yellow eyes like he was waiting for some kind of reaction.

"Um...that's real sad," I managed. I was starting to feel really uncomfortable.

He just continued staring at me. I suppose he was hoping for a more stereotypical response to the news of the death of one's father.

He didn't get it.

He shrugged, walked uninvited into the room, turned and sat himself down on our faded blue couch, looking terribly out of place with his crisp suit and somber expression.

I finally relinquished my grip on the umbrella and tossed it down on a side table. I looked at Mom for some indication of what I should do next, but she looked as lost as I felt. After a few more nonresponsive moments, I slowly sat in a chair across from the stranger intruding in my living room and my life.

The silence in the room was as thick as a late-April thunderstorm that refused to break, crackling with pent up electricity, gagging the thunder that wrestled to break free.

It scared me.

It thrilled me.

"On his deathbed your father made me swear that I would find you," my father's brother finally said. He paid no mind to my mom who looked as if she were about two seconds away from jumping up and driving the umbrella through his heart.

"You have a right to know who you are. You have a right to know your father's family. It is a right your mother stole from you."

"Okay, hold it!" I exploded out of my chair and into his face.

Something inside me snapped. I stormed towards him with balled fists. Not that I expected to do much with them. It's not like I have a black belt in karate or jujitsu or anything. But no one insults my mom. Not to my face. I was fiercely loyal to my family and she was the only family I had. At least she was until this guy showed up.

"No one talks about my mom like that! She has stolen nothing from me. She has sacrificed everything to make sure I have a good life!"

My uncle held up his hands in mock self-defense. The expression on his face clearly stated that he was trying to appease a cranky, ill-mannered child.

"Your mother sacrificed for herself, Leeowyn, not for you. She was selfish."

He spoke as if my mom wasn't two feet away from him. I couldn't believe she wasn't snapping him in two right then. She was not the type of woman to take disrespect lying down.

"Please, sit down," my uncle said. "Give me a chance to explain."

His voice softened. The compelling look in his yellow eyes made me swallow the quick retort that had leapt to my tongue. It was the same look I always saw in my mom's eyes when she looked at me; like I was a hidden treasure, and only she knew my worth.

It was creepy.

"I'm sorry, but we're in the middle of a birthday party."

My mom had finally found her voice, snapping me out of my state of confusion. The cake in the kitchen was long forgotten and I had no desire to revisit it. My party was the last thing on my mind at the moment.

I disliked this man for the way he talked to my mom. Yet even though he was a complete stranger, his presence pulled at me, taunting my curiosity like raw meat dangling in front of a lion's cage.

All my life I had lived without a father. I squashed all my questions out of respect for my mom. Now I had a chance to get some answers. Was I really going to pass that up?

"Mom..."

I turned my face toward my mom, knowing what I was about to do would betray everything she had ever done for me.

"I'll be back in an hour."

Chapter 2

I walked towards the door; the stranger - my uncle, my father's brother - followed me.

I expected some kind of outburst. I expected my mom to forbid me to go. I expected...something. What I didn't expect was the complete and absolute silence. She wouldn't even look at me.

It killed me to see my mom like that, but I had to know. I stepped out the door without looking back.

I had no idea what I was getting myself in to.

We lived right next to the beach, so my feet led me there without even thinking. We walked in silence, my uncle and I. I tried to think of something witty to say, but how do you start a conversation after something like that?

"Sorry my mom kidnapped me from your brother and hid me so well for the past ten years," I blurted out. "Do you think it would be okay if you just kind of forgot that?"

Silence.

Well, that went over well.

We continued walking over the moonlit beach while my mind sorted through the various phrases I could say to cut the tension. I risked a glance at him, and then burst out laughing.

He paused and cocked an eye at me.

"I'm sorry," I breathed between fits of laughter. "You just look so out of place in those clothes."

I stifled a chuckle and managed to get myself under control.

"I thought I was dressed quite nicely," he commented, giving himself a quick once over.

Oh great, not even ten minutes in and I've offended him.

"No, no. You...you are dressed very well. Just not for the beach, you know?" I stammered, wondering if there was any way I could possibly make even more of a fool of myself.

"Ah."

He started walking again.

"We don't have beaches where I'm from."

He looked out over the ocean, breathed in the sharp salt air. A look that was something akin to awe crossed his eyes. I knew the feeling. I got it whenever I took the time to actually contemplate the vastness of the ocean.

I wanted to ask him where he was from. If it was the same place I was from. If it was the same place my father was from. But I didn't want to mess up this conversation any more than I already had.

Instead of talking, I decided to sit down and let him take it from here. He had sought me out, after all. There must be something he wanted to say.

The ocean usually calmed me down. Whenever I was going through some emotional upheaval thing, I would walk down this beach, watch the waves break on the shore, and let the vastness of the universe put my petty problems into perspective.

The ocean's usual hypnotic effect wasn't working on me today. My mind was racing too fast, in too many directions, to be taken in by the soothing sounds of the surf on the beach.

He chose not to sit down on the beach; probably didn't want to mess up that nice, three-piece he was wearing.

"I'm here to take you back, Leeowyn."

My uncle's flat declaration cut the silence like a meat cleaver.

I didn't look at him.

I'm not sure what I had expected from this conversation. My mind wasn't really ready to take in anything he was saying.

"You have a right to..." he started, but I held up my hand, cutting him off in mid-sentence. He seemed a little bemused by my sudden demanding action after all my ungraceful attempts at civility.

"Look, I'm sure that my dad wasn't exactly thrilled at what my mom did – stealing me away, and all. But no matter what you say, I know she did it out of love for me."

He opened his mouth to continue, but I held up both hands and added my patented glare to stop him again. I'm sure I looked ridiculous, but no more ridiculous than a guy in a suit on a beach in Florida.

"I don't know why my mom felt like she had to steal me away. She never talks about it and I've learned not to ask. It doesn't really matter. What's done is done."

I softened my voice, "Regardless of why my mother did what she thought she had to...   I agree with you."

Those last words tasted a lot like betrayal.

"I'm not going to lie and tell you that a day hasn't gone by that I haven't wondered what it would be like to have a father," I said, the words spilling out of their own volition.

"Quite honestly, months at a time have gone by without me even thinking about having a father."

My words trailed off. I stared out over the ocean again, wishing it would work its familiar magic and still my racing mind.

"Recently, I've awakened in the middle of the night. It's happened several times. Not startled awake, like you see in movies. Nothing so dramatic. Just, one second I was asleep, and the next I was standing at my window looking out. In those moments, I had this intense…longing. I'm not sure for what or who. Just a feeling like there was a part of me that was missing. I don't know why I'm telling you this. I've never mentioned it to anyone before; not even my mom. Because I knew that the part of me that was missing was the part of me that was my father's."

I looked up at him as I said this, trying to gauge his reaction in those yellow eyes of his.

Slowly, he lowered himself down and sat beside me. It may have been meaningless to anyone else, but I could see a peace treaty in the gesture.

He may as well have said, "You give me a chance, and I'll stop hating your mom."

We sat in silence for a few minutes, interrupted only by the sound of the ocean. Even the gulls seemed to be giving us some space. I absentmindedly began digging my toes in the sand, watching as little grooves followed the motion of my toes.

"You like the ocean."

His comment was an awkward attempt at making conversation.

I nodded. I didn't think he really expected me to reply, but I didn't want to seem rude.

"I have a proposition," he stated.

"Nice transition," I said. I tilted my head and looked at him, waiting.

He merely stared at me.

"You look so much like him, you know?"

He brushed a strand of my deep auburn hair behind my ears.

"Yeah? Well, I mean, I guess so," I murmured. "My mom never talked about my dad. I never found any pictures of him around the house. But I assumed I must look something like him, what with mom being all blonde hair and green eyes and all. She was always able to get this great tan if she even thought about going out in the sun, while I just burn. With this hair, my pale skin and these eyes, I kind of figured I got my looks from my dad."

I scooped up a pile of sand and let it sift through my fingers. I always needed something to do with my restless hands.

"Seeing you confirmed my suspicions, though. Red hair, yellow eyes, pale skin. Doesn't take a rocket scientist, you know?"

I stood up and dusted myself off before offering him my hand.

"By the way, we haven't really been properly introduced. I'm Leeowyn. Leeowyn Blake. My friends just call me Lee. It's easier to remember."

I knew that he already knew my name, but giving it to him seemed to somehow make our meeting a bit more civil. And I still didn't know his name.

"I'm Cyle," he replied as he took my hand. "Cyle Blake, with a C. And my friends call me Cyle." He smiled at his own joke.

"Nice to meet you, Cyle, with a C."

We shook hand, a truce of sorts.

"So, what's this proposition?" I asked.

Chapter 3

A cool ocean breeze danced across my skin as I walked back to my house, bringing with it the familiar, briny scent of salt water. I stopped outside of the faded green steps that led up to my front door. I couldn't make myself go up those steps.

For as long as I could remember my mom had been my whole world. There was nothing she wouldn't do, wouldn't sacrifice to keep me happy; to keep me safe. Once I walked up those steps and through that door, I would be throwing that all away.

Cyle asked if he could walk me home. I assured him that as nice a gesture as it was, it would hurt more than help. This was something I had to do myself.

I took a deep breath, closed my eyes, and tried to let the comforting scent of the ocean calm my frazzled nerves.

No use. It wasn't working.

"Here goes nothing." I muttered, taking the stairs two at a time.

Treat it like a band-aid, one quick motion.

I took one more deep breath before opening the door. Any courage I had built up instantly went down the drain when I saw my mom, sitting near the window in her old wicker chair, looking at her favorite picture of me.

I knew that picture well. She had taken it with the first camera she could afford to buy after she left my father.

I was eight years old and covered in ice cream. We couldn't afford ice cream very often back then, so when mom bought a carton of Death by Chocolate, it was a treat. I'm not known for my willpower when it comes to stuff I like, and I really liked Death by Chocolate ice cream when I was eight years old. I still do.

When my mom got home from the store with her brand new camera, the first thing she saw was the freezer door open and an entire tub of Death by Chocolate ice cream melted all over the floor and myself.

I had expected her to be furious. Instead she just pulled out that camera and snapped a picture. That photo was like a beacon to her. It was a reminder that no matter how hard things got she could always make me happy. She looked at it when she was feeling low.

Well, crap.

"Hi mom," I said quietly, shutting the door behind me with a soft click.

"Mom, I have something to tell you."

I walked over and sat down in the chair next to her, reached out and took the picture away, and then took her hands in mine.

"I know," she said.

She was smiling at me, but the smile didn't reach her eyes like it always did. It wasn't a warm, momma smile. It was a sad, I'm-losing-you kind of smile.

"I knew the moment Cyle walked through that door that you were leaving me."

"No, mom! I'm not leaving you!" I lied.

She shook her head, still smiling sadly.

"You've always been so much like him."

She reached over and stroked my hair, holding a strand between her fingers for a moment before pushing it behind my ear.

"I've kept you safe for so long, shielding you from anything that might harm you."

"I know, and I'm a horrible daughter..." I began, but she put a finger to my lips, hushing me like she did when I had come crying to her as a child every time I did something wrong. I was never able to keep anything from her for long, and it always tore me up inside when I hurt her.

"I shielded you from everything, because I was afraid," she continued, caressing my hands in hers. "But you are so much like him. Everyday I see him in you, more and more. I've guarded you too much, Lee. You are his daughter just as much as you are mine. You deserve to know his life; his family."

I sat speechless. My mom rarely said anything about my father or his family, and when she did, it was something bad. Where had this come from, this open acceptance of all things *Dad*?

I pulled back and held her at arms length.

"Mom, are you sure you're okay with this?" I asked, waiting for the bear trap to snap shut on me.

She nodded, this time the smile reaching her eyes.

"Oh darling, I knew this day was going to come. I've always known. I've been preparing myself for it. I just hoped it wouldn't come this soon."

She patted my cheek as she stood up. I watched her leave the room, stunned. I sat there staring out the window, for how long I have no idea.

There was a soft rap on the door. I didn't have to open it to know it was my Uncle Cyle standing outside, waiting.

I walked out to the front porch.

"How did she take it?" he asked.

I turned and looked over my shoulder to make sure she hadn't walked back in the room.

"Pretty well, all things considered," I said. "Really well. Too well."

I turned back and searched his face for answers to questions I didn't even know how to ask.

"I was expecting tears, and rage, and forbidding. What I got was...not my mom."

I hugged myself as I leaned against the doorframe, feeling suddenly very alone.

"Your mother has just finally accepted the inevitable," Cyle said, giving me a reassuring smile.

I nodded and shrugged. His answer didn't make me feel any better.

"Don't worry too much about it, Lee," he said as he turned to go.

"Wait!" I said, rushing down the stairs to him. "So, what happens next? Will I hear from you? Don't you need my phone number...or something?"

He smiled and pulled me into a quick, fatherly sort of hug.

"Like I said, Lee, don't worry about it." He let go and walked away.

"Just be packed and ready to leave by the first week in September," he called over his shoulder.

"September? But it's November. September isn't for another year!" I shouted to his rapidly receding backside.

My uncle, my father's brother, just waved at me over his shoulder and kept on walking until he was swallowed by the night. He could have been a figment of my imagination for all the evidence I had of his existence.

I let out a confused huff, turned and stomped into my house, up to my bedroom, popped open my

laptop, pulled up the calendar and scrolled to *September* of the next year. Clicking the *New Event* icon, I typed the words, *My Life Changes.*
    I had no idea how right I was.

Chapter 4

Cyle frowned as he continued down the boardwalk, uncharacteristically muttering to no one in particular.

He had been careless with the girl. Careless with her mother. He had underestimated just how much Leeowyn might care about her mother. It was a stupid mistake. A dangerous mistake. He couldn't afford to be that careless again. They needed Lee too much.

He berated himself for the thousandth time for not finding her sooner. There were only four years left before her eighteenth birthday. Four short years; and there was so much she needed to learn. He couldn't tell if she was even strong enough. There was simply no way to tell at this late stage. All he could do was hope.

An older woman wearing a full-length black cloak fell into place beside him, keeping pace with him. Cyle gave her a quick, acknowledging nod, and the pair walked on in silence.

A few passers-by stared openly at the older woman's striking appearance. Jacksonville was not known for people who wore full-length black cloaks. A stern glare from the woman was all it took send the curious scurrying to the other side of the street.

"How is she?" The woman asked finally, her voice as frigid as her gaze.

"She's everything we expected." Cyle answered. "She's a lot like him. I just wish we had more time."

The woman patted his arm lightly.

"We all do, Son." She said. "We all do. But it can't be helped. Time does not stand still in any of the seven realms. We'll just have to make do with the time we have. If she's as much like him as you say, she'll do just fine."

"She has to." Cyle stopped, turned and stared back at the light that still glowed in Leeowyn's window. "Because if she can't...God help us."

Chapter 5

"Lee!" Cyle shouted from the curb.

I jumped back to awareness. I had spaced out by the sunglasses booth, lost in the endless variety of tinted shades. I handed the man behind the counter a twenty and waited while he made change. I had just scored the best knock-off pair of designer shades that money could buy. At least I'm pretty sure they were knock-offs, or counterfeit. No designer I knew sold their sunglasses for twelve bucks from a corner street vendor in Jacksonville, Florida.

I shoved my change into my purse, grabbed my bag, and skipped over to where Cyle was waiting with a good deal less patience than he needed when dealing with at 17-year-old girl.

Winter was approaching again, and I was going into my fourth season of staying with Cyle. It was strange, even though I had technically spent less than two full years all total with Cyle, I felt as if I had known him my entire life.

"You need to be more aware of the world around you," Cyle chided me as he took my bag and stowed it away in the trunk of the luxury sedan.

It had taken me my entire first season with my uncle's family, and a good deal of the second, to get used to the vast wealth on my dad's side of the family. My mom had certainly never mentioned anything about them being loaded. As much as she struggled in those early years, she must have really had some powerful reason to leave without even asking for child support.

"Sorry."

I gave him a quick peck on the cheek.

"I was busy thinking about the first time we met. Shotgun!"

I plopped into the passenger's seat. I don't know why I always called out 'Shotgun!' It's not like anyone else ever made the trip with us.

I put the newest addition to my sunglasses collection on my face and studied myself in the mirror that was cleverly fitted into the sun visor.

Cyle just rolled his eyes, started the engine, and pulled the sedan into traffic.

"I'm going to do it this year, Cyle," I declared. "I'm going to stay awake on the ride to your house."

I opened my purse, revealing a super-sized stash of Red Bull. The last three times I had made this trip, I found it impossible to stay awake the entire ride. No matter what I did, I always seemed to fall asleep before we even crossed the state line out of Florida.

It wouldn't be that big of a problem if I just knew where we were going. But it was all some big mystery.

I felt like a mushroom; kept in the dark and fed...well...you know.

Ew.

I shuddered as I grossed myself out.

When I visited my father's side of the family, no matter how many times or how nicely I asked, they never revealed the location of their home. They would say something about security, and how it's for my own good, and yada, yada; blah, blah.

I guess sometimes being rich isn't all it's cracked up to be. Not if you have to hide from the world.

I was suspicious that first year. Maybe even a little scared. I decided I could figure it out on my own. I was pretty good at digging out whatever information I wanted on the Internet.

Easier said than done. The only computer in the house was mine, but there was no Internet connection to be found. My cell phone got no bars no matter where I went in the house.

It was like living on some desert island. A very well appointed desert island, but a desert island, nonetheless.

I never asked my mom about it. I was pretty sure she knew exactly where I was going every winter, since she apparently ran way from it. But still, I couldn't bring myself to ask her.

When we were together during the summer months we both pretended that nothing had happened, and life went on exactly as it always had. But each year as September drew closer I could see the sorrow churning just beneath my mom's eyes.

My mom had always put my happiness above everything else as far back as I could remember. I was determined to do the same for her, now. So, I never told her about anything that disturbed me when I lived with my father's family. I never told her how little they told me, or how much they kept from me. She would only worry.

I didn't want her to worry.

Okay. I admit it. I also knew if she knew how much I was keeping from her about what they were keeping from me, she would start freaking out and demand I stay home in Florida.

And I didn't want to stay home. In Florida.

But I can still pretend I was doing it 100% for her.

The only thing I knew about Cyle's house was that it wasn't really Cyle's house, a fact that he constantly reminded me of anytime I referred it as 'Cyle's house.' I continued to refer to it as 'Cyle's house' out of some perverse sense of rebellion.

Cyle's house was actually the Blake family estate, and as near as I could figure out, it belonged to his mother – my grandmother.

Cyle's house was a huge Victorian-style mansion that could have fit our little Florida condo into its 'Parlor.' On the outside it looked exactly like something you would see in a black and white horror film. Faded black stones surrounded the numerous windows that stared at you as if the house were a many-eyed monster.

Chimneys and turrets poked out, complete with stone gargoyles that spewed water when it rained. Thick, dark ivy tried for a stranglehold on the house. And, of course, it was surrounded by the thickest, darkest woods I had ever seen.

Any thoughts I might have of exploring those creepy woods was quickly squashed by Cyle. On my very first night at Cyle's house, he informed me that I was forbidden to ever step foot in those woods.

No big deal. I could obey the rules. I was never a particularly rebellious child. Well, not over anything important. If Cyle wanted me to keep out of the woods, I could keep out of the woods. There was nothing in those woods I had any interest in seeing.

Besides, there were some really strange noises that came from those woods at night. I'm not sure how to describe them, but hearing them made me feel like a child, quivering under my covers as my imagination ran wild.

No, I'm good leaving the woods to themselves.

But I digress.

Cyle glanced at my bag of energy drinks and gave me one of his half smiles. Just the corners of his mouth would turn up and the ridges around his eyes would wrinkle a bit. I had come to recognize it as his way of laughing when I did something that he found amusing...or stupid.

"Come on, Uncle Cyle!" I joked, knowing he hated when I called him *Uncle*, apparently it made him feel old. "Have a little faith in me."

I cracked open the first of many drinks.

"I have nothing but faith in you," Cyle said quietly in a voice that made me pause, with the can of Red Bull half way to my lips.

I pulled my sunglasses off and stared at him, trying to decipher what was behind that comment. I had come to know Cyle pretty well over the past three years. At least as well as he would let me get to know him.

Cyle Blake was a somber man, but that did not mean he was unhappy or cruel; just...guarded.

He noticed my stare and it seemed to make him uncomfortable somehow.

"Stop trying to read my thoughts, Lee."

I was always able to tell when he was keeping something from me, even if I never could figure out what it was.

"Put your sunglasses back on and start moaning about how much you are dreading the coming months like you always do," he said.

"Cyle! I don't dread these months," I said, taking a big gulp from my Red Bull. "I just miss the beach when I'm away from it. And I miss my mom."

I looked down at the half-empty can in my hand and couldn't see it as half-full.

"I just wish the people at your house would be honest with me," I muttered under my breath.

I glanced at him again, this time through the corner of my eyes, expecting him to protest, swearing that he always told me the truth, the whole truth, and nothing but the truth.

Instead, he just continued to stare dead ahead at the road in front of us.

"Fine," I said, sucking down the remainder of the energy drink in a single swallow. "Keep your secrets."

I set the empty can in the cup holder where its constant metallic rattle was sure to irritate Cyle, and slipped my earbuds in.

Cyle wasn't one to crank up the tunes while he drove down the road. I, on the other hand, preferred to let the music take me away on long, boring road trips.

I leaned my head back and turned up the volume, hoping the pulsating beat would keep me awake. The sign flashing past said the state line was only 59 miles.

I didn't even notice when my eyes closed.

Chapter 6

The forest was deep and dark. Mist collecting around my feet. Cold bit at my bare legs like a ravenous dog. I wrapped my arms around myself, trying to generate some warmth, and shivered as I plunged through the woods, tears streaking down my face. My heart was racing.

"This isn't real. They're lying."

I kept repeating it to myself as if repeating it would make it true. My feet were cut and bruised from forging through the woods without shoes. I paused a moment, considering going back and gathering my things.

Shoes. Shoes would be good right now.

Pausing was a mistake.

I heard it. The low rumbling sound could only be the growl of some wild beast that inhabited these woods.

My heart sped up. My mind screamed at me to run. Run! But I was frozen.

A branch snapped behind me. I could feel its hot breath on my neck.

The car door slammed and I almost screamed. I jerked upright in the passenger's seat, my hand at my throat, searching for Cyle.

The next moment my door opened and Cyle was standing there, extending his hand to me. My mind finally caught up with my body as I realized that we had reached our destination.

"I fell asleep. Again."

I was all too aware of his familiar half smile.

"Better luck next year," he said.

I stepped out of the car, batting his hand away. I was grouchy because he hadn't awakened me.

Not that I thought he would. Not that he ever had. He seemed to take pleasure in proving me wrong.

I grabbed my purse and slung it over my shoulder as I slammed the car door with more force than was absolutely necessary.

It was a childish gesture. I knew it. I wasn't even all that mad that I had fallen asleep. But that dream had me on edge.

It *was* a dream.

Still, I couldn't shake the feeling that dream had left me with. It was so real. I could still feel the cold digging into my skin. I could still feel the hot breath of that beast behind me.

I shivered at the thought.

Cyle paused, noticing my shiver.

Cyle didn't ask a lot of questions. He knew if I had something on my mind, something that was really bothering me, I would tell him. But if I didn't offer the information, he didn't pry.

I liked that about Cyle.

He seemed to know that I liked that about him.

He waited a brief moment, sensing I wanted to tell him something. I just stood there in the gravel driveway, looking out at the deep, dark woods that surrounded that great, big house that belonged to my father's family.

Cyle nodded.

"Come on, your Grandmother is making dinner."

I had been a little confused when I found out that Grandmother did some of the cooking. I had assumed that with a house this big, there would be an arsenal of servants and cooks to do everything for you, but apparently Grandmother insisted on doing most everything herself.

Probably something about wanting it done right the first time.

Cyle picked up my one bag and walked toward the house. I took a deep breath.

"It *was* only a dream," I whispered to no one at all before rushing to follow him inside.

My Grandmother was a tall, slender woman. Her name was Josephine, although I had been instructed upon meeting her to only ever call her, *Grandmother.*

She was to be called Grandmother. Not Grandma, Gran, MawMaw, Nanny, Grannie, or any other derivative. And she was certainly never to be addressed by her Christian name by a person of my age.

I had smiled the first time I heard her name and compared her to Jo from *Little Women.* I tried imagining my Grandmother cutting off her hair and acting very unlady-like indeed. It was a ridiculous image, but one I always thought about whenever I saw her.

Her silvery hair was always pulled back in a tight bun. Her eyes - golden-yellow, like Cyle's; tawny, like mine - were just as sharp as if she was a woman half her age.

She always wore long, formal dresses that started at her neck and extended all the way down to the floor, revealing nothing but the tips of her shoes. She was stern and never joked.

At least not in my hearing.

And she believed in formality.

She had the same guarded air around her that Cyle had. I figured it must run in the family, and wondered if my dad had been as distant. And if he was, what did my mom - who was always so vivacious and outgoing - ever see in him?

The only time I ever saw my grandmother display any significant maternal emotion was one night when I happened to be walking by her room. I saw her holding an old photograph as a stream of tears dripped down her face. She didn't even bother to wipe them away, as if she was unaware that they were even there.

I never asked her about it. But it made me like her more, knowing that she was human; knowing that she had her weak moments like everyone else.

I came back to the present as she greeted me at the front door like she always did, with a curt nod.

"Leeowyn. Welcome."

She insisted on calling me by my full name, even though I had begged her to just call me Lee.

"Nonsense," she had said. "Names have power, Child. I refuse to be the one to take power from you."

She was a great one for saying cryptic things like that.

I never questioned her about it. I had learned long ago that my questions rarely earned a straight answer around here. I felt like a little kid asking where babies come from, with all the adults answering every question but the one I asked.

I resigned myself to hearing her call me "Leeowyn," knowing it was a losing battle to try and change my grandmother. It would have been like trying to make an oak bend in half by sheer force of will.

I walked up to her and gave her a quick hug, which she warmly returned. For all my grandmother's curt words and strict rules, I could tell she loved me, even though I suspected I wasn't quite what she hoped I would be.

I walked into the grand foyer and paused to wave at Reynolds, the butler. He was the only servant in the whole house.

I often wondered if Reynolds ever slept. The house was always spotless, the food was always hot and served on time, and the grounds were always beyond reproach. He was the only help Grandmother ever seemed to want, or allow.

Reynolds wasn't much of a talker. At least he didn't talk to me very much. I often wondered if Cyle and Grandmother forbade it, because whenever he did talk to me, he would always say the strangest things.

Half the time I couldn't understand what he was talking about. It was almost as if he was speaking another language; similar but different, like talking to someone from England or Australia.

Sometimes, though, he would speak of my father.

"You look so like him, you know," he said one winter night last year.

I was curled up next to the giant window in my room. It was snowing outside. Having been raised in Florida I don't recall ever having seen snow until the first year I came here. I loved to lean my forehead against the cool glass of the window.

It never failed that the first snowfall was at night, and they had to all but chain me to a chair to keep me from running out in it. I wasn't allowed outside after dark.

"Hmm?" I mumbled. I hadn't been paying attention. Reynolds looked up from the fire he was tending and I swear I saw his eyes flash silver. I blinked several times, rubbing my eyes, and when I looked back at him the effect was gone.

"Your father. You look exactly like him."

He walked over to me and cupped my face in his hands. Then he just stood there and inhaled, his eyes closed. I froze, unsure of what was going on, but I was afraid if I moved he wouldn't tell me more.

Even though Cyle had searched the world to find me at my father's request, no one here would tell me anything about him.

I knew that I looked a great deal like him.

I knew that he had loved my mother and me very much, and it almost killed him when he woke up to find us gone.

Beyond that I never found out anything.

After another moment or two, Reynolds finally opened his eyes, a wry smile playing across his face.

"Yes," he mumbled, patting my head as if he were soothing a fussy toddler. "You'll do just fine."

He turned and walked toward the door to leave. I started to call after him, but he turned around and placed his finger to his lips.

"Shh," he said. "It'll just be our secret."

He turned and left, and never mentioned it again.

I stayed up the rest of the night trying to puzzle out what he meant. How was I like my father? What would I do "just fine" at? What secret were we supposed to be sharing?

I wondered if I had really just imagined the silver sparkling in his eyes.

Chapter 7

I ran up the staircase that stood at the back of the foyer. It looked exactly like the kind I had seen in movies, with plush, red carpet and gilt with antique gold on the railing and banister. It split halfway up, and both sides curled around and attached to the second floor.

I chose the right side and skipped the steps two at a time. I turned right again and walked down the long hallway that circled the entire second story.

My room was at the very back of the house, which meant I had a long way to walk to get there.

I had expected the house to confuse me the first time I stayed here, but it never did. I almost felt like I had lived here my entire life.

It sometimes scared me how little I was bothered by this sudden intrusion on my life. It never occurred to me to hate being dragged away from my school, my friends or my mom. Of course I missed my old life, my *normal* life, but it just felt so...right...to be here.

I trailed my hand along the wall, letting it run over whatever wall hanging or portrait happened to occupy that bit of wall space. The house reminded me of a penthouse from the 1920s; like something you would see in an old gangster flick.

My first year here I had spent a good deal of time tilting pictures and pulling on candlesticks, trying to find some secret passage to a speakeasy or something equally as crazy, like Dr. Frankenstein's laboratory or something. I don't know.

I paused only a moment in front of the giant, oak double doors that led to my room. I grabbed the brass handle that was shaped to look like a leopard about to pounce and pulled the doors open.

It was exactly as it had been when I left it to return to Florida last spring. Well, almost exactly. I was not the housekeeper that Reynolds is, so my room was a little bit messy at times. At least when I occupied it. Can I help it if I like a room to have that 'lived-in' look?

Now my room was spotless, of course.

Reynolds, no doubt, had been here.

When I showed up that first year, my Grandmother had tried to stick me in a much larger room, closer to the front of the house. I instantly asked for a smaller room.

I never brought much besides clothes with me, so I only ever brought one suitcase. There was no reason I needed a bedroom the size of my mom's condo. I don't know what the opposite of claustrophobic is, but that room made me feel that way. Besides, I liked the solitude of this one better.

My room was the only place in the house that didn't look like it was stuck in the distant past. Cyle told me I could make myself at home, so I did. I painted the walls a bright green.

My Grandmother had pursed her lips at that, but she never said anything about it.

I had to lock Reynolds out of my room to keep him from trying to take the job from me. Truth be told, he probably would have done a much better job of it than I did. He probably wouldn't have spilled and spattered as much paint on the floor as I did.

But I like my room a little messy. It reminds me of my life.

Besides, I like to paint.

Besides the green walls, and partially green floor, my room had a combination desk and bookshelf. It was already stocked full with every book I had at home.

I was shocked to find that Cyle had asked my mom what I liked to read and she had given him a list of my entire book collection.

I didn't even know they talked to each other.

Having my books there did make me feel a little more at home.

Cyle was always doing little things like that. There was an oversized, antique dresser and a gianormous walk-in closet, which was a complete waste of space since all of my clothes didn't even come close to filling the dresser.

"If you wore dresses more often, you would have need for more room for hanging things up," my grandmother had commented, sniffing ever so slightly. I came to recognize that sniff as her sign that she disapproved of something, without actually flat out saying that she disapproved.

I had just smiled and shrugged. I was a jeans and T-shirt kind of girl. Forget the lace and pearls and stiletto heals. Converse and cotton were good enough for me.

I grabbed all my toiletries and walked into the adjoining bathroom, once again feeling dwarfed by the sheer size of everything. Besides having a giant mirror that looked to be made from crystal, set above double sinks, there was a linen closet that was full of giant, fluffy white towels. They were even bigger than beach towels. I heard my mom called them bath sheets.

One look and it was obvious I had no need of the toiletries I had brought. All the shampoo, cream rinse, lotions, cosmetics and stuff I would ever need were neatly arranged on a shelf in the closet.

For all the old-fashioned décor, the house had some ultra modern amenities. My bathroom had a shower that doubled as a sauna, and a Jacuzzi bathtub that was big enough for me to lie down completely in and not touch either end. I could swim in that thing.

Not that I'm complaining. I'm a girl. I love soaking in a hot bath. And no matter how long I stayed in the shower, this place never seemed to run out of hot water.

I could definitely get used to that bathroom.

Reynolds brought my bag up and deposited it in the middle of the floor. He tried to unpack for me, but I shooed him away.

I could unpack my own stuff, and I didn't like people going through my clothes. Just the thought of it creeped me out.

After I put my things away, I walked to the window, grabbed the cord and gave it a good yank. The drapes drew back revealing the backyard.

I often wondered how the yard would look during the spring or the summer. It was always autumn when I came. All the vegetation was already well on its way to its winter state. Only the evergreens provided any relief from the dreary grays.

We didn't have much of an autumn in Jacksonville. While I liked the change of the seasons here, I never quite got used to the continual lack of color in the landscape. I could just imagine the trees in full bloom; the withered bushes that surrounded the house bright and lively.

Still, as much as I would have loved to see this house during the summer, I could never bring myself to ask.

Yes, it felt right being here but, by the time spring rolled around, I was always ready to go home. I mean, to go to my mom's house.

I wasn't really sure where *home* was anymore.

I had friends back in Jacksonville, but I always missed my mom desperately.

It was so strange, almost like I was two people; my summer self and my winter self.

My winter self fit in here, as if I had lived here all my life.

But my summer self ached for the beach, the heat, the ocean.

Perhaps that is why I always bought sunglasses before I came here each autumn; as if my summer self was yelling, "Hey! Don't forget about me!"

I can't say I didn't feel a little like Persephone, dragged away from her mother every winter. Not that I ever equated Cyle with the ruler of the Underworld, and this house was far from Hades.

My thoughts continued to churn as I stared out over the back lawn. That's when I saw Cyle walk out the backdoor, accompanied by a man I had never seen before. I leaned over to get a better look.

"Lee! You're here!"

Chapter 8

A bundle of pure energy and excitement burst into my room, threw itself at me, and caught me in a strangling, bear hug.

"Hey, Peach," I gasped when I was finally able to untangle myself from her arms. I returned the hug with just as much enthusiasm.

Peach was my best friend.

Before my arrival on my first visit here, I had been a little depressed at the thought of spending all of fall and winter stuck in a giant house with nobody but Cyle and my Grandmother to talk to. You can't really count Reynolds, since he rarely talked to anybody. I was too afraid to voice this fear to Cyle, though. I thought he might take it the wrong way.

I soon found out I had no need to worry. I met Peach on my first day here.

She has greeted me in much the same manner every autumn, although I usually never made it out of the car before that bundle of energy collided with me and tried to squeeze the life out of me.

I can't say I wasn't just a tad freaked out at that first meeting.

"Hi! I'm Peach! You're Lee!" she had bubbled.

My Grandmother walked up behind her and put a steadying hand on her shoulder.

"Leeowyn, this young lady, though she may sometimes forget that *is* what she is, is Perennial," my Grandmother said, giving Peach's shoulder a firm squeeze.

Peach rolled her eyes.

"Miss Josephine insists on calling me by my real name," Peach laughed. "Everyone else just calls me Peach."

"Names have power, child..."

"I know, Miss Josephine," Peach interrupted. "You refuse to be the one to steal my power."

"Take, Perennial. Not steal," my grandmother corrected her. "Some day I may decide to take your power, but I would never steal it."

"Sorry, Miss Josephine," Peach giggled. "*Take*, then."

My Grandmother greeted me with a brief hug before excusing herself. This had not been our first encounter. I had met her a few times before when she came with Cyle to visit me at my home in Jacksonville.

Those meetings had been tense, to say the least. My mom and grandmother pretty much pretended the other didn't exist. I don't think they said two words to each other.

"Perennial? Like flowers that don't die?" I asked as I walked into the house next to her.

Peach was unlike any girl I had ever met. Her hair was a shade of dark brown that was hard to categorize. One moment it looked as dark as midnight, but it shown like gold whenever the sunlight hit it. Her eyes were a sparkling emerald green.

Peach was shorter than me, and tiny to the point that she looked fragile. When she walked, it was as if her body couldn't be contained to something as mundane as walking.

She was wearing a flowing dress that swirled and floated around her as if she was under water.

Perennial fit.

She looked exactly like a delicate flower.

I liked her instantly.

"Yeah, my mom had a thing for flowers," she laughed.

I wondered if she found the whole world and everything in it funny.

She all but danced around me while I strolled at a slower pace toward the house. I noticed she talked about her mom in the past tense. I didn't mention it, though. I didn't really know her yet, and didn't think it would be polite.

"Anyways, call me Peach. Everyone does. Well, everyone but your Grandmother, who doesn't want to *take my power.*"

She said it like there were quotation marks around it.

Peach took it upon herself to give me the grand tour. She chattered as we explored room after room. She seemed to be pretty comfortable with the surroundings.

"I should be," she giggled when I commented on it. "I live here."

"Oh," I said.

Peach didn't mention her mother or father, and I felt too awkward to ask. After all, we had only just met. In the three years since it never came up again. That was just one more thing to add to the list of secrets in this house.

"So, Peach. You seem to know everything there is to know about this place. Where is everybody? Do I have any other aunts or uncles or cousins that live around here?"

"No," Peach said, and this time there was no laughter in her voice. "Your grandmother and uncle are all that's left of your family line. Well, them and you."

She gave me a sympathetic look, like she expected me to burst into tears or something.

I just nodded. It was hard to grieve for the loss of a family you had never known.

"Did you know him? My dad?" I asked.

Peach froze, which seemed impossible. She didn't seem the type to stop moving.

"Um, yeah," she said, then rapidly changed the subject.

It was like that with everyone I met. Everyone knew my father, but no one was willing to tell me anything about him.

Did I let it bothered me?

Of course.

I mean, Cyle brought me here every autumn because my dad had asked him to. I was supposed to get to know my dad's side of my family. So far the only thing I had learned was that they were experts at keeping secrets.

I learned that the hard way, by asking a lot of demanding questions which got me nowhere.

So, yeah, I was a little frustrated with it all. Not that it did me any good. I finally came to the conclusion that all things would be revealed in due time. So I kept my frustration bottled up, and bided my time.

Chapter 9

"When did you arrive?" Peach asked as she pulled away, bouncing towards the bed and perching on the edge, looking every bit like a cat ready to pounce.

"Just now," I answered, turning back to the window. "Hey, Peach, who is that man?"

"What man?"

Peach hopped over to the window as I pointing down at the lawn.

Cyle was shaking hands with a man I had never seen before. His hair was stark white, and it lay back on his head like a lion's mane. It reminded me of Andrew Jackson's picture on the $20 bill. It also looked mussed, like he ran his hands through it a lot.

The new guy was about as tall as Cyle, but he was larger; more muscular. His hair may have been white, but his face didn't carry any signs of age.

In fact, the only line that marred his face was a long scar leading from the edge of his left eyebrow and running down under his collar.

His eyes caught my attention, even from this distance.

They were golden.

"Am I related to him?" I asked, turning my head and looking at Peach.

Peach pushed me out of the way and pressed her hands and face against the glass. Following my pointing finger, Peach caught sight of the man...and froze.

I let out an exasperated sigh. Whatever she was about to say, she now was not going to say. If she said anything at all, I knew it would be a lie.

Or at least it wouldn't be the truth.

Peach always froze up for a few seconds whenever I asked a question that she couldn't - or wouldn't - answer. For whatever reason.

"Um, I don't know. Never seen him before."

Yeah, I didn't believe her, either.

"Hey! I think your grandmother has made a really nice dinner!" She was bubbling again.

Grabbing my hand, Peach pulled me along in her wake. I cast a final glance out my window, but the mystery man with the white mane was nowhere to be seen.

While I let Peach drag me out of my room, I mentally ran through a list of the few people I had met here.

There was Cyle, my Grandmother, Peach and Reynolds, of course. But the only other people who had ever come to the house while I was there were the tutors that Cyle hired to teach me.

Yep. I am a homeschooler now.

Nope. I don't wear a denim jumper, head scarf and sneakers, and I didn't own a goat. But I am definitely homeschooled, nonetheless.

I can't say I really missed the drama of high school. Junior high's cliques and social hierarchy had already cured me of any notion that I might be one of the cool kids. And I'm pretty sure the cool kids had their own set of problems. But the teachers Cyle brought in sometimes gave me the willies.

There was Mrs. Lynd. I sometimes caught her looking sideways at me; like she was afraid I might change into a frog or something. She didn't even bother looking away when I caught her studying me. She just continued to stare.

It was weird; unnerving.

But I came to expect weird, unnerving things here. It just came with the territory.

This new guy was something else altogether. Just the fact that he *was* a new guy made him interesting.

At least to me.

I always wondered why we didn't get more visitors. But neither Cyle nor my grandmother even mentioned the names of the people who left the house.

As if they only existed here.

As if there wasn't a world outside the borders of their property.

I know it's silly. After all, I have a life outside this house. I live it every spring and summer, in Jacksonville, Florida. With my mom and my friends and the beach.

Still, it struck me as odd that Cyle had this great big estate and was obviously wealthy, yet he didn't have anyone to share it with.

I always thought rich people had loads of fake friends hanging around all the time; Yes-Men and models in bikinis sipping some alcoholic beverage with little umbrellas in them, or something. Isn't that how it happens?

At least that's the way it looks in all the movies.

Not around here.

I asked Peach about it once. Not that I expected her to give me a straight answer. I must have caught her off-guard.

"There used to be more people here," Peach got a far-off look in her eyes. "This place was always teaming with friends and family. But that was before..."

Peach grew still. Not the stillness that she takes on when I know she's trying to avoid answering me, but something entirely different. I had never seen this side of her before.

I was afraid if I moved, or even blinked, it would shock her back into reality and she wouldn't continue.

Her eyes were unfocused, as if her mind was locked into a distant memory. In that moment she looked much older; much more worn; like the weight of the world rested on her shoulders alone.

I realized I had been holding my breath, and let it out quietly.

That was all it took, apparently.

Peach shivered, and the affect was over.

She was just Peach again.

I tried asking her what "before" was.

I asked why things were different.

What changed?

She just laughed and brushed my questions away like dusty old cobwebs, then expertly guided the conversation in a completely different direction.

I went along with her. No sense getting worked up over it. I knew by now that nothing more would be revealed.

But I still couldn't shake the feeling that something was up.

Why would Cyle and Grandmother, two people who obviously valued their privacy and lived their lives as virtual shut-ins, suddenly have a new friend show up on their doorstep?

And his eyes.

Golden. Tawny.

Like Cyle's eyes. Like my Grandmother's.

Like mine.

What did it mean?

Not for the first time since being at Cyle's did I wish that I wasn't so inquisitive. Life would be so much easier on me if I weren't.

Chapter 10

Dinner was a formal affair that night. My grandmother always insisted on a first class meal for my first night under their roof each autumn. It was a nice gesture, I'm sure, but it always made me uncomfortable.

Before coming to Cyle's house, my idea of a formal dinner was when my mom opted to cook a TV dinner in the oven instead of ordering take out. My grandmother's idea of a formal dinner included eight courses, fine china, crystal goblets and formal wear.

Frankly, I prefer take out.

As always, my Grandmother begged me to put on *something a little more refined*. As always, she got her way.

My grandmother was a hard person to say *No* to when she really wanted something, and she really wanted me in a dress.

I hate wearing dresses.

Not because I'm some tomboy who hates anything pink and fluffy and princess-like. I actually like pink.

I just hate the feeling that if I wanted to run, I couldn't do it properly. Jeans gave me so much more freedom.

I consoled myself by thinking that there was probably a slim chance of me needing to run at a family dinner party, so I showed up in a short, green cocktail dress.

I'm sure my grandmother would have preferred me in some tulle and taffeta monstrosity, but I could only bend so far.

I did at least make the effort to pull my hair into a semi-formal twist, rather than letting it fall down my back in a ponytail like I normally did.

My annual *first night back formal dinner* was reserved for family only. Just Cyle, my grandmother and me.

No teachers.

No Peach.

And I actually really enjoyed it. It was a great time to catch up with both of them. Yes, there did seem to be an ever-widening gap of secrets between us, but I adored both Cyle and my grandmother and relished our time together.

Besides, during these intimate gatherings, they might be a bit more likely to let a few secrets slip.

Imagine my surprise when I entered the dining room for our *family-only* dinner to find that strange man with the white hair sitting next to Cyle.

"Oh," I said, stopping in my tracks. "I'm sorry. I didn't mean to interrupt."

Cyle looked up from his conversation and beamed at me.

"Nice to see you looking like a lady," Cyle remarked.

"Nice to hear you sounding just like your mother," I replied.

It was snarky, I know, but he deserved it.

"So, who's your friend," I said, extending my hand to the man with the white hair.

"Yes, do be a proper host and introduce us, Cyle," the man with the white hair said as he rose to his feet and took my hand.

His voice was deep and carried a wisdom that even I recognized could only be achieved through age. Yet even with his white hair, this man looked much too young to be old.

"Lee, this is Rodrick." Cyle intoned formally. "Rodrick, this is my niece, Leeowyn Blake. She is Cecil's only child."

Rodrick inclined his head over my hand in a greeting. I thought for a moment he was going to kiss my hand, but he paused a bare inch from my fingers, then straightened. I awkwardly pulled my hand away, unease beginning to make its home in my stomach.

"Rodrick is your new tutor," Cyle casually commented as I walked toward my seat at the table.

"Nice to meet you, Roderick. Wait. What?" I snapped in mid-sentence, fixing Cyle with a glare. "So, what happened to Mrs. Lynd?"

I found myself balling my fists up so hard my knuckles turned white. I honestly don't know what set me off. Nothing about what Cyle said should have made me this upset or angry. It's not like I had any great affection for Mrs. Lynd. But something about the thought of spending hours on end with this Rodrick guy put me on edge.

The unease begun to churn and grow.

"Mrs. Lynd is a fine teacher to be sure," Rodrick said. "But she has taught you everything she can."

I walked forward and stood beside my chair, unwilling to sit down just yet.

"Rodrick will take it from here," Cyle interjected. "You can learn a lot from him. Trust me."

Cyle was holding the chair out for my grandmother who was busy giving me a disapproving look.

I flexed my hands so that they couldn't betray my mood more than they already had.

I needed to calm down.

Instead of turning and stomping from the room like I so childishly wanted to, I just flopped down into my chair.

"Your uncle thought it would be a good idea if you and Rodrick got to know each other a little before you started your studies this year, Leeowyn," Grandmother said.

Rodrick gave me a warm, friendly smile. The smile looked out of place on his face, as if it were unaccustomed to it, and friendly didn't suit him.

I just nodded, keeping my face blank. I had come to trust my feminine intuition, and right now my intuition was telling me not to trust this guy.

I stared at Rodrick, trying to find out why.

Stop staring.

I shook my head slightly, as if I could shake this weird feeling.

I was being silly.

I was tired.

There was no reason I should let some stranger ruin my annual *first night back formal dinner.*

I sat up a little straighter, deciding that I was going to force myself to enjoy this. It has been my experience that sometimes when you force joy it eventually turns into real joy.

In this case, it seemed just as likely as my grandmother coming to dinner in sweat pants and flip-flops.

Best laid plans of mice and men, right?

It wasn't like Rodrick was doing anything wrong. He was pleasant enough.

And polite.

And he genuinely seemed like he was interested in listening to what I had to say, even when I wasn't talking to him.

Which I wasn't.

I made a point of not talking to him.

By all rights I should have enjoyed the dinner. The food was excellent. The conversation was sparkling.

Instead, I was just on edge the entire time, waiting for something - I don't know what - to happen.

There was just something not quite human about the man.

I stopped there.

Not quite human? Inhuman?

Why did I think *inhuman?*

"Leeowyn, is everything alright?" My grandmother asked.

I looked up, noticing that I had completely frozen with my dessert fork midway to my mouth. I set my fork down as nonchalantly as I could and smiled like I had meant to do that.

"Yeah, just tired, you know, from the trip."

A trip I mostly slept through, I reminded myself.

I wasn't tired. Not in the least. I just needed to get away from this table.

"Of course," my Grandmother said, as though she knew just how much I slept on the way here.

I gave her a real smile this time. Like Cyle, my grandmother didn't ask too many questions, and she could always tell when I needed to be alone.

"Why don't you get some rest?"

I nodded and stood up.

Cyle and Rodrick rose to their feet as well.

I froze for a moment, then realized they were just showing good manners. Life in Jacksonville hadn't prepared me for that, and Cyle never did anything that silly around me.

"Allow me to escort you to your room," Rodrick said, extending his hand as he walked over towards me.

I was suddenly tense, wanting to run.

Stupid dress!

"No need," I forced a smile. "I can find it myself."

It was rude, I know. I didn't even have to look at my grandmother to know the look of disapproval that must be on her face.

Before anyone could say another word I turned and hurried out of the dining room as fast as I could without bolting. Once I was outside of the room, though, I did bolt.

One good thing about this house - when you needed a good run, there was plenty of room to do it.

I didn't slow down until I reached my bedroom door. Once inside, I closed it behind me, and leaned back against it, heaving as I tried to calm down my breathing and my heart.

What is wrong with you?

I had way overreacted and I knew it.

At least, I thought I knew it.

But there was just something about that man, that Rodrick, that didn't sit right with me. There was nothing I could put my finger on; no logical reason for me to want so vehemently to get away from him.

All I knew was there was a great sense of *unright* about him.

"Heh. *Unright.*" I muttered.

I really must be tired if I was starting to make up words.

I sighed.

"I just need some sleep," I said to no one in particular, since no one else was in the room. "That's all. I will go to sleep, and in the morning everything will be back to normal. At least as normal as things ever get around this place."

I started to feel a little better.

Rodrick was probably just some guy who was going to help prep me for the ACT and fill out college applications.

And Cyle was right when he said I didn't need Mrs. Lynd any more. I was so far ahead in all of my classes that I skipped a year and was now taking senior level courses. As a matter of fact, the only course I needed to graduate was one more credit in English.

Piece of cake.

My heart was finally starting to climb back down my throat and into its regular place in my chest when I heard voices from down the hall.

Cyle and Rodrick.

I cracked the door just a hair.

I don't normally eavesdrop, but I heard my name mentioned, so I figured I had a right to know what they were saying.

"...Couldn't get a good read on her, not without physical contact. You know that, Cyle."

That was Rodrick's voice.

"Do you really need to?"

Cyle's voice.

"I mean just look at her eyes. Can't you see it, Rodrick?"

I felt my hand absently touch my cheek, just under my eyes. What was wrong with them?

"I'm not doubting you, Cyle."

Rodrick again

"You have good reason to believe. But *we* are not so willing to put all our eggs in one basket until *we're* sure."

Their voices were growing softer. I leaned even closer against the crack in my door.

"That's what you're here for, Rodrick, so you can..."

Cyle's voice drifted away and I cursed silently.

I waited for a few more moments, but they had just entered a room, shutting the door behind them, cutting off their conversation from me.

I closed my door and tried to coax my heart back down into my chest again. It was a futile effort.

I methodically started getting ready for bed. I certainly wasn't going to get any answers tonight.

My mind was racing, trying hard to jump to conclusions. But I couldn't find any conclusions to land on.

And just what did my eyes have to do with anything?

I knew they were an odd color, but my mother had told me it was a family trait, one I certainly shared with my father, and Cyle, and Grandmother.

And Rodrick.

Why did Rodrick need a physical connection to know anything about me?

And just what kind of *physical connection* was he talking about. My mom had taught me how to handle boys who wanted to make a *physical connection*, but somehow I wasn't so sure it would work on someone like Rodrick.

No, Rodrick was creepy, but he didn't strike me as the kind of guy to try something. And I knew Cyle and grandmother would never put me in that kind of predicament anyway.

It had to be something else.

I crawled under my cozy comforter and switched off my bedside lamp, the room diving into darkness except for the light from the stars outside.

I looked out my still opened window drapes, wishing I were looking at the ocean instead of those same familiar trees. I could always think more clearly when I was by the ocean. Those trees just reminded me of a fence I was never allowed to climb.

I drifted off into an uneasy sleep, as I tried to convince myself that things would return to normal in the morning

They didn't return to normal.

And after my birthday nothing would ever be normal again.

Chapter 11

Last summer

I stood looking out over the ocean while the snow cone in my hand slowly turned into grape Kool-Aide. June was drawing to a close, which meant I had a little over two months left until Cyle came and whisked me away to his house.

I absentmindedly walked over to one of the many trash cans located around the boardwalk and dropped the half eaten slush cone into it.

The sun was starting to set, and as much as I loved watching the sunset turn the sky a bazillion shades of red, purple and azure, I knew I needed to get home. My mom had become super obsessive over me ever since I started splitting my time between her and my father's side of the family.

She always wanted me home as soon as possible.

She was afraid that she was losing me.

She was partially right.

There was a part of me, the part that I got from my father, which belonged with his family.

My mom made sure to remind me that there was still a part of me that belonged with her.

I smiled at the thought.

Of course I could never forget that. She worried too much.

I turned the corner to walk back toward my mom's condo when I ran smack into someone.

"Oh, sorry," I said as I stumbled backward, trying desperately to regain my balance.

Steady hands gripped my shoulders and stopped me from falling on my backside.

"No worries."

It was a smooth, deep voice that was attached to two strong hands. I looked up to see where that voice emanated from and blushed. I was captured by a pair of ice blue eyes that gazed into mine as if they could see straight through to the back of my skull and read all the thoughts in between.

It wasn't just the deep voice, strong hands and blue eyes.

Oh, no.

Those eyes were set into a radiant face that was framed by raven black hair and a smile that was both genuine and warm. And they rested on a frame that was at least six foot tall.

And that frame was not wearing a shirt.

"Uhh..." I responded.

Smooth, Lee. Charm him with your smokin' hot vocabulary and rapier wit.

He blinded me with another smile as he slowly let me go.

"You okay?" He asked.

Was I okay?

I didn't really know. I was swaying a little. And I giggled.

I giggled!

Slightly, but there it was. A no-joke giggle.

I at least had the presence of mind to turn that giggle into an unbecoming, but much more appropriate, cough.

He just kept on smiling.

If it were physically possible to kick myself, I would have broken my leg by now.

It's not like I had never seen a boy before. Even a cute boy. But I wasn't boy-crazy like so many of my friends.

I normally never showed a lot of interest in them. Consequently they never seemed to show much interest in me.

I have a pretty good self-image. I'm not fat, but I'm certainly no twiggy-thin size 2, either. I have no illusions about my looks. I'm not homely, but neither am I a great beauty.

I'm just...average.

Average height, average build, average face. Now you would think average would still make you a catch, right?

Wrong.

Guys don't seem to go for average. Trust me on this one.

Add flaming auburn hair, yellow eyes and pale skin to a Florida beach full of tall, skinny blonde-haired, blue-eyed, sun-kissed goddesses, and suddenly average equals invisible to high school boys.

But this guy was still gazing at me.

At *me*!

And I was standing there like a goat with my mouth hanging open.

"Um...yeah. I'm...good. Fine, actually. Great. Thanks for asking." I stumbled over my words, feeling like the world's biggest loser.

I chanced another glance at him, and he was still just smiling at me. He leaned against the wall, a picture of nonchalance.

Statues couldn't pull off that kind of calm.

"I should, uh, you know, get home."

I stumbled past him.

I was a ticking time bomb and the longer I stayed here, the greater the chance I would explode into a giant cloud of stupid. It wasn't until I had taken a few steps that I realized he was following me.

I stopped and turned to face him.

"What are you doing?" I squeaked.

There was that mind-numbing smile again and suddenly my train of thought ran off its track.

"I thought I would walk with you for a little way, just to make sure you're okay. That was quite a nasty little bump you just had. I've seen this kind of thing before. You could faint at any moment. I would hold myself completely responsible, and I can't afford for my insurance premiums to go up."

He needed to stop smiling; my mind didn't work when he smiled at me like that.

"Uh, oh. Umm...that would be...bad."

Stupid, stupid, stupid!

Here he was making quick-witted conversation while I was standing here braying like a mule.

I shook my head, trying to kick-start my brain. It was no use. My brain had checked out for the night.

"I have to get home."

I set off at a faster pace, but he quickly shot in front of me, grabbed my hand and shook it.

"Hi, I'm Alex," he said. "We haven't been properly introduced."

That's when he paused and looked down at the sticky hand he was shaking.

"Snow cone," I said, extracting my hand from his.

Stupid, stupid, stupid!

"Snow Cone?" he replied. "Well, that's a lovely name, although a bit unusual. So, were your parent's hippies or something? Is your middle name Grape, or Rainbow?"

He didn't even skip a beat.

"No, no, I'm Lee. Leeowyn Blake" I stammered, trying to regain a semblance of my dignity, and failing miserably.

"Snow cone...on my hand...the syrup..." I said, pointing to the sticky residue.

There was a flicker in his eyes when I said my full name. I could have sworn there was a...

No, it was probably just the glare from the setting sun.

Now he had that lost puppy air about him. I knew if I didn't throw him a bone, however stupidly phrased that bone was, he wouldn't leave me alone and I would never make it home. Mom would be frantic and have the cops out looking for me.

"Thank you for, um...steadying me, but I really do need to go home."

I inched around him.

He grabbed my hand again, apparently not bothered by the stickiness.

"Thank *you* for running into me," he said smoothly, locking his icy blue eyes onto mine.

I stuttered a few words that didn't even resemble English, yanked my hand away and rushed off.

I felt lucky that I didn't trip over my own feet.

I didn't stop until I was on the faded steps of my house, breathing heavily. I looked down at my hand, and decided one thing then and there.

I was never eating another snow cone for as long as I lived.

Chapter 12

Alex watched as Leeowyn Blake dashed away, an easy smirk creasing his lips.

Girls were always so easy to confuse.

Still, this one was different. He had felt it the instant he touched her hand. Power was coursing through her veins. It was almost overpowering. No wonder Cyle had snatched her up.

He permitted himself a brief, inward chuckle.

Cyle only had her for the winter months. That meant he had access to her all summer long.

As he turned to go, he encountered a young woman who had an air about her that was not young at all; whose feet barely seem to connect with the ground.

"You're breaking the rules," Peach snapped, her eyes crackling like lightning. "You shouldn't be here."

He pushed past her and continued on his way down the boardwalk.

"So, what exactly are you doing here?" he asked without bothering to turn back. He knew Peach would be right behind him.

"I'm making sure you don't do anything stupid," Peach snapped.

He ignored her until she grabbed his arm and yanked him around with a startling display of strength.

"She's not eighteen yet, Alex!"

He glared down at her hand on his arm, smirked, and casually shook his arm free of Peach's grasp.

"I know the rules as well as you, *pawn*," Alex spat. "Do you think it's fair that Cyle can force himself into her life while the rest of us don't have a chance? I don't."

Alex smiled down at the diminutive woman at his side and it seemed like the sun came out from behind a cloud. The smile failed to produce its desired effect on Peach, and Alex let it fade.

"You can tell Cyle that just because she's Cecil's daughter does not mean she's chosen a side yet."

Alex turned to face Peach head on. He grasped both of her shoulders and pulled her close, as if he were about to kiss her hard on the mouth.

With lips bare inches apart he whispered, "I don't intend to go down without a fight."

Alex pushed her back, raised a warning finger, then stalked off down the boardwalk.

Peach stood with balled fists planted on her hips. She contemplated going after him and teaching him some manners, but she knew she could do nothing of consequence with so many people around.

She watched until Alex disappeared into the sea of beachgoers and vacationers, then turned and stared in the direction of Leeowyn Blake's house.

I hope that girl is smart enough to stay away from Alex. Her life is going to be hard enough. She doesn't need his kind interfering and making things worse. Not now.

Peach walked into the setting sun, and disappeared.

Chapter 13

"May I join you?"

The voice was unmistakable.

I paused from my reading and glanced up.

There he was, looking like some beach god deigning to grace this tiny café with his presence.

He glanced over my head, through the café window, and a grimace clouded his countenance. I turned my head to see what had disturbed him, but I couldn't see anything out of the ordinary.

He slid into the seat opposite me before I had the chance to turn back around. His presence pulled my attention back to him. There wasn't even a hint of frown around his eyes.

"I haven't seen you around the beach recently," he said.

Now, I may not be the brightest colored crayon in the box, but I've been out of the box enough times to know a line when I hear one.

I decided to ignore him.

I looked back down at my book, but his hand suddenly extending into my line of vision, grabbed the book by the spine, and snapped it shut.

"What?" I snapped.

He just smiled that smile.

"Look, I've been thinking about our... encounter, yesterday..."

He was starting to make a witty remark, I could just tell, but I threw my hands up and pressed my fingers against his lips to cut him off.

"No! No sly comments or smooth phrases," I commanded. "I tossed and turned all night last night trying to puzzle out why would a guy like you be talking to a girl like me. The only thing I could figure is that somebody put you up to this, right? Some big joke? See who can bring the homeliest girl to the party?"

I talked fast, knowing if he flashed that smile my way again, my brain would grow fuzzy and I would lose my courage.

"So, whatever prank you're pulling, or whatever bet you lost, or whatever it is that you are up to, you can just knock it off! And give me back my book!"

A shocked and confused expression passed over his face for a moment.

Score!

But it was only a brief moment. Another quick glance through the window, over my head, and his ultra-cool composure and easy smile were firmly back in place.

He turned his attention fully back to me, and I knew I was in trouble.

"I didn't lose a bet, and there is no prank. No one has to bribe me in order to want to spend a little time with you, Lee."

He slid his hand over the table and gently placed it over mine.

I stiffened.

I couldn't think straight when he was touching me, even something as simple as his hand on top of mine. I knew my cheeks must have changed into thirty shades of red by now.

I jumped up, yanking my hand away from his. It took some effort.

"Did I offend you?" he asked.

The next thing I knew he was standing next to me; treating me like a scared doe, like I was going to bolt any second, which I probably was.

"Yes. No. I mean, umm..." I stammered. "I really need to go."

As I turned to leave, he gently placed his fingers on my arm, just above my elbow. Once again my thoughts turned to mush. I used to make fun of girls who did such stupid things when they were around cute boys. Now I understood. They made it impossible to think straight.

"Look, we obviously got off on the wrong foot," Alex reasoned with me. "No one put me up to this, Lee. I'm simply intrigued by you. I think you are cute and funny and I would like to get to know you a little better. That's all."

Alex let go of my arm and suddenly I could breathe again.

It was as if there was some kind of static pressure around him that sucked all the air from my lungs if I stood too near.

"So, give me a chance," he entreated me. "Give me one day to prove that my intentions are pure."

And then he smiled.

Let him prove that his intentions are pure? Who talks like that anymore? What is this, a Jane Austen novel?

I took a step back, continuing to watch him. I couldn't risk letting him touch me again. It would be all over if he did.

"Fine."

His smile, if possible, became even warmer, like the sun breaking through after a thunderstorm.

I took another step back, finding it hard to breathe again. He must know the affect he had on girls, yet he didn't tone it down a bit.

Then he glanced out the window again and a cloud passed over the sun.

"There are some things I need to attend to, first," he said. "Can we meet back here in, say, an hour?"

I nodded, then plopped ungracefully back down into the booth.

He traced my cheek with the backs of his fingers, replacing an errant strand of hair behind my ear.

My pulse raced. He had to feel it. He let his fingers linger on my face for a moment longer than was technically necessary.

"Until then," he said, and sauntered easily from the restaurant.

Girls in the restaurant and on the boardwalk leaned towards him like flowers aching for the sun. He didn't spare a look for any of them. When the door closed behind him, they all glared at me as if I had taken the last cookie from the jar without even asking if anyone else wanted one.

I opened my book and raised it in front of my face and bit my lower lip to keep from giggling out loud.

It took a few minutes for my heart to stop doing jumping jacks. It took even longer for my face to return to a normal shade. I glanced down at the hand Alex had covered with his and wondered how I was going to spend a whole day with him, when I couldn't even focus enough to inhale when he touched me?

Chapter 14

Alex walked down the street, alone with his thoughts. No blinding smile graced his face now; a dark thunderhead scowl settled into its place; his hands clenched into fists.

People took one look at his visage and hurried out of his path.

He stormed into an alley, pausing for a moment to listen. In the blink of an eye he pivoted on his heel, grabbed Peach, and slammed her up against the brick wall.

"Now who is the one breaking the rules?" he spat.

Alex gave her one more firm shove against the wall for good measure before letting her drop.

Peach appeared unfazed by the viciousness of Alex's attack. Not a hair was out of place and her enigmatic smile never left her face.

She advanced on him, her feet barely touching the ground.

"Are you judging me, *boy*?" Peach snapped back.

"You are the one who is using your...charms...to sway her, against all convention. And yet you think you can judge me for being on your territory?"

Peach reached out and wrapped her tiny fingers around Alex's wrist; her hands so small she could not encompass his whole wrist. But her grip held power, power that made Alex wince as she exerted more force to emphasize her words.

"Leeowyn Blake is not yet eighteen, Alex. What you are doing is wrong, and you know it. You always were far too arrogant and dismissive of the rules to hold the position you do. You should be stripped of your authority."

Peach squeezed his arm harder, her eyes flashing silver.

"Choose your words carefully, *pawn*. You don't want me for an enemy," Alex threatened between clinched teeth.

Peach relaxed her grip and Alex yanked his arm away. Deep purple bruises were forming where her fingers had gripped his skin. He rubbed circulation back into his wrist.

"You are on my world, now," he said, "and I don't take threats lightly."

Peach held up a warning finger and fixed him with another glare before backing up and leaning against the wall. She casually crossed her arms beneath her breasts, looking suddenly young and vulnerable.

She let out a sigh.

"We need her, Alex."

"Everyone needs her," Alex snapped back. "I need her."

Peach opened her mouth to speak again, but Alex cut her off.

"Leave. Now," he commanded. "I've suffered Cyle's visits. I will not suffer you watching me like some guard dog. I know the rules. I'm not treating her any differently than I treat any of the others. No rules have been broken. Now leave and do not tread in my world again without invitation. Unless you're looking for a very nasty fight."

Alex moved close to Peach, like a tiger stalking its prey; or a lover enticing a maid. His lips were a breath from Peach's ear.

"And believe me, *pawn*, I would love nothing more than the opportunity to fight dirty with that frail little body you have chosen for your own."

His whispered threat caressed Peach's ear like a sweet lover's promise. Peach knew his powers, but appeared immune to his siren call.

"Such a temper, *boy*."

Peach reached up and stroked the side of his face with her tiny fingers, an electrical storm flashing silver in her eyes.

"You should be careful when you play with fire, Alex. Little boys can get burned so easily."

Peach withdrew her hand from his face, smiled, and turned without another word. She casually tucked her hands into her pockets, whistling a playful tune as she strolled into the sunlight of the main street, looking for all the world like she had just come from a carnival.

Alex glanced at his watch. It was time he returned to Leeowyn Blake.

Yes, he knew the rules. He wouldn't sway her. But he was definitely going to make sure she knew that she had options.

Chapter 15

I spent the rest of that day with Alex.

And the next.

And the next.

He insisted that I had promised him a day. A day was twenty-four hours, he said, and he expected to get twenty-four hours with me all to himself.

I knew within the first two hours that I wanted to give him the full twenty-four.

Or forty-eight.

Or as many as he wanted.

Being with Alex was like coming up for air after being under water too long. Once I got comfortable with him I found I could easily breathe around him, as long as he didn't touch me too suddenly. If I was expecting it, I could prepare for it.

Yes, he was gorgeous. But beyond that, I found him easy to talk to.

About anything.

About my life.

I've never been a big fan of talking, especially about myself. I was a much better listener. But Alex always wanted to know more and more about me. It was like he couldn't get enough of me.

He coaxed me into sharing more about myself with him than I had with anyone, other than my mom.

He seemed particularly eager to know what I wanted to do with my life.

We sat on the front steps of the condo one evening, enjoying the cool ocean breeze and the tangy scent of the salt water, talking of nothing in particular.

He asked me what I wanted to be when I grew up.

It was my last night in Jacksonville for the year. The following morning Cyle would show up in his limo, and off we'd go to...well...wherever it was that Cyle's house was. I was lost in thought, contemplating maybe even asking Alex to come for a visit during fall break.

Kinda hard to do when you don't know where to invite him to.

Alex's question took me by surprise and shook me from my reverie. For some reason I couldn't explain, it made me laugh out loud.

"The second I know what I want to be when I grow up, I'll let you know," I said.

I've always felt a little like a compass without a needle when it came to what I wanted to do with my life. From the time I was just a wee tyke, my mom taught me to never make a rash decision; that I had all the time in the world to figure it out. I was never pressured into really thinking about it, so I didn't.

"I guess once I go to college I'll get a better feel for what I want to do with my life," I mused aloud. "Mom wants me to go to Florida State. That's her old Alma Mater. I assume my Uncle Cyle wants me to go to whatever college my dad went to, but he's never mentioned it."

Alex got very still when I mentioned Cyle. He always got still when I talked about my dad's side of the family. It reminded me of the way Peach acted when I knew she was trying to hide something from me.

Alex was better about camouflaging his reactions than Peach, but I still noticed; maybe because I paid such close attention to him.

I had learned to stay aware of his every move, so that he wouldn't take me by surprise. If his hand brushed mine, or if he even so boldly took my hand in his, which he did occasionally, it could take my breath away. So I was keenly aware of when he stopped moving.

"Has your Uncle Cyle ever asked you what you wanted to be?" Alex asked.

He was staring straight ahead, a distant look in his eyes. I studied his face, trying to read his suddenly stony features.

"No," I replied, as honestly as I could. "My uncle never really talks to me about anything of any great importance."

Alex relaxed back into his normal posture, a half smirk creasing his lips. He brushed the tips of his fingers across my hand, slowly enough that I could see it coming and prepare for it.

I suspected that Alex knew just how much his presence affected me, and he was trying to make it easier on me by being deliberate in his movements.

"Well, I hope you pick some place warm. Someplace close."

His voice was soft, like a purr, as he continued to brush my hand. The lines of our friendship blurred when he made small gestures like that, touching my skin so softly.

"I would like very much to be near you," he whispered leaning toward me.

I was frozen, his closeness making me unable to move or think. The air around us hummed and crackled with the same static electricity that I felt emanate from him that first day we met.

He paused, a mere breath away, and my heart beat so hard and fast I thought it would explode. Being this close to Alex was painful and exhilarating all at the same time.

He reached a hand up and pressed his fingers to my lips, them pressed them against his own. He pushed a stray strand of auburn hair back behind my ears, then leaned back, giving me the same lazy smile that shot fireworks into the sky.

"Of course, the choice is yours," he said.

Alex glanced down at his watch and I sighed inwardly. He only ever looked at his watch when it was time for him to go.

He stood up and offered me his hand, which I ignored. I wasn't going to risk another heart implosion.

Instead, I used the railing to help hoist myself up.

I never touched him if I could help it. It was too intense, and I ended up babbling like an airheaded blonde joke after any kind of contact with him.

"I should probably be getting to bed."

I turned to go inside.

Before I knew what was happening Alex had turned me around and kissed me full on the mouth.

It was like all the static electricity that built up around him exploded inside of me; lightning bolts cascading through me, burning me to a cinder. His hands were holding my face, and where he touched me, it burned. I wasn't sure my body could contain the kind of fire that was his touch.

All too soon it was over.

He pulled away, though he continued to look at me with those sun-bright eyes.

If I made a sound, I don't remember it.

Alex took my hand and raised it gently to his lips, kissing it softly.

His kiss seared my flesh. I half expected to see an imprint of his perfect lips burned into my hand, and was surprised to see it was not so.

"That's so you don't forget me," he said, catching and holding my gaze for a precious moment before he dropped my hand and walked away.

I stood there, like a lovesick mooncalf, watching him leave. I continued to stare long after I could no longer see him.

This was going to be the longest winter ever.

Chapter 16

I didn't see Rodrick any more that first week back at Cyle's. I wasn't sure if I was glad about that or not.

Keep your friends close, and your enemies closer, my mom had always said. At this point I wasn't sure if Rodrick was the enemy or not, but I preferred to keep my perspective enemies in sight.

Not that I actually thought he was an enemy, but he certainly wasn't a friend.

I spent a great deal of time that week just hanging out with Peach. She was a constant, overflowing fountain of energy and it was often contagious.

We were outside roaming the grounds one bright fall day, being careful to avoid the scary, forbidden woods, when I got up the courage to tell her about Alex.

I had never really been close with any girls my age. Oh, I had a few friends back in Jacksonville who were almost as bubbly as Peach. They did more than enough talking, so I was usually relegated to the listening department. For me, "girl talk" had always been "girl listen." I wasn't used to being on the talking end of "girl talk."

I re-lived my last moments with Alex, particularly that explosive kiss, over and over again in my mind and I just had to share it with someone.

Peach was dipping her feet in the fountain that was in the center of the courtyard behind the house. I opened my mouth several times to tell her, but the words just wouldn't come out. I wasn't sure how to say it.

"Spit it out, already," Peach demanded.

"W-What?" I stammered.

Her eyes had been closed the entire time as she sat leaning back, her face upturned towards the bright sunlight, soaking it in. She popped one eye opened and smiled at me.

"You've been dying to tell me something, ever since you got back from Jacksonville. So, just spill already, before you bust a gut."

She opened her other eye and turned to face me, a wicked grin playing across her face.

I sighed.

"Why is it that everyone around here seems to be able to tell everything about me, and yet I never know anything more than what they decide to tell me?" I whined.

"Come on, Lee," Peach encouraged. "Give!"

"I, um, kind of...kissed a boy. And I *liked* it!"

I felt my cheeks grow hot as I conspicuously avoided looking at Peach, focusing all of my attention on the stream of water splashing from the fountain.

Peach squealed in an octave range that started out ear piercingly high and then rose to a level that only dogs could hear. She started clapping her hands and dancing in the fountain.

"Who is he? What's he like? Is he cute? Are you a couple?"

The questions spilled out of her mouth faster than my mind could register them. I paused a moment, letting the memory play out in my mind again, getting lost in the dizzy feeling that washed over me every time I lingered on the thought.

"He's a guy I met on the boardwalk in..."

A loud commotion around the corner of the house cut off all conversation.

I cast a questioning glance at Peach who was now standing on the edge of the fountain, her eyes trained in the direction of the sound. I quickly stood up and started towards the noise.

"I wonder what's going on?" I said aloud.

Peach was by my side in an instant. Her tiny hands gripped my arms with that unsettling, unnatural strength she had.

Not for the first time, I wondered how such a tiny form could hold so much power.

"Hey, you know what? It's hot out here. Why don't we go inside?" Peach forced a smile and started to drag me indoors.

With more than a little bit of effort I shook free of her grasp.

"Are you kidding me? I've been bored out of my skull around here lately. I'm not passing up an opportunity for a little excitement."

I continued walking toward the noise but, faster than should have been possible, Peach was in front of me again.

"I don't know, Lee. It doesn't sound like anything we need to be involved in. We might get in trouble."

Peach cast a quick glance over her shoulder at the noise.

I narrowed my eyes.

What was up with Peach? She was normally all for sneaking around and listening at keyholes. Why was she trying to avoid this obviously juicy bit of drama?

"Peach," I begged.

She just looked at me with those pleading, puppy dog eyes of hers, but made no move to step aside.

"Come on, Leeowyn, let's just go back inside. Anything happening over there isn't our concern."

Her voice was soft, yet unyielding. And she had used my full name. We locked eyes for a long moment as a silent battle of wills took place.

I must have blinked first, because I sighed and turned around.

"I wish people around here would trust me," I spat, investing more of my frustration into my words than I intended.

I expected Peach to quickly assure me that I was trusted; that this was nothing; that everything was just hunky dory.

She didn't.

And she wouldn't meet my eyes as we walked slowly back towards the backdoor.

"Lee!"

It was the last voice I expected to hear at Cyle's house.

I turned to see Alex walking towards me, with Cyle no more than a step behind.

My heart skipped a beat at the sight of Alex, but my blood ran cold when I saw Cyle's face.

I had never seen Cyle really and truly angry before, and now he was in a state of complete, unadulterated rage. His yellow eyes took on the shade of molten gold, the veins on his neck popping out and his hands were clenched into fists that looked like Zeus getting ready to hurl lightning bolts.

"Alex!"

I rushed towards him, but slowed and stopped a few paces in front of him when I felt the tension in the air rise to a boiling point.

"What are you doing here?" I asked, suddenly very suspicious. "How did you even know where *here* was?"

I looked from Cyle - who appeared ready to spit sparks - to Alex, who looked to be the calm before the storm. It didn't take a psychological meteorologist to know that an interpersonal hurricane was about to make landfall.

I just didn't know why.

Cyle sometimes treated me like I was his daughter rather than his niece; but seriously, no dad acted this crazy just because a boyfriend showed up.

A crimson flush crept up my throat and colored my face at the thought.

Alex isn't my boyfriend; we're just friends.

Aren't we just friends?

That fateful scene of Alex burning me with his kiss replayed in my mind, blurring the lines of *just* friendship.

"Your uncle invited me over to spend some time," Alex explained calmly, smiling at me as if Cyle wasn't giving him the death glare. "It turns out, Cyle and I are old friends. We go way back. Isn't that right, Cyle?"

Alex didn't even turn to acknowledge Cyle's presence.

If looks could kill, the look Cyle gave Alex would have undone his birth. I shivered at the pure hatred that radiated off Cyle.

Old friends? Way back? Alex didn't *look* all that old. I was confused.

Suddenly Cyle was smiling like he had just encountered a long lost son. But his smile was somehow worse than his glare. At least the glare felt honest.

"Yes," Cyle remarked. "Your mother told me about your new little friend here."

Cyle said the word *friend* like you would say *serial rapist.*

"So he called me up and invited me to spend the winter here," Alex never took his eyes off me. "Wasn't that kind of him?"

I gave him a half smile. I was torn between excitement that Alex was here, and a horrible sense of foreboding that a bloodbath of mythic proportions was just around the corner.

"Peach, why don't you see if you can find a room for our new house guest. I'd like to speak with Lee privately," Cyle said, holding his hand out for me.

I walked slowly towards Cyle, pausing beside Alex for a brief moment, flashing a quick smile that I hoped conveyed how glad I was to see him.

He rewarded me with one of his own dazzling smiles; the kind that sent my mind reeling and made me go all week in the knees.

Before the moment could take root, Cyle took me by the arm and, with more force than was absolutely necessary, pulled me away from Alex.

The mind-numbing fuzziness that usually accompanied any time spent with Alex lifted at my uncle's stern touch. I gave Cyle a shocked look and he eased his grip on my arm slightly.

Alex had already started to make his way towards the house before I could even say, 'See you later.'

Cyle watched him go, drilling holes in his back with his gaze.

And here I was thinking this was going to be a long, boring winter.

Chapter 17

Cyle felt him on his land before he saw him. His skin prickled as his anger began to boil.

"He wouldn't dare," Cyle whispered.

But he knew Alex would dare.

Cyle stood from the desk in his study and walked towards the big bay windows, pulling the curtains aside. There Alex was, acting as if he had a perfect right to be here. As if he owned the place.

Alex started walking toward the back of the house.

Where Lee was!

Cyle was out of the house and striding towards Alex before he could form a coherent thought.

Can't fight him. Not here; not in front of Lee. Clever boy. Alex knows that. That's what's given him the boldness to make his move now.

There was no way to force Alex to leave without revealing things to Lee that she wasn't ready to hear.

Still, he wasn't going to allow this pup to pull Leeowyn to his side without a fight.

It wasn't fair.

It wasn't right.

And it wasn't going to happen in his house.

"Hello, Cyle," Alex said, without turning around. "How have you been? It's been too long. How's your mother?"

When Alex finally turned to face Cyle his face wore an impassive expression that belied the danger behind it.

"Get out," Cyle ordered.

"I don't think so, Cyle. No, I really don't think so. What? You send your watchdogs to my land, my home, and you think I'm just going to stand by and take it?"

Cyle struggled to contain his fury. Alex had pitched his voice just loud to carry to the back of the house. Loud enough that Lee would hear it.

"I figured one good bending of the rules deserves another."

"Alex, you have no right to be here!" Cyle growled.

"And you had no right to be on Earth!" Alex shouted.

Cyle grabbed the younger man's jacket with both hands and lifted him from the ground. Cyle shoved him up against the side of the house.

"If you let something like that slip around Leeowyn..." Cyle's voice dripped venom.

"I've let nothing slip," Alex cut him off. If he was ruffled by Cyle's outburst, it didn't show. "Oh, my, what's that sound? Do I hear Lee on her way around the house?" Alex smirked.

"I have no intention of telling her anything before she comes into her inheritance," Alex continued. "But I also have no intention of rolling over like the dog you think I am. I have just as much right to try and win her as you do. So, unless you are ready to do some extensive explaining, which I'm pretty sure you're not, I suggest you play along."

Pushing past Cyle, he once again started around toward the back of the house.

Cyle swore; his mind racing. There was nothing he could do right now. Alex had outmaneuvered him, and he knew it. Anything he might try to force Alex away would have serious repercussions.

Lee's birthday was less than two months away. He couldn't afford to have her angry with him.

He couldn't risk losing her.

He was going to have to follow Alex's lead. At least for now.

Chapter 18

I sat in Cyle's office, watching him pace.

He had been pacing for sometime now, not saying a word. I would have asked him what was on his mind, but he had the disposition of a rattlesnake with a toothache. It just didn't seem like the right time to interrupt him, no matter how bored I was starting to become.

Besides, it seemed like he was finally getting ready to reveal some fresh tidbit about my family history. So, I sat back and continued to watch him stalk from one end of his study to the other, muttering to himself.

After a while sitting in one position got to be too much for me. I sighed and stretched.

I wasn't trying to attract Cyle's attention, but he glared at me like I had interrupted him in mid-sentence or something.

I froze in mid-stretch.

"Look...Lee..." he started, slowly walking in front of his desk, then leaning back against it. "This boy, Alex..."

I waited.

"What about him?" I coaxed.

"I'm not sure how much you should trust him," Cyle let out an exasperated breathe, as if there was some obvious truth that I was missing.

"I shouldn't trust him," I repeated. "But, you trusted him enough to invite him here."

Two plus two wasn't equaling four and I was starting to get just a smidge put out with it. From all appearances, Cyle hated Alex. So, had he just invited him here to have him killed or something?

That thought was absurd, of course, but it was the only thought that made any sense at all. I sat up straight.

"Wait...you didn't bring Alex here to kill him did you? 'Cause that's taking the whole over-protective uncle routine to an extreme, don't you think?"

I hoped to break the tension with a joke. Of course, the joke would have worked better had it not seemed so much like a reality.

Cyle just gazed at me.

"Oh, god, Cyle, no. You can't kill him!"

This time Cyle did chuckle.

"No, Lee, I'm not going to kill him."

I let out a sigh of relief that really did feel like relief.

Cyle walked toward me until he was close enough to touch my face. For a moment I felt the presence of the father I never knew.

"I promised your father I would take care of you, Leeowyn. That includes protecting you from... boys."

Cyle held my gaze for a long time with a tenderness I had not seen before. I tried and failed to read the expression that was locked behind his eyes.

"So, just be careful, okay?"

"Okay," I smiled. "I promise."

Cyle allowed a suddenly sad smile to crease his lips. A far off look clouded his eyes, as if a distant memory rose unbidden. Just as suddenly it was gone and his features resumed their normal guarded façade.

He turned back towards his desk.

I stood.

"So...is Alex really staying the entire winter?"

I hoped the question wouldn't spark Cyle's anger again, but I needed to know something of what was going on around me.

Cyle had his back to me. I saw him clench his fists, but he showed no other sign of aggression.

"So it would appear," he answered.

"So...he'll be here for my birthday?" I asked, not being able to keep the excitement out of my voice.

It was stupid to get so excited about the thought of Alex being there for my eighteenth birthday, but I couldn't help it.

Once again, Cyle tensed up, clenching his fists even tighter. He didn't even answer. He just nodded.

I took that as my cue to leave.

I closed his office door behind me, happy to be out of the war zone.

A smile tickled the corners of my mouth as I walked down the hall toward my room.

I had the whole winter to spend with Alex!

We could research different colleges together. Cyle was a reasonable man. Surely he would get over whatever piddly little grudge he had against Alex, and then this winter would be amazing.

I would be surrounded by my family, my best friend and my boyfriend, all at the same time!

My boyfriend!

I blushed at the thought.

Maybe the winter wouldn't be so long after all.

Chapter 19

She looked at the body in front of her and smiled. It was perfect, truly perfect.

Newly dead, so there was no sign of decay, the poison that stopped his heart had left no nasty, gaping wounds.

She ran her hands through the dead man's hair. Humming a soft melody from her childhood as she rolled the body over onto its stomach. Her silvery blonde hair fell in front of her face, hiding everything except a lovely pair of blood red lips that pulled into a smile.

Picking up a dagger, she positioned it on the back of the dead man's neck. Applying surgical precision, she cut a short, deep line at the base of his hairline.

She drew the dagger from the dead man's flesh then, lifting it to her left palm, cut an identical wound, giggling as she watched the blood ooze from her hand.

She laid her bleeding palm over the cut on the dead man's neck as she resumed humming the sweet, soft song.

The body twitched.

She stopped humming and watched as the twitches grew into spasms, and as then body began flailing. Sucking air into its lungs, it let out a blood-freezing scream. It would have flopped off the stone table had it not been for the girl's firm hand on its neck, holding it down.

In one quick motion, the girl leapt onto the dead man's back. She giggled aloud as she was rocked back and forth by its thrashing spasms.

She started humming again, louder this time.

She reached behind her and drew a sewing needle from the dead man's thigh. It was, in fact, the needle she had dipped with poison; the needle she had shoved into the dead man's leg when he was still among the living.

Ignoring the dead man's spasms and whimperings, she plucked a strand of her silvery blond hair and threaded it through the eye of the needle.

With the deft touch of a master seamstress, she stuck the needle into the wound on the dead man's neck and stitched it closed.

With each stitch, the dead man moaned and flailed less. By the time she knotted the final stitch, the man who was no longer dead, but was not quite alive, was still once more.

The girl leapt to the ground, laughing at her handiwork.

She extended her hand out to the thing. It slowly sat up and took her hand.

The girl's laughter took on a ragged edge of madness, pitching higher and higher until anyone hearing it would call it a screech.

She quieted as she studied her creation. She leaned forward, and whispered into its ear.

"Kill her."

The not dead man stood up and turned.

"Wake up!" A girl's voice screamed. "Do not let them see you, Little Bird!"

Chapter 20

I gasped for breath, jumping out of bed before I was even aware of what I was doing. My bare feet thumped on the floor and I had my bedroom door half opened when I stopped.

Why was I running?

It was a dream. A horrible, disturbing dream; but a dream, nonetheless.

I sighed and leaned my head against the door, trying to get my heart to stop doing jumping jacks inside my chest. I could still hear that girl - *that thing* - humming.

I shook my head, trying to erase the memory of the sound. I turned to go back to my bed, closing the door behind me.

Then I saw her.

A girl was standing inside my room, in front of my window, looking at me. The moon beyond the window was veiled behind wispy clouds, but I could see her curly hair that reached just below her chin, framing her face. She appeared to be around my age, though shorter and slighter of frame.

Her dress was indistinct in the muted moonlight, but it must have been ripped and tattered, because it was casting odd shadows on the floor around her feet.

She just stood there, stroking something in her arms that twitched and struggled to be free.

I reached for the light switch, but her voice stopped me.

"You must wake up, Little Bird," she said.

It was the voice from my dream.

I was still dreaming.

I *had* to be dreaming.

"There is no time." The girl's voice took on a pleading insistence. "You must wake up."

I finally found my voice.

"Who are you? What are you doing in my room?"

"You must wake up, Little Bird," she repeated. "You must wake up! WAKE UP!"

She was screaming, now and moving toward me. I stepped back, tripping over my own feet. I fell flat on my back, knocking the wind from my lungs.

Before I could catch my breath, the girl was kneeling beside me, leaning over me until her face was bare inches from mine.

I gagged.

The stench of burnt flesh and death rolled off of her.

Whatever the girl was holding twisted and contorted, desperately seeking escape. She placed her hand on my cheek as the moon broke through the clouds, casting its bright, silvery light over her.

She looked like a refugee from a war zone. Her clothes were torn and soaked in blood; her eyes wide, terrified. The hand that rested on my cheek was stripped of flesh, with nothing but bone remaining.

Still, I couldn't catch my breath.

I was finally able to recognize the thing in her arm as it let out a bone-cracking screech. It was a raven. But something was wrong with it. Its head swayed from side to side as it struggled and fluttered in the girl's grasp.

Its neck was broken. Yet it was still alive.

I would have screamed if I could have just drawn air into my lungs, but terror choked my throat.

"There is no time," the girl snapped.

The bony fingers of her flesh-denuded hand grasped my face and forced me to stare hard into her eyes. Her eyes had the look of someone holding tight to their last strand of sanity.

"WAKE UP!"

And then she was gone.

I was finally able to draw a breath deep. I rolled onto my belly, then struggled onto my hands and knees. I searched frantically around me. The moon had disappeared once more behind a thick veil of clouds, plunging the room into dark shadows.

I found my feet and staggered to the wall, flicking the light switch on, flash blinded by the sudden brightness in the room.

The light chased the shadows away, although it took several painful moments before my eyes could adjust enough to see clearly.

I searched in every nook and cranny of the room - in my closet, under my bed - for any faint sign that the girl was there. Or that the girl had ever been there.

There was no sign that anything had been in my room that night... except for myself.

I took several deep breaths trying to stave off hyperventilation. I touched my hand to my cheek. I could still feel her skeletal fingers pressing into my flesh.

Tears started streaming down my face. I knew I was crying; I may have been screaming. I don't know. I couldn't focus on anything but the feeling of her hand on my cheek.

And her voice kept playing in my mind.

You must wake up!

Chapter 21

I took a shower.

Then I took another.

And another.

No matter how much I scrubbed, or how much hot water I used, I wasn't able to get rid of the feeling of her fingers on my cheek.

So cold.

So hard, like...

No! Don't think about it.

I shivered and closed my eyes, forcing my mind to think about something else; forcing my mind to think about nothing at all.

Back home, in Jacksonville, whenever I had a nightmare, I refused to cry about it. I had trained myself to deal with it myself. I couldn't bring myself to go crying to my mom. She had more than enough to worry about without me bringing silly dreams to the table.

She already worried about me more than I liked.

Instead of burdening her with a nightmare that she could do nothing about, I taught myself to just take a deep breath, empty my mind of the frightening images and rationalize the whole thing away.

It usually worked.

It didn't work this time.

I found myself staring blankly out my window as the sun rose. I let my mind wander wherever it wanted while I watched the dying leaves playing ring around the rosie as they fluttered off the trees to the ground.

Ashes, ashes, all fall down.

The nursery rhyme felt ominous to me, but I couldn't get it out of my mind.

I had gotten no more than three hours of sleep, but there was no way I was going back to bed.

Not after *that* nightmare.

Stupid.

It was just a dream. No one had been in my room.

I kept telling myself that, over and over again.

There was no way some girl straight out of a Freddie Kruger movie, holding a dead bird that wasn't dead, had just waltzed into my room and tried to wake me up.

I was in that in-between stage of asleep and awake. That's why it felt so real.

Yeah, that makes sense.

So, why don't I believe it?

I don't know how long I stood in front of my window.

I don't know how long it took me to notice that Peach had been standing next to me.

It was strange that she wasn't chattering away at me. It was strange that she hadn't burst into my room with her usual energy.

But then, maybe this was a day for strange.

I pulled my gaze away from the window and met her eyes.

"You okay?" she asked.

Her sharp eyes roamed over my face.

I mumbled some answer. I don't remember what it was. I shrugged, turned and walked over to my dresser. I pulled a T-shirt and a pair of jeans from the drawers.

"What time is it?" I asked, dropping my bathrobe on the floor.

"A little past noon," Peach answered as I dressed. "Cyle was worried about you. It's not like you to miss breakfast."

"Yeah, well, I didn't get much sleep last night," I replied, with only a hint of bitterness in my voice.

"Cyle says Rodrick wants to meet with you."

I sat down at my vanity and tried valiantly to pull some of the tangles out of my hair. It was a loosing battle.

I sighed.

Of course, today would be the day Rodrick wants to start meeting with me.

I don't know what it was about that guy that put me off, but I just didn't trust him.

"Hey, Peach..."

Peach looked at me expectantly.

I shrugged and forced a smile.

"Never mind."

I gave up on my hair and pulled it back into a frizzy ponytail.

"Reynolds saved you some breakfast if you want some," Peach said, opening the door and holding it open for me.

She looked like her normal, chipper self, but I could feel her eyes studying me more intently than normal. Thankfully she didn't ask any questions about my zombie-like state. I wouldn't know how to explain it to her.

I didn't know how to explain it to myself.

If I could just get that dream behind me and forget about it, I would start feeling better. I was sure of it.

I grabbed my bag of schoolbooks and slung it over my shoulder.

"I'm not really in the eating mood," I answered, the memory of cold, dead fingers stroking my cheek...

Stop that!

Peach walked with me down to the library, which doubled as my primary schoolroom. She chatted about superficial things on the way, which I appreciated. It was nice to just listen to her voice and let my mind wander without giving a thought to what she was chattering on about.

I was so unfocused that I didn't even hear Peach as she shouted "Look out!" seconds before I ran headlong into Alex.

This was getting to be way too much of a habit.

"Are you okay?" Alex asked.

I barely noticed his question. I was much more interested in his hand which was holding my wrist to steady me.

I could still breathe.

Back in Jacksonville, whenever Alex would touch me unexpectedly, it was like I was in outer space and all the oxygen was suddenly sucked out of my lungs.

But I could breathe.

I looked up into his eyes, shocked to discover that my mind wasn't filled with the familiar hum and buzz that always distracted me when ever I was near him. He didn't seem to radiate that human embodiment of summer when I looked at him.

He seemed to be, in every way, just a normal guy.

I blinked several times and kept gazing at him, completely ignoring his questioning looks.

He was still ungodly handsome, no doubt about it. And he was still way out of my league. But I did not feel that irresistible pull toward him that I had this entire summer.

I slowly extracted my wrist from his grasp and let it flop at my side. I stared at him, waiting for the affect to switch on and make me babble and sputter like an idiot.

"Leeowyn, what's wrong?" Alex asked.

He reached for me again.

I shied away from his touch, sidestepped him, and continued on towards the library.

Alex turned, watching me go. Neither of us spoke another word.

I couldn't answer him right now. I simply did not know what was wrong.

It was that dream. It has to be.

That dream had left me with more than the normal foreboding that any other *normal* nightmare had. I could still hear that silver-haired girl's evil laugh echoing in my mind, and my cheek had yet to forget the feel of those bones...

Stop thinking about that!

I was just sleep deprived, that was all.

I needed to get a nap, or something, and everything would feel right again.

I sighed as I reached the library door. I was already on edge and in no mood to deal with a man who would no doubt put me even more on edge. Unfortunately I was in a classroom of one. When you're the only student in the school, the teacher will definitely notice if you cut class.

"I guess I'll see you later," Peach said.

Startled, I jumped, bumping into the library door. I let out an exasperated sigh and leaned my head against the door.

"Jeez, Peach, maybe make a little noise when you walk so I know you're still beside me."

I wasn't sure how many more scares my poor little heart could take.

Peach looked at me with a quizzical expression on her face.

"I've been talking the entire time," she said.

I turned toward her voice and caught her out of the corner of my eye. I could have sworn she was floating an inch above the floor.

I blinked once and turned to look at her fully.

There she was, standing with both feet planted firmly on the ground, just like normal.

"I..." I started to say something, but anything I would have said would have just sounded crazy.

I gave her an apologetic look.

"Yeah, I'll see you later."

I pushed the door open and walked into the library.

Sleep deprivation. That's all it was.

Chapter 22

Everyone called it 'the library,' but it wasn't what I assumed a library in a really old mansion would look like.

When Cyle had first taken me to the library, I had expected to find something straight out of *Beauty and the Beast*, with winding staircases and books filling every nook and cranny.

Instead he opened the door to a room that was only slightly larger than my bedroom, which I suppose is still pretty big as rooms go.

The library had four tables in it, each surrounded by four, red leather chairs. One wall was top to bottom filled with books, but there was a thick plate of glass between the books and anyone who might want to read them.

There was a lock in the glass, but I had no idea where the key was and I had never seen anyone unlock it.

The tutors Cyle hired had always supplied me with whatever books I needed for school.

No one talked about the bookcase.

No one even acknowledged it.

And I never asked about it. It just didn't seem like something I was supposed to ask about. I can't explain it.

I was initially curious about the books, and, the first few times my tutors had left me alone in the library, I had wandered over to the bookcase and tried to read the titles on the bindings. I wanted to discover some hint as to why they were so obviously forbidden.

The problem was that none of the books had any writing on their binding. Nothing at all.

No title.

No author.

No Dewey Decimal system.

Nothing.

After a while I just lost interest.

The only other thing of any real interest in the library was the fireplace. Located on the very back wall, it was unlike any normal fireplace I had ever seen.

Not that I had that much experience with fireplaces, being from Jacksonville and all.

Honestly, none of the fireplaces in Cyle's house were what you would call, 'normal.' They all had fireboxes that were big enough to roast an ox in, with stonework decorated in ornate designs etched into it that looked like gold. The mantels were all constructed of marble or some other equally expensive material.

The fireplace in the library, though, was different.

Its firebox had to be seven feet tall, reaching more than halfway to the room's 12-foot ceiling. It appeared to be carved out of the purest white marble I had ever seen. Four people could stand abreast inside it, and it was deep enough for me to walk in with my arms stretched from the back to the front and not touch either end.

But the oddest thing about the fireplace in the library - the thing that gave me the creeps - was that, whereas all the other fireplaces in Cyle's house were embellished with dramatic carvings, this one was bare.

I had never once seen a fire inside the fireplace in the library. Probably a good thing, since there was also no chimney leading from the firebox.

I asked Cyle about it, once.

"You're father liked fireplaces," he answered without even looking up from his book.

My father liked fireplaces?

"Did my father also like to fill the house with billowing black clouds of smoke?" I had asked, totally not satisfied with Cyle's answer.

Not that I expected any additional information.

But Cyle sighed, set his book down and gave me a calculated look.

"All fireplaces have their uses," he said. "This one has its use. One day I'll show you, but this is not that day."

He sounded for all the world like Aragorn from *Lord of the Rings*. I almost laughed, but his eyes looked so serious.

"Right now, I'm reading," Cyle said, as if that was sufficient for anyone.

He picked up his book and very obviously ended the conversation.

It wasn't much of an answer, but it was as much as I was going to get.

So, when I entered the library for my lesson with Rodrick and found a fire roaring in the fireplace, I was more than a little disconcerted.

I dropped my bag and rushed toward the fire, frantically trying to find something to put it out with. All the lessons my mom had taught me about fire safety came rushing through my head, but before I could get close enough to do anything about the fire, it was gone.

I stopped short.

There was no fire in the fireplace.

No charred remains of wood.

Not even the smell of smoke that I swear had greeted me not ten seconds before.

It was all gone. As if I had imagined the whole thing.

What in the name of all that is holy is going on today?

Sleep depravation. It has to be.

"Ah, you're early," Rodrick said from behind me.

I jumped and let out an undignified squeak.

I turned toward Rodrick's voice, placing a hand on my chest in a futile attempt to coax my heart back down from my throat.

I needed to stop acting like a scared rabbit if I didn't want to have a heart attack.

Rodrick stood there, staring at me as I forced myself to calm down and breathe slowly.

I stared right back at him.

Now, generally I don't like to openly stare at people like a creeper, but I didn't trust my eyes today. I had seen too many things that obviously didn't exist. I wanted to know if Rodrick had grown a third eye or anything.

Nope.

He looked just the same.

Same white hair.

Same ageless face.

Same odd scar.

And the same sense of unease I always felt around him.

Nothing had changed, so why could I feel the hairs on the back of my neck rising to attention. My heart started to flutter again as I tried to quell the fight or flight reflex that was welling up inside of me.

He was not right.

I watched Rodrick like a hawk as I walked back to pick up my bag and place it on the nearest table. I opened it and started pulling books out and setting them on the table, but never took my eyes off him.

There was no way he couldn't pick up on my absolute distrust of him. He might have been creepy, but I was pretty sure he wasn't stupid. But he didn't say a word. He merely continued watching me as I set out my school supplies on the table.

"So," I said when everything was out of my bag and I could stall no longer.

Rodrick put his hands behind his back and advanced towards me.

I grabbed hold of a sharpened pencil as if it were a dagger. I had no idea what I intended to do with it, but it made me feel a better holding it, nonetheless.

When Rodrick was within a few inches from me, he reached out and took my face in his hands, tilting it up and looking into my eyes.

"Hey, let go!" I shouted.

I tried unsuccessfully to yank away from him.

He was every bit as strong as he looked. He continued to hold my face, peering into my eyes. I could tell struggling would get me nowhere; his hands holding my face were like vices. I just gave up and stood still, though I kept my grip on the pencil.

If his hands went anywhere else I was ready to put his eye out.

"You're not ready," he said. Releasing my face, he turned and walked towards the door.

"What do you mean?" I shouted. "Where do you think you're going? Aren't you supposed to be teaching me something?"

I dropped the pencil and stomped over to him. I planted my fists firmly on my hips and gave him the death glare that my mother was so good at.

"Well, aren't you?"

Rodrick stood looking at me for a moment. I couldn't tell if his expression indicated irritation or amusement.

He opened the door. "I have nothing to teach you. For now." He left.

I stood there gaping like a codfish as he walked down the hall.

Great. So what am I supposed to do now?

I stomped back over to my bag and began slinging my books into it.

What do you mean you have nothing to teach me? It's not like I'm too stupid to learn. You teach me something and I'll learn it, Buddy. Just you try it and see!

I was ahead in all my classes, but I wasn't that far ahead. I still needed a credit in English to graduate, and I wanted to get a jump on college level algebra.

"So help me, if that man keeps me from graduating because he thinks he can't teach me anything, I'll...I'll..."

I slung the bag over my shoulder and stomped to the door.

I paused to give the fireplace one last look.

I shook my head, and slammed shut the library door. I turned and walked away before I could waste another thought on it.

Chapter 23

"She's beginning to change," Rodrick said as he flipped through a book in Cyle's office.

He studiously avoided looking at Cyle, who stood facing the window, his back to Rodrick.

"Did you hear me?" Rodrick asked when Cyle failed to respond.

"Yes, I heard you."

Cyle sighed, staring out the window at nothing in particular. "It's too soon."

"We knew this was a possibility." Rodrick set the book down, stood and crossed to stand beside Cyle.

"Yes, but we didn't think it would be this early," Cyle responded. "She's not ready. The change could kill her if it comes before her time."

"She's stronger than you think, Cyle. She'll make it. It'll be tough, but she'll make it."

Cyle nodded, his eyes focused on an oak leaf that refused to relinquish its hold on a lonely branch, even though the wind buffeted it mercilessly.

"I just wish we had found her sooner. We could have kept a better eye on her, maybe even convinced the Council to let us train her early."

Rodrick gave a rueful laugh.

"The council would never have allowed it," he said. "Or, rather, they would have insisted you give her to them, and let them do the training."

Cyle nodded, walked to his desk and sat.

"We need more time, Rodrick. I need more time; more time for her to trust me completely, so when we do tell her everything, she won't cut and run. Wouldn't Alex love that? Then he would have all the time in the world to win her over."

"Alex? What's that little prick got to do with it?" Rodrick asked.

Cyle ran a hand over his eyes and answered.

"That *little prick* is apparently Lee's boyfriend of sorts. He has forced himself upon us and refuses to leave. I assume it's because I sent Peach to Jacksonville to watch over her. He apparently feels that gives him the right to come here to...protect his interests."

"The girl's smarter than that. She won't be taken in by him."

Rodrick turned to leave the room.

"She already has..." Cyle mumbled. He looked up as Rodrick opened the door.

"Rodrick...how was it? I know you've just returned from there."

Rodrick was silent, his eyes staring straight ahead, as if seeing something that wasn't there.

"Dead. Everyone and everything." He whispered.

Rodrick shook his head, trying to dislodge the demons that pranced before his eyes. He turned back to Cyle, the anguish evident in his gaze.

"I'll keep searching, but..," the words caught in his throat. "But I fear there's not much hope of finding Bethany."

Cyle nodded and dropped his eyes back to his desk. He paid no attention to the click of the latch as Rodrick left the room. There never was much hope that they would find Bethany. Not alive, anyway. But he could never quite allow himself to believe she was really dead.

He opened his desk drawer and pulled out a photograph of a young woman with curly blonde locks and big, bright yellow eyes. She was holding a birdcage that was almost as big as she was. A raven with feathers as black as midnight resided inside.

Cyle ran his fingers over the girl's face. His expressionless features revealed the depth of emotion that churned just beneath the surface to anyone who cared to look.

Chapter 24

"Cyle, what is going on around here?" I banged open Cyle's office door and marched in without waiting for an invitation.

Cyle shoved something into his desk drawer and looked up at me in surprise.

"Oh. Um, sorry." I said. "Am I interrupting?"

Cyle cleared his throat.

"No, no. Of course not. So, what's on you're your mind?"

Cyle focused his attention completely on me as I threw my book bag across the room. He didn't even flinch when the contents spilled out across the floor.

I flopped into a comfy leather wingback chair opposite his desk is a most unladylike fashion that Grandmother would have scolded me for had she been there to see.

"First, I'm having all these weird dreams. Then I'm being visited in the night by this weird girl. And everyone around here is being all weird because they are so much *less* interesting than they normally are. Oh, and this morning; I swear I saw Peach floating. Yeah, floating. A couple of inches off the ground."

Cyle rested his elbows on his desk and steepled his fingers in front of his face. If anything I told him caused him any alarm at all you couldn't prove it by his expression.

"I don't know," I muttered, as much to myself as to Cyle. "Maybe I'm just tired. But I *know* I saw that fire. I saw it! It was a real fire, in the fireplace in the library that has never had a fire, and I saw it, and it was there!"

I couldn't control the flow of jumbled words that spewed from my mouth.

"And then that jerk of a teacher you hired for me has the gall to tell me that he has nothing to teach me. What is that supposed to mean? Is he calling me stupid? Like I'm too stupid to live? Like he's so brilliant I wouldn't understand anything he has to say? Jerk!"

I crossed my arms in defiance of any defense Cyle might offer. I was totally prepared to be disgruntled the rest of the day. I waited for some kind of reply, but Cyle never said a word.

I finally took the time to really look at him, forgetting that I was trying to be in a foul mood.

"Cyle?"

His eyes shot over to me, as if he were startled; as if he hadn't even known I was there.

"Oh, yes," he managed, like he hadn't heard a word I said. "That does sound awful, but everyone has a bad day now and again."

Cyle stood, walked to the door and held it open for me.

"Leeowyn..."

I knew something was up when he used my formal name.

"I've got a lot of work to do. Would you mind terribly if I asked you to do your homework in your room?"

"That's just it, Cyle," I tried hard to keep the sting out of my voice. "Your white-haired buddy didn't give me any homework."

"Well. Good. So you have a nice day off."

Cyle stared at me for a moment as he held the door open.

I met him stare for stare, but I guess I blinked first. I pushed myself up and took my own sweet time as I slouched out of the room.

"You forgot your books," Cyle called after me.

"I don't need them!" I shouted over my shoulder. "I have a *nice day off*, remember?"

I stormed down the hallway, looking for any person, place, or thing to take out my sea of confusion and anger on. No one had been fully truthful with me here since the day I arrived. I knew that. But *this* was taking it to a whole 'nuther level.

They were purposely trying to make life harder on me. I was sure of it.

You're over reacting.

I stopped and leaned against a wall, trying to will my mind into some semblance of its happy place.

I *was* over reacting.

No one was being any more shifty than usual. Maybe I was just more aware of it, for some reason that I couldn't fathom. Maybe there was something wrong with me; something wrong with my eyes.

"Lee?"

It was Alex's voice.

I turned to see him standing a little more than an arm's length from me. He had the look of a man facing down a starving leopard; one wrong move and you get your throat ripped out.

I gave him a half-hearted smile to show that I meant him no harm.

Alex hadn't changed since the last time we met.

No luster.

No inhuman aura of greatness surrounding him.

Just a regular, better-than-good-looking male.

"Are you...better?" he asked as he tentatively stepped towards me.

"No," I answered simply. "I'm not."

I turned my body towards him, trying to give off a more welcoming sense than what I was feeling. Truth be told, I didn't want to be around anyone right now.

I especially didn't want to be around someone whose mere presence was a constant reminder that everything I was seeing was wrong.

But, I also had my fill of diva moments for the day and I didn't particularly feel like causing any more drama. No sense in making a big fuss over something I couldn't explain.

Alex reached out slowly and allowed the tips of his fingers to glide across my arm.

"Is there anything I can do to help?" He asked.

I dunno. Can you make my eyes see normal stuff again?

"No."

I closed my eyes and paused for a moment.

"Well, yes."

I opened my eyes again.

"That guy Cyle hired as my new tutor? He's not doing the best job of teaching. So, if you wanted to keep me company while I studied, I guess that would be helpful. I mean, if you want to."

Rodrick may not think he could teach me anything, but I still had plenty to learn. I was pretty sure the state of Florida would take a dim view of my senior year report card with straight F's. The state home school board would not be amused and my mom would throw the mother of all hissy fits.

Alex gave me one of his trademark sparkling smiles, the kind that would have sent me reeling a month ago. Today, it just felt like a wall of fog rolled over me.

"I would love to," he replied.

I graced him with as much of a smile as I could muster and started back towards the library. Before I could take a second step, Alex grabbed my arm and pulled me into a soft embrace.

"I hope you're alright with me coming to visit you," he breathed into my ear.

My heart failed to skip a beat. My face didn't flush. The temperature didn't rise and the birds didn't start singing sweetly in the trees. He simply had no affect on me.

"No, of course not," I answered, pushing him away a little more forcefully than was absolutely necessary.

I could see the hurt look in his eyes for a split second, but he covered it quickly with another smile.

I wish I could hide my emotions that well.

"Good! Then lead away to the library," he bowed and extended his arm like a musketeer from an old storybook.

Chapter 25

I absentmindedly turned a page in my ACT prep book, but my eyes stayed trained on Alex.

He was engrossed in a first-edition, bound copy of Robert Frost's poems. He was ready to help me if I had a question about anything.

So he said.

I had lots of questions I wanted answers to.

None of them had to do with anything covered in the ACT.

Funny; just a few days ago I felt like I could talk to Alex about anything. He was now just like everyone else in this house - all knowing and untelling.

Untelling?

I needed to stop making up words.

"Did you need something, Lee?" Alex asked.

I startled and dropped my test prep book. I had been spacing out and didn't notice when he started looking at me.

"Huh? What? Um, no."

I scooped my book back up and flipped it open.

"Just reading."

"You always read upside down?" Alex asked.

I glanced down at the book and, sure enough, I was holding it upside down.

"Um...yes. Yes, sometimes I do."

I turned the book over.

Why did I suddenly feel like Alex was a foreigner? Like he was the enemy?

Even worse, why did I feel like my own family was the enemy?

I felt the book suddenly being tugged out of my hands and Alex was kneeling in front of me. He set the book aside and put his hands on my knees, catching and holding my gaze like you would hold a butterfly - soft enough to not hurt it, but firm enough to keep it from flying away.

"Lee, this is me. Alex. You can talk to me. What's wrong?"

His voice was low and comforting as he softly rubbed my knees. His visage was kind and welcoming. I found myself desperately wishing I could just curl up in his arms and forget that I was probably losing my mind.

But all I could focus on was the fact that his touch wasn't affecting me at all.

"You're different," I mumbled.

It took some effort, but I managed to tear my eyes away from his. His hands paused and I felt his grip tighten slightly, almost imperceptibly.

"What do you mean?" he whispered.

I didn't meet his eyes. I couldn't.

"You're just...different," I said. "Everyone is. You all look and act exactly the same. But you're not. You're different. You used to be a blazing sunset. You used to take my breath away. Touching you was like reaching my hand into a bag of full of lightning that was stolen from a thunderstorm. I touch you now and I don't feel anything. Except fear. And confusion."

I stood up and walked away from him. I started to rant as I paced. Finally, someone was listening to me and I wasn't going to miss my chance to vent. Who knows, I might even get some answers.

"And I'm having these dreams," I snarled at the memory.

"Dreams?" he asked.

"More like waking nightmares," I snapped back, for no good reason. "There was a girl in my room this morning."

"Wait, what?" Alex asked. "Who was in your room? Was it Peach?"

He rose to his feet, obvious concern was etched on his face as he watched me continue to pace.

"No! Stop talking. It wasn't Peach. I don't know who it was. It was someone I've never seen before. And she was horrible. She was shouting things at me, and I think it was because of the other silver-blonde haired girl I had been watching who was killing a man..."

"You saw someone kill a man?" Alex gasped.

"I said stop talking! And no, I didn't see anyone kill anybody. Not really. At least I don't think so. No, it wasn't real. Or...well. It *felt* real. But it was a dream. It had to be a dream."

I paced back and forth, the length of the library.

"And then that other girl was there; the one who was in my room. And she was covered in blood."

I don't know when it started, but I was crying. Tears were streaming down my cheeks and I couldn't stop myself.

"And she touched my cheek." I shivered at the memory.

"But her hand...her hand..."

I couldn't make myself finish, I couldn't relive that moment.

"And everyone is different, and no one will tell me anything, and I feel like I'm going crazy and everyone knows why and no one will help me!"

All the unease and anger I had held in check came galloping out and I was powerless to hold it back.

Suddenly Alex was holding me, stroking my hair, whispering soothing words into my ears. I don't know how long I wept like a baby, but eventually the tears dried up and I was able to breathe normally again. I pulled away enough to turn my face up and look at him.

"Lee..." he started to say something, but his voice trailed off.

"You *know* something," I stated.

I could feel the anger starting to rise again. I pulled away from him completely.

He looked around to make sure we were alone, then nodded once.

"Then why won't you tell me..."

"Because I can't."

His voice was pitched low enough that it wouldn't carry past my ears.

He put a hand over my mouth and looked around once more before pulling me closer until his mouth was next to my ear.

"Meet me at the edge of the woods tonight when everyone is asleep. I'll explain as much as I can."

He pushed me back to arm's length, released me, and strode from the room without looking back.

I stood there, shaking. My heart pounded in my chest like that gooey little alien creature in the movie, trying to explode with excitement.

I was finally going to get some answers.

Chapter 26

Are you the one responsible for starting the fires in all the rooms?" I asked Reynolds as he poked and prodded the wood in my bedroom fireplace until it was a sufficiently roaring blaze.

Reynolds smiled and nodded as he closed the screen in front of the fireplace and dusted his hands together.

"Oh, yes," he replied.

I slowly positioned myself between Reynolds and the door, trying hard to not make it look like I was trying to cut off his exit.

"Oh," I said. "So, you are the one who started the fire in the library this morning?"

His eyes met mine evenly. There was a surreptitious smile that crinkled the edges of his mouth. He tapped a quick finger to his nose and winked at me.

I furrowed my brows and leaned back against the door. At this point I really didn't care if he knew I was blocking his way.

"That's not really much of an answer, Reynolds," I chided.

Reynolds just continued to smile. He walked until he was standing directly in front of me. We stood facing each other without speaking for an uncomfortable moment.

"Things are changing," Reynolds finally broke the silence. "If you please?"

He nodded toward the door and I reluctantly slid out of the way. Reynolds opened the door and started to leave, but he turned at the last moment and gave me a quixotic look that I couldn't read. I wasn't sure if it was concern or pride, like a parent watching his little girl go off the high dive for the first time.

"*You* are changing," he said, then shut the door behind him.

I felt cold, despite the fire that roared just a few feet away. I looked down at my hands. They were shaking.

Changing?

Is that why I feel so different?

I rushed into my bathroom and examined myself in front of the full-length cheval mirror.

I looked the same to me.

Height, build, hair color, eye color - all normal.

I hadn't sprouted any horns or tails that I could see, so that was a plus.

You're changing.

I shivered as I walked out of the bathroom.

You just need to calm down.

I picked up the notebook I used for writing letters home to Mom, and allowed my thoughts to flow into the ink and onto the paper. At least I tried to.

Dear Mom,

I stared at the paper, willing the words to come. But they wouldn't. I finally gave up, threw the notebook onto my bed and let out an exasperated sigh.

What could I possibly say that would make any kind of sense without completely freaking her out? I didn't want to lie and tell her everything was normal and I was fine. *Dear Mom. Having a wonderful time. Wish you were here.* But...

I glanced at the clock on the wall.

I still had a few hours until everyone would be asleep. I ran my hands through my hair, and not for the first time wished that there was any kind of Internet here.

4G. 3G. Heck, I'd have been happy with dial-up.

No such luck.

Twenty-six successful five-star Sudoku puzzles and five failed crossword puzzles later, and it was finally time to meet Alex. I pulled on my black zip-up jacket and turned the lights off in my room.

Somewhere in the back of my mind that old theme song from *Mission: Impossible* was playing. My hands began to shake.

Pull yourself together, woman!

The hallways that linked my bedroom to the front door were dark as midnight. Luckily I had wandered these halls enough over the past few years that I knew the locations of all the side tables by heart. I knew where the creaky boards were, too.

It didn't take long for me to get to the front door. I hadn't made a sound, but my heart pounded so loud I was sure it would wake up the whole house. The last thing I needed at that moment was someone running out to find out what all the commotion was about.

My hand was on the doorknob, yet I paused.

This moment had the eerie feel of weighty importance, like I was standing at the proverbial crossroads of my life.

One road would lead me to answers. But somehow I knew those answers would change everything, and not necessarily for the better.

The other road would lead me back to the safety of my room. But in that safety there was only confusion and darkness.

I made my decision.

I took a deep breath and opened the door.

Answers were better than darkness, no matter how much it might change things.

Mission: Impossible gave way to *James Bond* theme music playing in my head as I crept across the courtyard. While I knew the hallways of the house by heart, it was impossible to avoid crackling twigs, crunchy leaves, and noisy patches of gravel underfoot.

It was all I could do to keep from breaking out in fits of nervous hysterical laughter.

I panicked when I saw a window light up and I ducked behind a bench.

I had no idea who belonged to the room with the lighted window, so I wasn't sure who was awake. A silhouette walked to the window and peeked out from behind the curtain for a moment. Then the light went out and the after image from the lighted window floated in front of me in the sudden darkness.

I waited a few more moments to regain my night vision, and to make sure no one was coming outside, before I stood up and made a mad dash to the woods. Adrenaline fueled my legs and I sprinted like a cross-country runner smelling the finish line.

I no longer cared about noisy gravel or crunchy leaves. I leaped over logs and fallen trees like a gazelle, not even breaking my stride. I didn't slow down until I was safely into the tree line.

I grabbed onto a slender poplar tree and contemplated my situation, just outside of the line that separated the backyard from the forest that I was never allowed in to.

I breathed heavily. That sprint revealed that I wasn't in nearly as good a shape as I thought.

I looked around, trying to decide which way to go. Alex hadn't really been too specific about where to meet him, and I hadn't seen him since the incident in the library in order to ask him.

To the right? Or to the left? Time to flip a coin.

Luckily, it wasn't left up to my judgment.

"Lee."

I stifled a scream, although an undignified squeak still managed to escape my lips.

I turned to see Alex a few feet deeper into the woods. He waved for me to join him.

I couldn't make myself move. The adrenaline that had fuel my actions was depleted; the beginnings of fear sewed my feet to the ground.

Alex sighed, muttered something under his breathe about *'girls,'* strode forward, grabbed my arm and yanked me into the woods.

"Do you want someone to see you?" he hissed as he pulled me through the trees and brambles, ignoring the times I whimpered or yelped as a thorn or stray branch jabbed at me.

When we reached a small clearing in the woods, he let go of my arm and rounded to face me.

I flinched. He looked angry, and for a moment I thought he was going to hit me.

I had no idea what I had done to offend him so deeply.

I waited in silence.

Alex started pacing.

And I waited some more.

Finally I could stand the waiting game no longer.

"So, not that I don't love standing in the deep, dark scary woods in the middle of the night, but was there a reason you literally dragged me in here?"

At the sound of my voice, Alex stopped pacing and looked at me as if he had forgotten I was even there.

Typical.

He strode towards me and I started to tense up. The look on his face was deadly serious, and I wasn't sure if it was directed at me or something else entirely.

Alex stopped and, taking my hand, he led me over to a fallen log and sat me down on it.

"Okay, don't interrupt me," Alex commanded, "because I'm not sure just how much I can make myself say."

I nodded once to show I was listening.

This was it; I was finally going to get some answers.

"So, you need to know right off the bat that there are some things I cannot tell you. It's not because I don't want to. There are rules."

"Rules?" I asked.

"Stop talking and listen," he snapped, and I clamped my mouth shut immediately.

"There are rules preventing me from telling you certain things. Rules, and some very powerful people who would probably disembowel me if they ever found out I was here with you."

He chuckled as if he had made a joke, but his laugh carried a hint of truth that said he was whistling in the wind.

Alex took a deep breath to steady himself, then continued.

"First things first. This place we are right now; this isn't Earth. These people, your family, they're not human."

Alex looked me square in the eye and said, "Lee, you're not human."

I'm not the prettiest girl in the class, and I know I'm not the sharpest crayon in the box. But I've had at least a few guys try to get me into the woods alone with them at night.

I knew a line when I heard one.

I stood up and stomped towards the edge of the clearing, and I was being none too quiet about it.

"Where do you think you are going?" Alex snapped.

"You're a jerk!" I exploded. "I came to you for answers, and now you're playing some stupid mind game with me? I'm not one of your simpering little beach groupies, Alex, and I'm not an idiot. You're going to have to try a little harder than that if you want to make me look like a fool."

Bile rose in the back of my throat making me what to throw up. I turned around and walked back towards the house.

"Lee, I'm not lying!"

Alex rushed after me, grabbing me by my arm.

I yanked it away in one smooth motion as my other hand caught his face in a full-bodied slap. I turned away from him.

If he was startled, or hurt, he didn't show it. He merely took my shoulders in his firm grasp, turned me around to face him and said, "Leeowyn, look!"

Suddenly the clearing was bright as day, stinging my eyes. I put my arms over my face to shield my eyes from the stark brightness.

"Turn it off," I spat. "Someone will see!"

"Leeowyn; open your eyes," Alex commanded.

I gingerly lowered my arms and opened my eyes to the light. I blinked, rubbed my eyes, and opened them again.

There was no searchlight. There was no firelight. It wasn't the dawn.

It was Alex.

He was emitting light.

I stood gaping as the nimbus that surrounded Alex slowly faded to a dull aura. He walked towards me, his hand outstretched, showing me he wasn't holding anything.

I backed away. I wanted to run, to hide, but my legs wouldn't cooperate. Tears started to well up in my eyes, from fear or wonder, I don't know.

"How did you do that?" I whispered. He was like a sun, embodied.

"Leeowyn," he called my name and it was a cool breeze over gardenia blossoms. "I'm not human either."

Alex touched my arm and it was summer caressing my skin.

"Let me explain."

Chapter 27

I watched Alex slowly dim until he was just Alex again.

My mouth was hanging open like a trout out of water, but I was powerless to close it. I dug my nails into my palm, expecting to wake up in my bed at any moment.

This isn't real.

This *couldn't* be real.

Alex fixed his eyes on me, making sure I was watching, as if I could possibly tear my eyes away. He held his palm out over the ground. Leaves and twigs began to float up towards his palm, as if they were caught in a tiny tornado. They continued to float and spin, intertwining and coalescing until they formed the shape of an orb; then the orb assumed the shape of a miniature planet earth.

Alex extended a palm to me and the mini-earth floated towards me.

I sucked in my breath as it stopped and floated right in front of me.

"It's real, Leeowyn," Alex said.

I looked up at him and then back at the globe that floated in front of me, gracefully turning on its axis.

I reached out a finger and poked what would have been Asia.

It *was* real.

"How?"

It was all I could think to ask.

I put my hands on either side of the globe. I held it in my hands, turned it over and examined the leaves that had formed to the exact outlines of earth's oceans and continents.

"I can't tell you."

Alex took a couple of paces forward and stood beside me.

"Not yet."

Alex took the miniature world from my hands and tossed it into the air where it burst into a hundred pieces, each one floating peacefully back to the ground as if nothing had ever happened.

Alex never took his eyes off of me.

"Things are changing," he said.

I frowned.

"Reynolds told me that earlier tonight."

"Of course he did." Alex pasted that trademark smirk across his face, but he didn't sound happy about it.

I wanted to ask him what he knew about Reynolds, or my family, or anything, but I couldn't find the words. My mind was racing way too fast, yet it was completely blank at the same time.

I still couldn't believe what I had just seen; what I had just touched. I reached my hand out and took one of Alex's. I turned it over and studied it. It looked perfectly normal.

Everything looked perfectly normal.

Nothing about Alex, or his hand, said that he had just super nova-ed, or created a planet out of the forest floor.

"You're not going crazy," Alex said.

"I'm not?"

I could feel the tears forming behind my eyes. Alex had just tapped into my biggest fear - that I was going stark, raving mad.

"There is a reason no one has been completely honest with you."

"The rules you mentioned earlier?" I asked.

Alex nodded.

He pulled his hand from my grasp, and placed it on my cheek, soothing me like I was a little girl who had skinned her knee.

"Lee, you are important to everyone here. I can't tell you how important."

Alex looked at me with such intensity, I was amazed I could hold his gaze without bursting into flame.

"Just, hold out for a few more weeks, okay?"

I frowned.

"What happens in a few more weeks? I mean, besides my birthday?"

Alex rewarded me with a sunburst smile.

"Wait," I said. "My birthday? What's so important about my birthday? I mean, to anyone other than me, and maybe my mom."

"You are turning eighteen," Alex said. "You are coming into your inheritance."

Alex let his hand drop from my face. He turned and started walking towards the edge of the woods.

"Alex, wait! I have questions, and you haven't explained anything."

I followed him toward the edge of the clearing. I wasn't even sure which direction led back to the house.

"I know, and I'm sorry, but I've explained all I can. I can't risk saying anything more."

Alex took my hand and led me to the line of trees that marked the edge of the backyard.

"Now things get tricky," Alex breathed as he studied the house for any movement.

"This part is very important, Lee. You can't say anything to anyone about this. You have to act like nothing ever happened, do you understand that?"

I nodded.

Alex smiled, leaned down and kissed my forehead before leading us out of the woods. We hadn't taken two steps into the yard when we were interrupted by a very angry, very familiar voice.

"What have you done, boy?" Peach snapped.

Alex's grip on my hand tightened until I was sure my hand would break. I stifled a whimper and was able to slip my hand from his grasp while keeping my eyes on Peach.

She was fuming.

I had never seen her so mad.

"She was going crazy," Alex said between clinched teeth. "She had to know something. Besides, I broke no rules."

Peach walked forward, her hair flickering around her as if caught in an electrical storm. I was sure I saw tiny sparks flying from the tips of her locks. Her eyes were shining, glowing, brighter than they should have, illuminating the total darkness that surrounded us.

She looked beautiful.

She looked dangerous.

She did not look human; not in the least.

"You were always too impatient," she snapped at him.

Peach rounded on me, an odd dichotomy of anger, pity, and anguish roiling in her eyes.

"Lee, I'm so sorry," she said.

"Sorry about what?" I asked.

Peach stopped in front of me, and touched the side of my head.

Chapter 28

I opened my eyes to bright, cheery sunlight flooding into my bedroom. I sat up, in bed and looked around my room.

I had the strangest feeling, like I was forgetting something, but I couldn't remember what.

Which I suppose is the definition of forgetting something.

I had a vague impression of being in the woods, which was sheer foolishness. The woods were strictly off limits.

And Alex was there.

And Peach.

Or were they?

The harder I tried to remember, the faster the images faded from my mind.

I yawned and stretched.

Nope. All gone.

I hated it when I couldn't remember my dreams. Now it was going to bother me all day.

Chapter 29

"What?" I asked for the third time.

Peach had been staring at me from across the breakfast table and it was starting to creep me out. She paused for only a moment before breaking out into an easy smile.

"Oh, nothing," she chattered. "Just excited about getting ready for your birthday."

I gave her a look that clearly said I didn't believe her before turning my attention back to my eggs.

My birthday was tomorrow and everyone seemed to be exponentially more excited about it than I was.

Yeah, sure, I was happy to be turning eighteen and all. Woohoo, now I get to vote. So what? It's not like turning sixteen when you can finally get your driver's license. But everyone around here was acting like it was *the* milestone event of my life.

The past couple weeks had been some of the strangest I had ever experienced at Cyle's house. More than once I woke up with the weirdest feeling that something big had happened, but I couldn't remember what. Normally this would have bothered me. A lot. But, for some reason, I just let it slide.

I was letting a lot of things that would normally bother me slide, come to think of it. I felt like a zombie, walking around in a haze and barely noticing anything.

At least that's how I think zombies feel. I've never actually talked to one, so I don't really know.

Peach was my constant companion, never straying too far from my side. I could forget even hoping to get any alone time with Alex.

I blamed it on my grandmother. I didn't think she would be overly thrilled with a good-looking boy that I was obviously interested in staying in the house, but I didn't expect her to overreact the way she did.

It was like Alex had committed some unforgiveable sin by wanting to date me.

I had walked into the library once to find my little, old grandmother standing toe to toe with Alex, staring him in the eye and pointedly jabbing her finger into his chest.

"...find out you talk to her one more time, Boy, I will report it to the Council. And don't give me any of your guff about not breaking any rules. I don't care if you've not technically broken any rules."

Alex opened his mouth to say something when my grandmother turned and saw me. She gave Alex a look that would wither an oak tree, turned and walked out without so much as a glance at me.

"What was all that about?"

I had started walking towards Alex when suddenly Peach appeared out of nowhere to stand by my side. It was like some sensor had gone off in her head, like, *'Ding! Ding! Ding! Lee and Alex are alone together! Get over there now!'*

"Hey, there you are, Lee!" Peach chirped as she grabbed my hand and steered me from the room.

I had just enough time to shoot Alex an apologetic look over my shoulder before Peach pulled me out of the room and into the hallway.

I saw Rodrick every day, and every day it was the same old story. He would look into my eyes, then tell me he had nothing to teach me.

Again, this should have bothered me, but instead I just shrugged my shoulders and continued to study on my own.

Once, while doing my school work on my own – *Thanks, Rodrick* - I had looked across the table at Alex and Peach, who regularly flanked me like sentinels. It occurred to me that they were the same age as me, yet they never did any school work.

"Hey, Alex," I asked, "how is it you are able to miss so much school?"

Alex and Peach gave each other a look that screamed, *Busted!*

Alex coughed to buy himself a moment, then said, "Oh, I've already graduated."

"Decided to forego college, then?" I asked, setting my book down and looking at him steadily.

I could have sworn he told me he was in my grade, but the more I tried to remember, the fuzzier the memory got.

"I'm taking a year off," he said. "You know, a gap year, to find out what I really want to do with my life."

He gave me a reassuring smile.

I nodded and picked my book back up.

It was an obvious lie. I should have been bothered by it. I *knew* I should have been bothered by it.

Instead I just shrugged and continued to study.

I didn't have any more nightmares, which was partly due to the fact that I rarely slept. I spent a good deal of the night roaming the halls. It was a ritual that I had come to enjoyed immensely.

At night there was no chance of me running into someone who looked feverishly happy. Or walking into a room with people who looked as if they had just been caught talking about me.

At night, alone in the halls, I could think. Or not think, which I think I preferred.

I always woke up in my bed with no recollection of how I got there. One moment I would be roaming the halls, the next moment I was waking up to a bright stream of sunlight washing the gloom from my room.

If I didn't know my family better I would suspect that they were drugging me.

My forkful of eggs paused halfway to my mouth.

Just how well do I know my family?

What if they were drugging me?

What if those patches of my memory were suddenly just gone because I found out too much?

I laughed out loud.

Sometimes I think crazy things.

"So, is there anything special you want for your birthday, Leeowyn?" Grandmother asked.

She was making a list of all the things she and Reynolds needed to do in preparation for the "Big Event." I begged her not to make a big deal about it, but no one seemed to really listen to my requests when it came to things like this. I wasn't too surprised when she ignored me.

"Um, no. Not really." I said.

I wasn't a very picky eater and I didn't have a lot of favorite foods. Food was fuel, so I ate whatever they put in front of me. Besides, anything Reynolds and my Grandmother made was generally amazing.

My mind drifted back to the last birthday I spent with my mom, and I felt my eyes sting with tears. I missed her more than ever this year. My mom might not have been super-mom, and sure, money was tight sometimes, but my mom never lied to me.

She never told me about my dad.

I excused myself and walked to my room. I was glad to see that Peach didn't immediately jump up and follow me.

I sat on my windowsill and started writing out a letter to my mom. Like always, I found it hard to give her a good amount of detail about my stay here without making her worry.

I was sure she had noticed how nondescript my last few letters were, but she never said anything in her responses to lead me to believe she was worried about me.

I was glad for that.

Everyone here is making a huge deal about my birthday. Of course, I'm sure you would, too. I miss the cakes you used to get at the store for me. Maybe when I get back we can celebrate my birthday again, just you and me.

I scribbled a few more lines of superficial fluffy stuff, just to make it sound less depressing, then licked the nasty tasting glue on the envelope and sealed the letter.

Grabbing my school bag, I stood and walked down stairs to Cyle's office. I knocked on the door and poked my head inside.

"I've got a letter for my mom," I said, waving the letter in front of me as I walked over to his desk.

He smiled and took the letter from me.

"You've been sending out a lot of these lately," he said.

I shrugged.

"It'd be a lot quicker and easier if you'd just get Internet," I responded, only half joking.

I turned to leave.

"Lee, are you happy here?"

I paused, staring at my hand on the doorknob. I pondered his question. I'm not sure I had really thought about it until that moment.

Was I?

I thought I was. Or at least I think I *had* been. But recently, everything was so fuzzy. I wasn't sure what I felt.

"I don't know, Cyle," I answered truthfully. "I miss my mom. A lot. And I miss being trusted more."

I whispered the last part, and I wasn't sure he had heard it. I turned around and looked at him.

"Why?" I asked.

"I just want you to be happy here. You'll be eighteen tomorrow," Cyle said.

I laughed as I opened the door and stepped out.

"I know. Everyone keeps reminding me."

I shut the door and headed off toward the library, ready to face another day of Rodrick telling me, *I can teach you nothing.*

I entered the library expecting to find Peach and Alex, but the room was empty.

I set my bag down on the table we always used for studying and sat down.

This is weird.

After enduring the last few weeks of constant surveillance, to suddenly find myself alone during daylight hours felt wonderful. And I felt like someone, somewhere, was watching me.

Chapter 30

Cyle looked around his study, fixing his eyes on everyone as they settled in.

Alex leaned against the back wall, separated from the rest of the gathering. He was an outsider there, but he refused to relinquish his right to be present.

Peach and Rodrick sat in front of him.

Everyone waited for Cyle to speak.

"Tomorrow," Cyle said.

The others nodded.

Cyle raised his eyes to meet Alex's brooding stare. There was burnished fire in those yellow eyes.

"I hope we won't have any more outbursts from you?" he asked.

Alex held up his hands in submission.

"No, of course not, I'll just keep lying to her like the rest of you, while little Miss Pawn over here keeps wiping her memory clean."

"Damn it, boy, stop being a fool!" Rodrick roared.

The white haired man pounded his fist on Cyle's desk and stood to confront the younger man.

"You have your own agenda," Peach joined in the fray before Rodrick could get in another word. "You're trying to win her over to your side, so you can stop it with all your holier-than-thou crap. Man up, and quit pretending that anything you've done has been for Lee's benefit."

The heat in her glare should have set the air between them on fire. And it might have, if Alex hadn't matched it with a glare that was as cool as ice.

"Enough!" Cyle stood behind his desk, authority rolling off him like a hot, August thunderstorm.

Peach swallowed, nodded and sat.

Rodrick shook his head and strode over to stare out the window.

Alex merely crossed his arms and leaned back against the wall, cooler than James Dean on a good day - but he didn't say anything else.

"As I was saying," Cyle placed his hands on his desktop and leaned forward, accentuating his presence in the room, "tomorrow Leeowyn Blake comes into her inheritance. None of us knows at what time that will happen, so someone needs to be around her at all times."

Alex started to raise his hand.

"Not you!" Cyle snapped, but Alex would not submit without a fight.

"What? You and yours are the only ones with the chance to sway her?" he barked.

"This is *still* my land." Cyle spoke quietly, dangerously. "As long as you're here, you will abide by my rules."

Drawing himself up to his full height, Cyle folded his hands behind his back and walked toward Alex with slow, measured steps. A nimbus glow pulsed around him; barely contained power threatening to burst free. He stopped inches from Alex and paused for a moment before continuing.

"Please understand me, boy. I've endured your insolence these past weeks because Leeowyn wasn't ready to know the truth. I couldn't afford to compel you to obey. Well, that time is past. Now, you *will* obey, because there is no reason for me to keep my temper in check. Do we understand one another?"

Alex opened his mouth to say something, thought better of it, closed his mouth and nodded.

"Good," Cyle's smile didn't reach his eyes. "Of course, if you find my rules too... difficult...you are free to return to Earth."

"When will you give her the necklace?" Peach broke the tension in the room.

Every eye in the room turned to the rectangular box on Cyle's desk.

Cyle marched back to his desk and picked up the box carefully, as if it carried the weight of the world, or housed a poisonous asp.

"After dinner, hopefully," Cyle replied. "If the change doesn't occur before then."

He ran his hand through his hair.

"Tomorrow," Cyle breathed.

"Everything changes tomorrow."

Chapter 31

The smell of burning ash choked my throat and stung my eyes as I stumbled across the beach towards my house. Black plumes billowed into the sky. I wished, rather than hoped, that they were the result of a festival bonfire. But they originated right where my home should be.

No! Please no, please no, please no.

My heart ached as I got closer and closer to my house.

The new, white pearl pendant banging against my throat as I ran reminded me that everything that had just happened was not a dream.

I rounded the corner of the street to see my home, my mom's home, engulfed in flames.

My lungs were too sore from running to scream.

I startled awake and managed to stifle the scream that was still bubbling up in my throat.

I was still in the library. I didn't remember falling asleep, but I must have. And I must have slept for a long time. It had been morning when I opened my books to study, but now the sun had set. I was sitting in pitch darkness. I could barely see my hand in front of my face.

I tried to remember what I had seen in my dream that made me so jittery; that filled me with foreboding.

But it was no use. It slipped through my mind like water through a sieve. I sighed and felt for my book bag while my eyes adjusted to the blackness.

Then I saw her.

She was sitting across the room from me.

The same blood stained clothes.

The same dead, not-dead, bird struggling in her hands.

I froze.

Everything inside of me screamed for me to move, to run, to get out of that room, to find some light! But I couldn't even force myself to blink.

"You're waking up, Little Bird. But there is not much time left," the girl whispered to me. "So very little time."

She continued to pet the flailing bird with soothing strokes of the hand that was still covered in flesh. She opened her mouth to speak again when someone turned the lights on, and she was gone.

"Why are you sitting in the dark?" Peach asked.

She walked into the library with Alex at her heels.

I sat staring at the chair that not two seconds earlier had held a girl with a raven.

Did I dream her? Was I dreaming now?

"I, uh...asleep." I mumbled. "Yeah, I must have fallen asleep."

I gave myself a shake and turned my attention back to my study materials. As I packed my stuff into my bag I couldn't stop my hands from quaking.

"So, where were you guys today?" I asked.

Peach give Alex a sideways look before answering.

"We were making birthday plans!"

Great. My birthday. Again.

I stifled a groan as I pulled my bag onto my shoulder and walked out of the library with the two of them.

"I really don't want any big to-do," I insisted for the fortieth time, as Peach linked arms with me and led me down the hallway towards the dining room.

"Of course you do. Everyone does," Peach responded.

She continued chattering on about cake and presents as we walked towards the dinner table.

I started to feel a little dizzy and was thankful when I was able to finally sit down. I was sure I was still just a little groggy from falling asleep so early in the day. I hated long, afternoon naps because they always left me feeling more tired than before I took them.

This feeling was different, though. Maybe I was getting sick.

I barely paid attention to anything throughout the entire dinner. I took whatever was offered to me, but ate almost none of it.

Dizziness spread from my head throughout my entire body. I know that sounds weird, but I don't know how else to describe it. It felt exactly like my entire body was dizzy.

I lifted my fork, but my hand was shaking so badly that I quickly set it back down before anyone could notice. I was less than thrilled with the amount of attention I was getting already. The last thing I wanted at that moment was one more reason for people to fawn over me.

Dinner took longer than normal.

At least it seemed that way to me.

I kept glancing at the clock, hoping someone would notice that it was well past eleven and time to call it a night, but no one did.

Everyone's voices kept ringing in my ears until I could no longer distinguish one from another. I nodded at all the right times; at least I hope I was nodding at the right times, but I could barely keep a smile on my face. I tried my best to keep out of the conversation. I was sure I would make no sense to anyone if I tried to talk.

Sweat started trickling down my back between my shoulder blades.

I had to hold my hands together between my knees under the table to keep them from shaking.

I was afraid I might throw up at any minute.

I wanted desperately to run to my room.

I didn't want to move.

I wasn't sure my feet would be able to hold me up.

My throat was on fire.

My eyes were stinging.

I glanced at the clock again.

Eleven fifty-three.

Would this dinner never end?

How could people still be eating?

Then I realized no one was eating. The plates had all been cleared from the table.

When had that happened?

Eleven fifty-five.

I began shaking violently, and there was nothing I could do to hide it.

I tried to say something; tried to get someone's attention; but my throat was too dry.

I only ended up croaking.

Eleven fifty-eight.

No one in the room was talking.

Everyone in the room was staring at me.

I grabbed the edge of the table with both hands and forced myself to stand.

The room was deathly silent, and everyone was staring at me.

Surely they could tell something was wrong with me.

Why was no one helping me?

They all just kept looking at me; eagerness, expectation etched across their faces.

My legs were shaking too much. I knew I wouldn't be able to stand much longer.

Eleven fifty-nine.

My legs gave out.

I think I may have shouted something that sounded like a plea for help.

My eyes were clouding over.

I was burning up.

I was on fire, I was sure of it. I would be consumed by it at any moment.

I lost all control of my limbs.

I couldn't see anymore.

I couldn't talk anymore.

I couldn't feel or move or know.

I was dying.

I was in Hell.

Midnight.

Chapter 32

I wasn't dead, but I was screaming.

My eyes were open, but I couldn't see anything.

Strong hands held me as I thrashed and flailed, striking out at anything within reach.

The fire that had been burning me alive was slowly fading to an ember; or maybe I had just lost all my nerve endings and I couldn't feel it any more.

I blinked, and slowly the world started coming back into view.

At first it was only blurry colors and indistinct outlines. The blur that was holding me forced some cool liquid into my mouth. I swallowed gladly, relishing the cool sweetness that quenched the fire in my throat.

The cool liquid was gone too soon.

I wanted to ask for more but I was afraid that I couldn't speak, and I didn't want to risk it.

My vision sharpened and the blurs slowly came into focus. The blur holding me was Cyle. He was saying something to me. I could see his lips moving, but I couldn't make out the words. The ringing in my ears was too loud; too distracting.

I closed my eyes and waited. Eventually the ringing receded enough for me to understand him.

"Can you stand?"

I nodded slowly, an action which caused the room to lurch around me for a moment. Cyle helped me to my feet and immediately maneuvered me into a plush chair where I sat down.

I was still shaking, but even that was fading. Only the aftermath remained now.

I felt a weight around my neck that hadn't been there before. I looked down to see a white pearl pendant hanging from a chain, resting against my skin.

It was vaguely familiar. I tried to remember where I had seen it before.

Had someone been wearing this before?

Yes.

Who? Was it someone here in the house?

No.

I remembered a flicker of me running on the beach, this necklace, this white pearl pendant, bumping against my throat.

My dream.

I had dreamed this.

And then I remembered...everything.

Alex in the woods, glowing like the sun, creating worlds out of the dust of the earth like some kind of god.

Peach catching us.

And not just once, it had happened several times.

Each time Peach caught us, she did something to me. She made me forget. She made me forget what Alex told me.

This place isn't Earth.

They're not human.

You're not human.

I'm not human!

"No. No. No. No. No!" I gasped, standing, pushing myself away from Cyle's steadying hands.

Everyone was standing in a circle around me; all wearing expressions of mixed worry and concern.

Or was it fear?

I saw Peach, floating inches above the floor. The air around her was shimmered and sparkled like the aurora borealis. She appeared thinner, frailer than I had ever seen her before.

Not human. They're not human.

"What's happening to me?" I asked when I could finally work some spit back into my mouth. "Who are you people? Or should I ask, *what* are you?"

Everyone cast a disparaging look at Alex.

He was glowing too, but not like when we were in the woods. Not like the sun. This time it seem like only a dull candle burned inside of him.

"You should have kept your mouth shut," Rodrick snapped.

"She deserved to know," Alex snapped back.

"It is harder now on her than if she had remained unknowing," Cyle declared, silencing Alex's retort with a commanding glare.

"Would everyone just stop fighting and explain things to me?" I shouted.

Pain seared through my raw throat.

Everyone turned and looked at me.

I rubbed my throat and returned their stares. No backing down now. My memories of my meetings with Alex came crashing back. But the little he had confided in me was only enough to whet my appetite. There was more for them to tell, and this time I wasn't taking *No* for an answer. I had been ignored for long enough.

"Leeowyn, you may want to sit down," Cyle said, holding his hands out to me.

He stepped toward me, but I flinched and backed away.

Cyle looked hurt.

I didn't care.

"I'd rather stand," I said, but I walked back to the plush chair and sat down anyway. I looked down at my hands. They looked normal. I'm not sure what I expected to see. Green scales or something, I guess. Maybe I expected them to start glowing like Alex, or for things to start floating like Peach.

But my hands were human hands.

I am human.

Nothing had changed.

Everything has changed.

No one was talking, but everyone was watching me, waiting for me to acknowledge them. My grandmother stood next to Cyle. Both shared an expression of worry. It was a strange sight to see on my grandmother's face. I didn't think anything could faze her.

Peach was still floating.

She looked so foreign to me now. I waited to see wings flapping behind her, but all I saw was that faint shimmer that encompassed her.

Alex was looking at me with his sky blue eyes and flickers of light danced across the surface of his skin, miniature suns illuminating miniatures worlds in the universe that was Alex.

Rodrick hadn't changed at all. He stood behind Cyle and examined me like I was a puzzle that was missing the most important piece.

The white pearl pendant hummed against my neck, throbbing in time to the beat of my overactive heart. I lifted a shaky hand and touched the small droplet. The pearl reacted to my touch, like a flower opening its face to the sun.

I immediately dropped my hand to my side. I hated the feeling that the pendant and I belonged together; that we were made for each other.

I didn't belong here, I wasn't like them.

Not human?

Cyle drew my attention, speaking slowly, calmly, as if to a frightened colt that might bolt if he moved too quickly.

"We haven't been entirely honest with you, Leeowyn," he said.

Cyle's eyes whispered an apology that I wasn't ready to accept.

"That's the understatement of the year," Alex muttered under his breath.

If anyone else heard him, they didn't let on.

I stared into Cyle's eyes. Memories, dreams, vague impression all came crashing together in my brain, swirling around and twisting my reality.

"What is wrong with me?" I whimpered.

Tears leaked from my eyes and became an uncontrollable flood. I locked my gazed on Cyle, my eyes pleading. I felt like I was sitting in someone else's skin; and that these people around me were not my family, but wolves in sheep's clothing.

"Nothing is wrong with you, Lee."

Cyle allowed a smile to curl the edges of his mouth, and this time it actually reached his eyes. He placed his finger tips under my eyes and wiped away my tears, but I pulled away.

I couldn't stand anyone's touch right now.

Rodrick stepped forward, a cup of cool water in his hand.

I reached for it. My throat was dry.

"You're not on Earth, Lee." Cyle said.

I nodded as I sipped the cool water. Somewhere deep inside I had already come to terms with that part of Alex's story.

The whirlpool in my head was beginning to subside, and as it did my senses returned to their full strength.

I'm not sure I was all that thrilled about having all my faculties in top shape. Part of me wanted to remain deaf, dumb, blind and stupid. I wasn't at all sure I wanted to be able to understand anything right now.

"If this is not Earth, then where am I?" I asked.

I stared at my reflection in the cup of water. My eyes had always been tawny, a bright honey-brown color. They were brighter now; the color of molten gold.

Like Cyle's.

Like my grandmother's.

Like my father's?

"You're in the In Between; this place is known as The Mists." Cyle said.

"The In Between," I repeated. "The Mists."

I nodded, thinking I should have spent more time reading Tolkien.

Cyle ran a hand through his hair and took a deep breath.

"I'm sorry, Lee," he said. "This is difficult. I've been so used to..."

"Lying to me?" I interrupted. "Doesn't feel right telling the truth now, does it?"

Venom dripped off my words. The hurt look that clouded his expression told me I hit home.

"Lee, we had to..." he started to explain before I cut him off again.

"Why?" I snapped, cutting him off. "Why did you *have* to? Is there some law that made you drag me away from my mom, my home, my friends, and bring me to this God-forsaken house so you could lie to me for the past four years? Four whole years! Why couldn't you have just left me alone?"

I was so angry I was shaking. I felt anger resonate as the white pearl pendant seemed to reflect my anger. It was as if it was supporting me, cheering me on, and I hated it.

I stood up and grabbed at the chain around my neck. I tried and failed to find the clasp. I wanted to be rid of this pearl, this reminder that I wasn't right.

That I wasn't human.

"It won't come off," Rodrick said.

I turned and stared at Rodrick like he had grown a third eye. Of course it could come off. I could snap that flimsy chain with a single jerk. I grabbed the pendant and tugged to show him how wrong he was.

The chain didn't break.

My hands clawed furiously at the pendant. It had no clasp. And the chain wouldn't break.

I paused; dropped my hands to my sides.

"Why?" I asked.

Rodrick nodded toward Cyle and I reluctantly turned my attention back toward him. Cyle held up his hands in a calming gesture.

"Please, just let me explain before you jump up and start shouting again," Cyle said.

I nodded once.

"Would you like to sit back down?"

I nodded again and dropped into the plush chair, grateful for the support. I felt like I was sitting next to an enemy now, but I was still too weak to stand for long.

The pearl kept humming against my skin, soothing my nerves, calming my racing heart.

"Earth is not the only reality," Cyle started. "There are many different realms."

Memories of things Alex had told me, that Peach had wiped away, tickled the back of my mind. The pearl pendant hummed away the anger until only curiosity remained.

"This place, The Mists, is a kind of bridge between those realms."

I gave him a blank stare. I understood the words, but they weren't making any sense to me.

"Think of it like a road map," Cyle continued.

He stood and walked to his desk, pulling a notepad and pen from his top drawer before coming and sitting next to me. He drew several lines that zigzagged across the paper, crossing at various points.

"There," he said, pointing the pen at a point where the lines crossed over each other. "This is the crossroads; two separate roads leading to two different places, but at this one spot they take up the exact same space. That's what this place is; except instead of roads crossing, it's worlds crossing."

I pinched the bridge of my nose, trying to force the concept into my brain. Or maybe trying desperately to keep it out of my brain.

"So, you can get to another world from this place?"

I hated that what Cyle was telling me made so much sense to me. I wanted my brain to be foggy, and slow, and refuse to understand him.

"Yes. Kind of," Cyle replied.

"Kind of?"

"The Mists is a special kind of crossroads," Cyle explained. "It's not just two realms that are crossing at this point. It's all of them."

"All of them?" I gulped. "Exactly how many is, 'all of them'?"

"Seven. That we know of."

I shook my head. This was unreal.

"Wait, wait, wait." I said. "If other worlds, other *realms*, are just a hop, skip, and a jump away, how come no one has ever met anyone from a different universe or whatever?" I asked.

"They have," Cyle said.

"Encounters happened a lot more frequently before we were able to figure out exactly where the intersections were. You may recognize the result of some of those encounters from your history books. The pyramids, the Roman aqueducts, those unusual statues on Easter Island, they are all the results of someone accidentally wandering through an intersection into Earth's realm. The ancient Greek and Roman gods? They weren't figments of their imagination or ancient astronauts. They were beings from one of the other realms that had wondered to earth from their own lands."

"But now you've found all these crossing points, these intersections?" I asked.

Cyle nodded.

"Well, not us. Our predecessors did. These points, these crossroads, they're guarded by a person from each realm."

"It sounds like there were some pretty cool things going on back then. What's with the guards at the gates?" I asked.

"Not all encounters ended well," Cyle explained. "Little things like slavery, the Black

Plague, Mt. Vesuvius. Those were all the result of encounters gone wrong."

There was an intensity in the room that was palpable. The pearl pendant warmed with it. Cyle was about to reveal something important. Something I wasn't sure I wanted to hear. Something I had waited all my life to hear.

"Those who watch over the crossroad are called Guardians. They have certain powers and abilities that allow them to protect their worlds. Most come from the same family line. Their powers get passed down from one generation to the next. Each new generation of guardians is more powerful than the last. That is important, since the worlds they are charged with protecting are constantly evolving, changing and growing."

Something about "absolute power corrupting absolutely" tickled the back of my mind.

"So, if these Guardians are so powerful, how come no one has tried to abuse their power?" I asked.

"They have. Several times, actually," Cyle answered. "In their wisdom our predecessors formed a Council with representatives from each of the seven realms. These representatives established the rules and laws that we are all bound by."

I looked at all the others in the room and shivered.

"Are they Guardians too?" I asked. "Do they have all those special powers?"

I trained my eyes on my bare feet.

They still looked normal.

I still felt foreign.

"Not all," Cyle said. "Guardians aren't the only ones with abilities, and Guardians are not allowed to be on the Council."

I turned and looked at Alex, my face blank.

"But you are, aren't you? You are the Guardian for Earth."

I asked even though I already knew the answer.

It didn't take a rocket scientist to figure it out. Alex had mentioned rules, people in authority who kept him from telling me things. He obviously wasn't part of the Council, which meant he had to be a Guardian.

Alex nodded slowly.

"You knew who I was when you bumped into me that first day we met on the boardwalk. You knew all along."

He nodded again, but this time he wouldn't meet my eyes.

I controlled the urge to jump up and slap him into the middle of next week, and turned my attention to Cyle. A black storm of anger began to rumble inside of me. The white pearl pendant pulsed with radiating power, matching my mood. I could feel it.

"So, what do I have to do with all of this?"

My voice grew sharp and I made no effort to blunt its edge. I wanted a good explanation as to why I had been lied to by my closest friends and my family for four long years.

"Am I supposed to be one of these Guardians? Am I supposed to guard this...this... Mistland?"

"No, Leeowyn," Cyle said quietly. "You not the Guardian of The Mists. You are the Guardian of all the realms."

My anger died in confusion.

"I don't understand? I thought you said each realm already had a Guardian. Why do you need with another one?"

"Yes, each realm has a Guardian," Cyle explained. "But occasionally, once every century or so as Earth measures time, another Guardian is born. This Guardian is invested with power not only from their own family line, but from the family lines of every Guardian from every realm. As such, this Guardian has a responsibility to all realms."

"There is no way to be sure who that Guardian will be until they turn eighteen," he continued. "That is when they come into their inheritance. It is a unique event. Most of us never dreamed we would live to witness it. We call it, The Awakening."

This is insane!

I wasn't some Guardian or whatever. I didn't have super powers or a secret identity or anything.

I was a high school student, for crying out loud. I couldn't solve an algebra problem without a calculator, much less figure out how to usher in world peace.

I was a normal girl, with normal girl problems. I had never once been able to do anything out of the ordinary, so why did they just assume it was me?

"And this Guardian; you think it's me?"

"We don't think you the Guardian, Leeowyn," Cyle's eyes bored into mine.

"We know."

Chapter 33

"We weren't sure until tonight," Cyle continued. "That is why we couldn't tell you what was happening."

"I don't understand," I said.

I seemed to be saying that a lot lately.

Cyle nodded, and Rodrick took up the explanation. "There are rules in place. They may not seem fair to you," he eyed Alex, "or to some others; but they are for your protection. There have been potentials before; young people, like yourself, who were trained from infancy to assume the mantle of the next Guardian of the Realms. Great honor would come to the family that birthed such a one.

"Unfortunately, training does not guarantee The Awakening. Eighteenth birthdays came and went, and most didn't take it very well. Many took their own lives, believing they had disgraced their families."

Rodrick related this information as if he were giving a lecture to a class of bored college freshmen. His expression, or rather his lack of expression, actually had a calming effect on me.

He was the only one in the room that wasn't looking at me any differently than he had before tonight. To him, I was the same old Leeowyn Blake, the one he couldn't teach anything to, and that was comforting.

"So, you see, Lee. We couldn't tell you until we were sure," Cyle said.

"But how can you be so sure that I'm this...Guardian? Just because I sicked up when the clock struck midnight?"

Cyle reached out his hand and touched the white pearl pendant that hung about my neck.

It didn't hum in response to his touch like it did to mine.

"How does it feel?" he asked.

It feels right.

I didn't respond.

I reached up and held the pendant in my hand. I could feel it throbbing under my touch, as if it were trying to send out comforting thrums.

Trust it.

I dropped the pendant like it was electrified.

Why was I thinking about the necklace as if it was a sentient being? It was just sand that had irritated an oyster long enough that the oyster had coated it over with some kind of special oyster goo that had turned hard over time. That's all. Nothing more.

Nothing more?

"Leeowyn," Cyle said, "that necklace wouldn't have stayed clasped on your neck if it wasn't right for you."

I knew he was telling the truth. Knew it deep in my bones. But I didn't have to like it.

That was why I felt so different, like some new kind of blood was coursing through my veins.

I looked at the expectant faces of every person in the room. They were waiting for something.

What did they expect me to do? Say, 'Thank you?'

"Leeowyn, that's not all," Cyle said.

Oh great.

"Could you please just call me, *Lee,*" I interrupted him.

I stood and walked toward the window that surveyed the front yard. I needed something to break the tension that was rising in my soul.

In the distance, even in the darkness, I could make out the thick woods that surrounded his house. I had always wondered what kind of world lay outside of those woods. Now I wondered if there even *was* a world beyond their borders. If this was some kind of inter-dimensional crossroads, did this world begin and end with this house?

"Things are worse now than ever before," Cyle said. "The Guardians aren't able to keep their lands safe like they used to."

Cyle cast a look around the room, as if looking for encouragement from the others. He took a deep breath and continued.

"There is a rogue Guardian on the loose. He has unimaginable power. He is destroying lands, killing thousands. He has to be stopped. Not one of the Guardians is strong enough to do that on their own, and no Guardian would consider leaving their realm unprotected to go and help another."

I leaned my forehead against the cool glass. I wished I could see the ocean right now.

"Except Alex, who is busy skirt-chasing in the Mistlands."

I'm pretty sure I didn't mean to say it as loud as I did. I'm also pretty sure, by the awkward silence that followed, that everyone in the room heard me.

Cyle kept on talking about whoever this one guy, this rogue Guardian, was. But I had stopped listening.

I saw her.

She was standing there, illuminated, as if by moonlight.

She held my gaze, and for once I wasn't panicking or scared. The bird in her arms wasn't struggling or flailing as it had before. She reached her good hand into her tattered shirt and pulled out a pearl pendant. She held it in her hand, the way I was holding mine.

She beckoned me.

As some point, I don't know when, Cyle had stopped talking.

There was a storm brewing inside of me.

"What do you want from me?" I asked without taking my eyes off of *her*.

"Lee, we need you," Cyle said.

Alex took a step toward me and said, "We're under attack; each realm is. Portals between the realms are opening without warning, and without our knowledge. We have to keep our homes safe, but none of us have the power."

"Except me," I stated flatly.

I didn't need to turn toward them to know they all nodded.

"You must make a choice, Lee," Rodrick said in that disinterested tone of his. "One Guardian alone cannot stand against this Rogue. Two Guardians, particularly one with extraordinary power, have a chance. But which realm to defend? That is the choice you must make."

She beckoned me.

The faces of everyone in the room flashed through my mind. They wanted to use me, each and every one of them. My family. Alex. Peach. They each wanted me to side with them; with their realm. Not one of them really cared about me.

Still, she beckoned.

I nodded to her once, then slowly started to walk from the room.

No one said a word as I closed the door behind me. By the time I closed the front door and heard their voices behind me, shouting my name, it was too late.

I was already running.

The storm inside me had broken and was raging.

How could they use me this way?

They were my family, my friends, someone I cared about. I thought of Alex and cursed myself for a fool. How could I have ever been stupid enough to believe someone like him could actually care about someone like me?

Then I just turned my mind off.

I didn't care any more.

I didn't want to care any more.

I just wanted to be near the ocean.

I crossed the yard in a moment and broke into the tree line before I even realized I had run that far. I heard voices in the distance, calling my name, but I ignored them.

The pearl hummed and thrummed against my chest. I reminded me of who I was. It reminded me of *what* I was. I hated it, but I couldn't take it off.

It felt so *right* having it on.

I felt *whole* having it on.

My cheeks were wet with tears. I cursed myself again. I needed to stop crying so much. I needed to be in better control of my emotions. I slowed to a brisk walk. I couldn't hear any voices behind me, but I wasn't taking any chances. I didn't want to talk to any of them right now. I forged on.

The forest was deep and dark; darker than the first night I met Alex here. Mist collected around my feet. Cold bit at my bare skin like a hungry dog. I wrapped my arms around myself and shivered, but I didn't stop. I plunged deeper into the woods, tears streaking down my face.

She was out here; beckoning me.

"They're lying," I kept repeating to myself. "I'm not some all powerful Guardian. I'm just a girl from Jacksonville. This can't be real."

But it had the feel of real.

My feet were cut and bruised. At some point in the course of the night I had taken off my shoes and, as it turns out, running through the forest in the middle of winter without shoes on may not be the best of ideas.

For a moment I considered going back and gathering my things; some shoes at the least.

That's when I heard it.

It started as a low rumble, but increased in intensity to a snarl. They had warned me to stay out of the woods; that the woods were not safe. There was something in the woods, they said.

Now I believed them.

Now that it was too late.

My heart galloped. My mind screamed at me to run! My legs were frozen to the ground.

Until a branch snapped behind me.

Until I felt its breath on my neck.

A cold sweat broke out over my skin as I turned to face my stalker.

It had the eyes of the creature from my dreams.

Chapter 34

I must still be dreaming!

It was as if the creature was made of pure-white, self-contained fire. Flecks of blue cascading down its back and over its legs; dripped off its snout and sizzled on the ground where they fell.

Its eyes were the deepest black of the night sky, swirling with constellations and shooting stairs. Flames on its lips pulled back in a growl as it bared its razor sharp fangs at me.

Though it blazed white-hot, it did not cast its illumination further than itself, as if it were composed of matter too dense to allow its light to escape.

I must be dreaming, otherwise I would be dead by now.

My heart, pounding in my ears, reminded me that I was *not* dead yet. I was still alive, and I could still move.

Thump, thump, thump, thump.

Was that my heart, or the pearl pendant around my neck?

Thump, thump, thump, thump.

The creature of white fire took a step toward me, a rumbling growl like a self-satisfied purr rattling in its throat. Black smoke arose wherever its foot touched the ground.

A tiny part of my brain remained rational enough to wonder why the whole forest wasn't on fire by now.

Thump, thump, thump, thump.

The pearl pendant began to radiate its own light; light that fed off the beast, reflected it, and competed with it. I felt the tiny weight against my chest began to heat. The pearl pulsed with light, and energy, and heat, and...*life!*

It burned me down to my soul; it engulfed me; threatened to consume me; to become one with me.

The beast of white fire snapped at me, then nudged me with its snout as if trying to herd me in another direction. It backed off a step and gazed at me with those midnight eyes.

It didn't occur to me that I should have been burnt to a crisp from contact with this creature. I didn't even wonder why it wasn't trying to eat me, right then and there.

I didn't wonder about any of these things because, quite simply, I was ticked off.

I was tired of people, dreams, waking nightmares, and things that go bump in the night trying to push me in a direction I didn't want to go.

I mean, I was in an insane state of angry!

I was exhausted beyond words.

I had just learned that I'm some kind of all-powerful Guardian and that I'm probably not even human.

And I was all alone in the dark, scary woods.

All I wanted was a moment to myself; just a moment to think things through, to process everything, you know?

And now this *thing* that should be having me for its main course was trying to direct my path.

The pearl pendant mirrored my mood; reflected it; enhanced it. It cheered me on as I took a step toward the beast.

What was I thinking?

I have no idea.

I had no weapon but I didn't care. I was angry and I was spoiling for a fight, even if it killed me.

I locked eyes with the fire creature, balled my hands into fists and advanced upon it. My skin prickled and sparked as adrenalin, or something more potent, flowed through my veins. All the tension, the emotion, the stress that I had been holding in check snapped as I lunged at the beast.

It effortlessly leapt over my head and landed behind me. As I turned I swear I saw it lick its lips as if smiling. Then it bounded away deeper into the woods.

Oh, no. You're not getting off that easy.

I took a moment to pick up a fallen branch to use as a club before I shot off through the woods after it without a second thought.

You better run if you know what's good for you, because if I lay my hands on you I'll...

The heat from the pearl spread across my chest; down my arms; into my legs. A tiny part of my brain registered that my body was glowing with the same white-blue light as the beast.

I didn't care.

I wanted this fight.

I *needed* this fight.

It didn't register that the creature's smallest teeth were the size of my forefinger. It didn't matter that, standing on all fours, it was as tall as I was and could look me eye-to-eye. I didn't care that it was obviously a predator and I looked very much like prey.

The beast bounded over fallen logs and ricocheted off standing trees, cutting great chunks out of their bark with its paws. It moved at an astounding speed, yet I matched it stride for stride.

I came crashing through the trees and skidded to a halt as I entered a clearing. I couldn't tell how far the clearing extended because a heavy mist covered the ground and obscured my vision.

It looked as if I had stepped onto a blank sheet of paper. Everything was white and swirling, glowing with an odd luminescence that seemed to come from everywhere, and nowhere.

I knew if I didn't stay near the trees I would lose them in the thick mist. I might not be able to find my way back.

At that moment I didn't care.

The white-fire animal sat on its haunches in the mist a short distance away. A low growl came from its throat and it licked its lips at me.

I advanced, more slowly than before; more cautiously. I lifted the branch and held it like a bat, ready to strike out. It had taken on the same pure white fire that now coated my body.

She stepped out from the mist and stood beside the beast. She scratched it behind its ears, and was not burned by its fire.

She was beautiful. The gown flowed like air over her body. Her blonde hair framed a lovely face. Her ruby lips curled into a satisfied smile. Her honey yellow eyes sparkled and shown like molten gold, and a nimbus, like a halo, surrounded her head. There was not a trace of blood on her and, I was relieved to see, her skeletal hand was clothed in flesh and normal looking.

With one hand she beckoned to me, as she continued to caress the creature the way you would pet a beloved dog.

The club fell from my hands and disappeared into the mist at my feet. I walked toward her in slow, measured steps.

There was a flicker, a shifting of the light, and the creature of fire became a sleek four-legged creature like none I had encountered in this world or my own; an odd cross between cat and a deer. It curled around her feet and purred a low hum that exactly matched the sound emanating from my pearl pendant.

I stopped within a few feet of the girl and her beast.

"You must go, now."

It was the same voice I had heard before, but different. Before her voice was tinged with insanity and panic. Now it rang out clear and strong.

"Go? I'm not going anywhere until I get some answers," I spat.

"This is no time for cowardice, child," she said.

"Excuse me? Cowardice? Child?" I snapped.

I had just run through the deep, dark woods chasing a fire-creature with nothing but a stick, and she was calling me a coward? Was I really getting chastised by this zombie girl who now looked more like an angel?

"What's this *child* crap? I'm just as old as you are. And I'm not going to go back there. I don't know who I can trust any more."

"Listen to me," she snapped. "I don't have much time! I said you must go. I didn't say you must go back *there*."

There was another flickering and shifting of the light that surrounded her. Blood start to seep onto her clothes from a dozen different unseen wounds. The pearl pendant around her neck continued to pulse, but each pulse was more dim than the last. Rips began to slash across the fabric of her gown.

"Now that you have awakened you are ready."

"Awakened?" I breathed. "Cyle said something about the Awakening. Is that what you mean?"

She nodded, her hair beginning to mat against her skull with sweat.

"This is Kahl'Nar," she said, indicating the creature that was now rubbing and twining itself around her legs.

The creature - this *Kahl'Nar* - eyed me, as if it could understand what she was saying.

"Leeowyn, Kahl'Nar *is* a portal," she said.

On cue Kahl'Nar took a step toward me, then melted into a puddle on the ground. It was suddenly no longer a four-footed, fire creature, but a bright, blue-white pool of liquid light.

"You must go," she said, her voice taking on that crazed, insistent tone of my earlier visions.

"You want me to step in that?" I asked, unbelieving. "What are you, nuts?"

"If you want to save your mother, you must go now."

My heart skipped a beat.

Mom?

"My mom has nothing to do with this," I shouted. "She is not involved."

"Everyone is involved," she replied as the skin from her hand crisped black and flaked off. "Everyone in every realm. And those we love are the most vulnerable."

I wondered briefly if my mom knew about everything my family had hidden from me, if that was the reason she stole me away in the first place.

"Leeowyn, you must hurry. He's coming."

"How do I find her? Who's coming?"

I didn't give a second thought to whether or not I trusted this girl. She said my mother needed me, and her words rang true.

"Kahl'Nar will guide you," she said.

"Kahl'Nar is a puddle of light," I replied, a bit more exasperated that I wanted.

She reached out and touched her pearl pendant, then reached out and touched mine.

"Kahl'Nar will teach you," she said.

"Wait, I thought you said that thing, that beast, was this Kahl'Nar."

I wasn't grasping whatever it was that this girl was trying to communicate. None of this was making a lick of sense. But I knew I had to hurry.

She walked forward, stepping onto the lake of stars and white fire as if it were dry ground. She turned back and faced me, placing her hand, her good hand, over her pearl pendant. I felt mine grow warm at the same moment. The glow on my skin faded in an instant until it was gone.

I looked normal again.

"Go. Save your mother. Then come back. Cyle will explain what I cannot," she said.

I opened my mouth to speak. I had more questions that needed answers.

But she was gone.

No bright light.

No puff of smoke.

Just, here one second and gone the next.

I let out a curse that would have made a sailor blush - I have no idea where I picked it up; my mom would have grounded me for a month if she heard me say it - then turned my attention back to the starry pool before me.

She had walked across it.

Was I supposed to do that too?

How was this supposed to get me back to my mother?

My heart constricted at the thought of Mom being in some kind of trouble; particularly trouble that I might be the cause of. I knelt down in front of the pool of liquid light and slowly poked it with my fingers. As I pulled them out of the pool, droplets of fire dripped off my fingers.

Okay, so it definitely isn't dry land. I wish there was just some kind of manual that came with this puddle thing that I could read and follow word for word instead of winging it.

Like I was about to do.

I closed my eyes, took a deep breath, counted to *three!*

And jumped.

I was falling through deep waters, but instead of the waters slowing me down, they were speeding me along. I was falling so fast I knew if I hit anything it would kill me on impact.

Did I mention I was running out of air?

My lungs were screaming at me to breathe. I needed some oxygen or I would pass out.

The waters around me had grown black and freezing. I was so cold I couldn't feel my arms or legs any more. I couldn't even tell if I was still moving.

I tried kicking my arms and legs, but it didn't help. I had no idea which direction to swim.

My only thought was of my mom being in danger. The girl said I had to hurry if I was going to save her, but I wasn't sure I could even save myself.

I fought to stay conscious, to find some way out of this abyss. In desperation, I kicked again, and this time I definitely felt myself moving upward.

I swam faster, using my arms and my legs. My lungs were about to explode. I could see light, like the moon rippling above me, an arm's length away.

Then I broke through the surface, sucking in great gasps of air; shaking the wet hair from my face and the water from my eyes, trying to figure out where in the world, or out of the world, I was.

This was real water; not liquid light. I had to continue kicking to keep my head above the waves. I turned 360 degrees in the water. Thankfully the moon was full. I could see a beach only a short distance away and started to swim toward it. The tide was on my side and pushed me toward my goal.

I stumbled onto the sandy beach and took a few precious moments to catch my breath and get my bearings.

Where am I?

I looked left, then right. There was the boardwalk, and the familiar stores, and the snowcone stand.

I was on Earth.

Not only on Earth but just a few blocks from my home.

Home!

My face split with the biggest grin I had permitted myself in the past six months.

Until I saw the clouds.

Big, black, menacing clouds were billowing up into the sky, with a base of red and orange flashes that could only be fire.

Fire!

Right where my house should be.

I ran towards my house, any tiredness forgotten in the adrenaline rush.

The smell of smoke choked my throat and stung my eyes as I flew across the beach toward my house, my mother.

I stared at the black plumes that threatened to blot out the moon, hoping and praying that they were caused by a simple bonfire and not my home.

Please no, please no, please no.

My lungs were close to bursting and my side ached as I neared my home. The white pearl pendant banged against my throat as I ran. It was real, tangible, a stark reminder that this was not a dream. This was real.

I rounded the corner to my nightmare.

My house; my mother's house, was engulfed in flames. The fire had already consumed almost everything. Most of the house was gone. The roof had completely caved in. Sparks fluttered into the air with the smoldering ashes like so many fireflies on a summer's night.

The smoke was thick and acrid, creeping into my lungs, choking me in its embrace like the Black Death.

Where is the fire department?

Why has no one called the fire department?

Where is everyone!?

A house fire draws onlookers like honey draws flies. But no one stood outside.

Steam rose from my soggy clothes as the heat from the flames licked the ocean water dry.

Mom!

I had to find a way into the house. If my mom was in there...

I couldn't make myself continue that thought.

She wasn't in there.

She couldn't be in there.

We have a smoke alarm. It would have gone off. She would have woken up and got out in time.

I looked for her; for a figure standing in a faded blue bathrobe, speaking rapidly into her cell phone.

She was always the first to report any kind of accident and make sure the proper authorities had been contacted.

Once, when our neighbor's house had been broken into, she had sat up all night, consoling the family, serving them hot chocolate, offering a reassuring smile, saying everything would be all right.

Where are those neighbors now?

She was nowhere to be seen.

I ran toward the house, trying to find a door or window I could climb though that wouldn't cave in on me. But it was no use. The flames were too hot, the exits cut off by falling, burning debris.

No, she's not still in there.

She got out.

I shouted for help. But no help came. I couldn't bring myself to walk away from my house, even to go bang on doors and demand someone help me. I had to stay by the house. I had to wait for my mom to come back and tell me she was all right; to tell me that everything was all right.

I needed to have her hold me. In the midst of my screaming, I heard laughter.

Despite the inferno before me, it chilled me to the bone.

Chapter 35

"There's something so cleansing about fire, don't you think?"

The voice came from behind me.

I turned to see a man shrouded in smoke and ashes walking towards me. His skin appeared to pulse, alternately glowing then fading, like he was an ember himself. As he drew closer, the affect faded; he was just a normal man, after all.

"Please, I need your help," I said.

In my anguish my mind did not process the amused smirk that tugged at his lips, or the glee that registered in his eyes.

Until he laughed again.

The sound echoed unnaturally in my ears. The Kahl'Nar's pulse intensified, beating out a warning against my skin.

The man stopped laughing.

His eyes locked onto the pearl pendant.

"Ah. So, you've come, after all," he said.

He advanced towards me, but there was a hesitancy in his step; a cautious look in his eye; as if he were unsure of exactly what dangers lay ahead.

I ignored the sense of trepidation pulsing through the pendant.

"We don't have time," I pleaded, gesturing wildly toward the house. "I have to find my mom and make sure she's alright."

"I wouldn't worry about your mother, if I were you," he replied, the hint of a crazed grin playing across his lips. "She has been asleep for hours."

"Asleep?"

The word didn't register in my mind.

"Oh, yes. Quite asleep," he said.

He reached his hand toward me, touching my arm. Pain exploded through my arm as I jerked away.

"I made sure she stayed safe and sound in her room while I put on this little show for her."

"Who are you?" I shouted.

The Kahl'Nar was now a steady, brilliant beacon, clothing me in light.

"Don't you know? Didn't they tell you?" he snarled, or laughed; I'm not sure which.

He reached for me with both hands, grabbing me by the throat, lifting me off the ground, pulling me to his eye level. I choked and kicked, struggling desperately to free myself.

"You are the best they have?" he laughed. "You are pathetic."

Then his words hit me.

My mom was in her room. In our house.

And this guy was responsible.

I felt my flesh heating up again; searing, burning where he touched me. But this time the energy flow was not coming from him. It was leaching into my flesh from the Kahl'Nar. The white light I had been coated with while in The Mists originated at the pendant, and was spreading over my whole body.

When the light reached my throat, the man's reaction was instantaneous. He jerked back as if he had touched a live electrical wire, and dropped me to the ground. I coughed and gasped for breath

The white light receded back to the Kahl'Nar as I lay panting on the ground. The man kept staring at his hands in unbelief. They were blackened, as if burned with a welding torch.

He gave me a look of pure hatred, before turning and walking into the billowing smoke.

I stumbled to my feet, willing all my anger and anguish into the necklace, and it responded with its now-familiar *thrum.*

My fingertips began shining with white fire. Without thinking I reached out toward the man, and arrows of white energy flew from my hands, slammed into his back and knocked him to the ground.

He struggled back to his feet and disappeared into the smoke.

"I'll find you!" I screamed after him. "I will kill you!"

I fell to my knees, completely drained.

The fire died from my hands.

The Kahl'Nar grew cold against my neck, once more just a lovely pearl pendant.

The man who had killed my mother was gone. I couldn't give chase even if I wanted to. I was exhausted beyond what I thought was possible.

And a grief as cold as the grave was spreading through me as reality began to sink in.

My mom is dead.

***

I don't know how long I sat there on the cold sand. The night grew darker as the flames that consumed my home and taken the life of the woman who had given up everything for me, died into gently glowing embers that crackled and popped behind me.

My mom was dead.

I was the only witness on the scene.   No one else came to watch the conflagration.

Not the neighbors.

Not the police.

Not the fire department.

Only me.

And that man.

I looked down at my hands, black from the ashes that fell like Lucifer's snow around me; hands that had failed to save my mother.

I was an orphan.

She tried to warn me. She told me to wake up!

Now that my rage was spent, an unfathomable sense of loss washed over me. I felt nothing when I learned my father had died. The knowledge that my mother was now dead was different. I had never experienced true grief before.

My hands were trembling. My arms began trembling, too. My legs began to quiver and my stomach knotted up. My throat clamped shut making it hard to draw a complete breath. My vision fogged over as the stream of tears that I had held back for so long began to gush out of my eyes.

Gasping, I leaned forward, curled my hands into fists and pounded the sand as I screamed my grief into the night. I screamed until my throat was too hoarse to create sound, and then I screamed silently.

Finally, completely spent, I tried to stand. The world swam before me, forcing me back onto my knees in the sand. My stomach heaved, emptying itself of its contents; then heaving some more, just to make sure.

I fell to the side, sobbing. I curled up, hugging my knees to my chest and surrendered to the sorrow.

Chapter 36

"Is there a reason none of us are going after her?" Alex asked, pacing the length of the living room.

He had felt her appear on Earth, which meant somehow she has learned how to use her Kahl'Nar, even though none of them had explained it to her.

"If you want to push her further away, more than we already have, then be my guest," Cyle snapped back. He rubbed his hands over his eyes. He was seated in the same chair he had occupied before Lee left.

Alex, Peach and Cyle were the only ones still awake. The rest had gone to bed, convinced there was nothing left to be gained by waiting.

"Maybe Alex is right..." Peach suggested.

She was seated across from Cyle in a high backed leather chair, curled up on herself like a cat.

"She's alone and confused, and we're the only ones who can help her."

Cyle pulled his hand from his eyes and regarded Peach for a long moment before turning his attention to Alex.

"You're sure you felt her on Earth?" he asked.

Alex nodded.

"There's no mistaking her power. It's like being hit by a semi. You just don't mistake something like that."

Alex stopped pacing and waited for Cyle.

Cyle leaned back, deep in thought, his fingers steepled together. This was a delicate situation. One wrong move and they could lose Lee forever.

They couldn't afford to make that one wrong move.

"How long has she been there?" Peach asked.

Cyle tilted his head to look at Alex, who shrugged.

"A few hours; maybe. She shouldn't be far from the crossing point."

"*If* she came out at the crossing point, Cyle pointed out.

"What if she accidentally fell into one of those new portals that have been opening up? What if she ended up in Spain or Rome or some place like that?" Peach asked.

"Can we not add more hypothetical situations that'll just serve to make us worry more?" Alex snapped.

"Well *excuse me* for trying to look at it from every angle and be prepared!" Peach spat back. "But I guess you just like to go in swinging, never even taking a few seconds to think something over."

"The real question is how she managed to use a portal at all," Cyle said, as if to himself. It was the question that troubled them all.

Alex went back to pacing while Peach watched him like a hawk. Cyle merely sighed, leaned back and placed his hand back over his eyes.

This was all on his head. He had begged the Council to allow him to find her. The Council was unaware that he had promised Cecil he would do everything in his power to protect his daughter. All the Council cared about was that Leeowyn was the heir to the mighty Cecil Blake. The blood that flowed through her veins virtually assured that she would be the new Guardian of the Realms, even though her mother was of Earth and had no ability at all.

"Why should we entrust you with this great responsibility?" Heril had asked, sitting in the front chair of the Council, as befitted his position of authority.

Heril was not fond of female Guardians. He was not fond of the very *idea* of female guardians. Heril was from Archend. In his realm women had no voice in politics. He didn't see why they should be permitted to speak in any realm unless first addressed.

"Because she is my brother's daughter," Cyle had answered. "Who better to raise her, to watch over her, without arousing her suspicion?"

Cyle knew Heril would dismiss his request if he could. Heril would say it was unlikely that a female would be the next Guardian of the Realms. Except for the fact that of the past ten Guardians, eight had been female. It was a fact that brought Heril endless frustration.

Without the approval of the Council, Cyle knew he would not have been allowed to even set eyes on Lee.

That was something that he could not allow.

He had promised Cecil.

So he had compromised with Heril, and he hated the man all the more because of it.

Cyle had managed to convince the Council that, when the time came, he would be able to explain everything to Leeowyn; to train her in her powers; to gain her ascent to her Guardianship.

He had been so sure that nothing would go wrong. He had not wasted the slightest thought on the "what ifs" of her leaving or refusing to help them.

He had been an idiot.

She *was* Cecil's daughter, after all, no matter that she had human blood flowing through her veins as well. Cecil had never backed down from a fight. But Cecil was never one to take anything at face value either. He was headstrong, obstinate, willful, and opinionated. And he had an unerring sense of right and wrong.

Leeowyn was a Blake, and that meant she could not be controlled.

But maybe she could be guided.

"Wait," Alex stopped pacing and stood stock still. "She's gone!"

"What? You lost her?" Cyle's frustration spilled out.

Alex shot him a dark look.

"I didn't lose her. She left. She's not on Earth any more. She was there a second ago, and now she's...just not."

Alex stormed out of the room and headed toward the front door, mumbling loud enough for everyone to hear, "Well, that's just great. Now she could be anywhere. If I had been allowed to go and get her in the first place, none of this would have happened. But, *no*. I had to sit on my hands and wait, like a..."

Alex flung open the front door, then stumbled back, his mouth hanging open.

Chapter 37

I had reached out my hand to take the doorknob when the front door jerked inward. It startled me for a moment as I stood on the porch, staring up into Alex's shocked face.

Water still dripped off my face, mingled with soot and ashes, leaving little trails of pale skin as they created tiny rivulets across my face and arms.

The numbness that had started outside the charred remains of my house had spread throughout my being and cut off my emotions. I had once wished for nothing more than to be able to hide my emotions. Now I couldn't even feel them.

I pushed past Alex without a word. I walked into the house without sparing a glance at Cyle or Peach, though I could feel their eyes.

My feet took me up stairs of their own accord. I didn't notice the searing and blistering on my neck where that man, or whatever he was, had tried to choke the life out of me.

But I did notice that the banister needed dusting.

Reynolds is falling down on his job.

It was a silly thought. An odd, mundane sort of thought. The kind of thought you have when the whole world crashes down around your shoulders and there is not a damned thinkg you can do about it.

At the top of the stairs I turned down the hallway and continued to my room.

It was my only room now; the only place I could call home.

I pushed the door open and stepped inside. I crossed to the window and stared into the darkness - so black just before the dawn.

Maybe I expected to see *her* there.

But I didn't see her.

I didn't see anything.

I wasn't sure what I intended to do here.

I didn't know what I intended to do now.

But I didn't know where else to go.

For all that they had kept me in the dark about who I was, about who they were, these people were my family.

They were all the family I had left.

I don't know how long I stood there, but a gentle knock rapped on my door, breaking my reverie. It was a comforting kind of sound. Solid, real. It was followed by a familiar voice.

"Lee? May I come in?"

"Yes," I said, my voice flat and devoid of emotion.

The doorknob turned and Cyle stepped tentatively into the room. He crossed to stand silently behind me.

"I met a man tonight," I said. "He killed my mother. He almost killed me. He knew who I was. He was expecting me."

I turned finally, and looked at my uncle. He stood there, an arm's length away, his eyes filled of sorrow.

"Lee, I'm so sorry..."

I held my hand up. I couldn't bear to hear this right now; I couldn't deal with sympathy and regret. There was only one thing I cared about at this point.

I needed to find that man...and kill him.

And I knew that Cyle could help me do it.

"Lee! What happened to your neck?"

In an instant Cyle was beside me, examining the wound. I watched him in the mirror on my dresser as he fussed over the throbbing red welts that held the shape of human fingers wrapped around my throat.

Cyle's eyes widened and he looked at my eyes.

"This man, the one who killed your mother, he did this with his hands?"

I nodded, the pain from the burn starting to seep through into my consciousness.

Cyle pursed his lips, a grim familiarity flashed in his eyes.

"You met him," he said. "You met Ruok."

I'm sure his words held some kind of significance, but my mind couldn't focus anything beyond my own need.

"Is that his name? Ruok?"

Cyle nodded.

"Good," I nodded in return. "I'm going to kill Ruok. But first I need to change my clothes."

I started fiddling with the buttons on my blouse, unsure how to make them work.

"Do you know where the washer and dryer are?" I asked.

Cyle took me by my shoulders and gently brushed the hair away from my face. He stared deeply into my eyes.

"Lee, you are in shock. I need for you to focus. I need for you to tell me everything that man said to you. Word for word. Can you do that?"

"He called me pathetic," I whispered. "I tried to fight back, but he was so strong. I burned his hands."

I'm sure it was my voice speaking, but I heard it from somewhere else in the room, like I was a casual observer watching a soap opera. I felt detached; disembodied.

"Lee, you fought Ruok? How?"

There was something akin to awe in his voice. At least it seemed that way to my numbed consciousness.

Cyle shook me slightly, snapping his fingers in front of my eyes, trying to shake the numbness out of me.

It didn't work.

"I need to take a shower," I said, looking up at him. "My hands are dirty."

I was beyond feeling and content to be so.

"Leeowyn!" he snapped, shaking me hard.

I jerked my eyes to his face. Cyle was angry now, though I could tell his anger was not directed at me.

Still, it frightened me.

The shell of numbness that surrounded me started to crack. Cyle shook me again and shouted something that I couldn't comprehend. Light from the Kahl'Nar started seeping through the cracks in my wall, forcing them open, forcing the light inside.

Cyle shook me once more, harder this time.

"Leeowyn, answer me!"

I slapped him. Hard.

"He killed my mother!" I screamed.

I struck out again and again, oblivious to who I was slapping or if I even made contact.

"He locked her inside of our home and he burned her alive!"

Cyle grabbed my wrist before I could hit him again. He pulled me to him, cradling me in a father's embrace while I shook with rage and sorrow. I struggled against him at first, but he was firm and resolute in his motions, trapping me in a warm, comforting hug.

I didn't want comfort! I didn't...

I was weeping again.

The wall of numbness that had protected me from vital emotions had been reduced to rubble, as charred as the remains of my home.

My knees buckled. If it hadn't been for Cyle's strong embrace I would have crumpled to the ground.

But he held me, like a father holds his little girl after her first heartbreak.

He didn't offer words of solace. There are no words for times like those. He just held me, allowing me to be weak in his strength.

When the well of my sorrow ran dry for a moment, I pulled back from Cyle. I gave him a grateful pat on his chest and turned to sit on my bed. I was glad to have something to support my weight.

I was suddenly just so bone weary.

"Lee," Cyle said quietly, in tones soft enough not to spook a deer. "You said you fought Ruok."

"I don't know who Ruok is," I said. "I fought a man."

"Did he appear to be a man who was made out of fire?" Cyle asked.

I paused, reliving the memory, watching a man walk out of the smoke like he was part of it, seeing him dissipate back into the smoke as he left, the pain in my neck as he burned me.

"Yes," I answered.

I absentmindedly reached up to touch the burn on my neck, wincing at the instant pain.

Cyle swore. I had not heard him swear before. Not like this.

"Is that bad?" I asked.

Is that bad? How stupid a question is that? The guy turned my neck into barbeque. Of course it's bad.

Cyle nodded.

"Remember how we told you that things were getting bad?" Cyle asked.

I nodded.

"Well, Ruok is the reason why. At least, he is one reason. Lee, this man has killed more mothers than just yours, and he'll kill many more if he's not stopped."

I nodded again, not really sure how to respond.

"How did you fight him? Can you remember?"

"I'll try," I said.

Memories of liquid fire, heat and light played leapfrog in my mind. The Kahl'Nar, my arms shimmering, sparks flying from my fingertips. None if it made any sense to me.

"I'm not really sure," I answered. I looked down at my open palms hoping to find an answer there.

I didn't.

My palms were as empty as my understanding of the events surrounding me.

"My skin was acting weird. It turned all white and blue. It was still my skin, but it was almost like I had some kind of liquid flowing over my skin. I wanted to hurt him. I *needed* to hurt him. Then suddenly, there was...I don't know, *something*...flowing out of my hands, rushing at him. It knocked him down. It might have hurt him, I don't know. He got up and walked back into the smoke."

A wave of self-pity washed over me at the memory.

"He's right. I am pathetic. I couldn't even avenge my own mother's death."

My hands balled into fists as tears started leaking down my cheeks again. I thought I had already exhausted my supply. It's amazing how the body just keeps on producing more as you need them.

Cyle didn't respond. He just stood there, looking at me like I was a character out of some graphic novel; a creature that he couldn't quite believe really existed.

"What?" I asked. His look was starting to creep me out.

A sweet and distant smile played across Cyle's face.

"I was just thinking how much you remind me of him."

"Of who?" I was more confused than ever.

"Your father," he said, reaching out to touch my cheek. "You have his eyes, his smile, his need for solitude and his obstinacy."

I smiled slightly, embarrassed. I felt like I had just been offered a remarkable complement, although I couldn't tell you why.

"And you have his giftings."

I pulled my face away from Cyle's touch and turned my face toward the wall. There was a question I needed to ask, but I wasn't sure I wanted to hear the answer.

I looked down my hands. They looked so normal; not at all like they were suddenly going to betray me. They didn't have scales or feathers. They looked like human hands.

"Alex said I wasn't human..." I started before my voice trailed off into a deep, unbroken silence. I wasn't sure how to even phrase the question. It sounded so strange to question my humanity.

Cyle sighed and shook his head, running his hands through his hair. He looked infinitely weary.

"That *boy*," he sighed. "He's always making things more difficult than they should be."

There was a moment of silence while Cyle gathered his thoughts, but I knew deep down inside, that this time he would not avoid my questions.

"No, Leeowyn," he answered. "Technically speaking, you're not human."

Chapter 38

I had prepared my self for that answer, but it still felt like a kick in the gut.

Cyle tried to lessen the impact of this revelation.

"You are no different than anyone else on Earth, anatomically," he continued, "but you are different, Lee. Because of the unique ability that you have. Because of the Kahl'Nar that's inside of you."

Cyle gave me a reassuring smile that didn't reassure me at all.

"Okay, I need to buy a vowel. This whole *Kahl'Nar* thing; is somebody going to explain that to me?" I asked. "Remember? Kind of new to this whole magic thing."

Cyle's face went from reassuring to disapproving in an instant.

"What?" I asked. "Why are you looking at me like that? I mean; it is magic, right? Some kind of spell or something? I mean, what I did, it isn't normal, right? There's nothing else it could be. Right?"

"Do you really want to get into all this right now, Lee?" Cyle asked. "You've already had an unimaginably horrific night; one I can't even imagine..."

I held my hands up to stop him, closing my eyes against the flood of tears that threatened to force their way past my eyelids. I paused long enough to compose myself, forcing my eyes to look up from the floor and into his.

"Please, Cyle. I can't talk about the night...about Mom. Not right now. I need a distraction, and if this Kahl'Nar is nothing else, it is certainly a distraction."

The sympathy and anguish on his face was almost too much to bear. The corners of Cyle's lips curled into a sad smile. He took a ragged breath, blew it out, and began.

"All right, Lee. Let's start at the beginning," he said. "What you do; what *we* do; it is not magic. Not in the witches and wizards and Harry Potter sort of thing you might think of. I'm not saying spells and magic don't exist. But, those are not natural. Spells and magic are practiced by people who don't have the ability to do anything else."

I gave him a blank look.

"I'm not seeing the difference," I said.

"But there *is* a difference," Cyle replied. "Think about it this way. Can an artist paint a picture?"

I nodded.

"Can a chef cook?"

I nodded again.

"Can you paint a portrait or prepare a gourmet meal?"

I laughed, shaking my head.

"The last time I tried to paint a picture, it ended up looking like someone threw up on the paper."

"But an artist can paint, and a chef can cook," Cyle continued. "Just because they can do something that you can't, does that make it magic?"

"Wait," I objected. "That's different. What they do is a talent; an ability."

"Exactly," he nodded. "Lee, what you and I can do isn't magic. It's just an ability. Some people are gifted musicians. Some are gifted athletes. Some are gifted orators, or scientists or writers. The gift we have - the gift *you* have - just happens to be a bit rarer than the ability to draw or cook."

An ability?

"So, if I have this *ability*, how come I've never been able to do any of this before?" I asked.

"Because, you're a Guardian," Cyle answered. "Others of our kind are born with this ability; this gift. It is evident at birth. But your gift is different from ours, Leeowyn. Your abilities have been growing, building up within you until you were ready to handle them. That's why we couldn't tell you. If your abilities had manifested before your body and your mind were ready to handle them, before your Awakening, they would have killed you."

I recalled the deep, sickening feeling like I was dying that had occurred only a few hours before. It seemed like a lifetime ago. It was strange to think that night hadn't extended for several weeks. It felt like forever ago since I sat down to my birthday dinner with Peach and Alex and everyone.

"How could you have been so sure about me? If I didn't have these powers until just now, you said yourself no one really knew, so how could you be sure it was me?" I asked

"Because of your eyes."

Cyle's answer struck me as odd. What on earth did my eyes have to do with anything? Then it hit me.

"Yellow eyes aren't just a family trait, are they?" I asked.

Cyle shook his head.

"Yellow eyes are the mark of someone who has an especially powerful gift," he explained. "You might think it is a family trait, like inheriting your father's red hair. But yellow eyes run in this family because your family just happens to be a very powerful family."

"With great power comes great responsibility," I whispered.

Cyle looked at me quizzically.

"Spider-man," I said.

Cyle still looked a bit confused.

"Nothing," I laughed. "Just a line from a movie."

"A wise saying, whether from a movie or not," Cyle smiled.

The conversation slowed to a stop, and there was an uncomfortable silence for a few moments. I examined my hands. They still *looked* human.

"So," I said. "I'm this Guardian, huh?"

Cyle nodded.

"And I have to decide which realm to defend out of all seven?"

Cyle nodded again, his face taking on a grim demeanor.

"But, I'm so ordinary."

I turned and looked at him like a child being dropped off on her first day of school.

"I'm clumsy. I'm not the smartest girl in the world, or even in the 12th grade. I say stupid things and I do awkward things and I'm pretty sure I'm not at all the right person to be in a position of power."

Cyle smiled and placed his hands on either side of my face.

"Now what about that makes you ordinary?"

He stood and walked toward the door.

"Cyle?"

He turned and looked at me, his hand resting on the doorknob.

"What's next for me?"

In that moment I could look back and see every road I had ever taken leading me to this point – yet there was one more crossroad that I had to choose.

Don't worry about making the wrong decision; it's just the rest of your life. And the fate of the universe.

Cyle smiled, a genuine, loving, comforting smile.

"Next, you sleep," he said. "We'll worry about the rest of it in the morning."

I nodded and allowed myself a tiny smile.

Cyle opened the door and walked out. But before he closed the door behind him he turned back to me and said, "Welcome back home, Lee."

Home.

My only home.

Chapter 39

If I was thankful for anything, it would have to be the pain in my neck.

Every time I started to dream about ravenous flames, thick black smoke and endless screaming I would inevitably toss in my sleep, which would send shooting pains across my badly burned neck, which would wake me up. However unpleasant it was, it was better than reliving that nightmare.

That reality.

By the time the sun was bathing my room with light, the burn on my neck had blistered and popped. I had kept a cold, wet towel on it for most of the night, not that it helped with the pain all that much.

Honestly, I didn't mind the pain. It gave me something else to focus on.

I think I was rounding the corner from extreme exhaustion to clarity. I was so tired that I was delusional, and so delusional that I was starting to make sense.

Or something like that.

Maybe I *did* need more sleep.

No one came to disturb me, so I took advantage of the opportunity to lounge in my bed until well into the afternoon. I only got up to rewet my towel to cool down the burning around my neck.

Even after I finally crawled out of bed, I stayed in my room, processing the events of the past couple of days.

Has it only been a couple of days? Feels like a lifetime.

The sun was beginning to set when I finally decided it was time to face the world.

I dressed slowly, my muscles protesting against movement. I didn't object to that pain either; it was a distraction from the pain in my neck. If I got enough injuries, I would soon be able to ignore everything and never have to face another unpleasant thought again.

I went into the bathroom to wash my face and got my first real look at the wound on my neck.

I've been burned in the past. Sunburn. Curling iron. That sort of thing. Nothing serious. I'm not exactly the most graceful person in the world. And if the truth be told, I've always kind of liked playing with fire. Yeah, I'm something of a closet pyro.

But I'd never been burned this badly.

Cyle was right. The burn was in the shape of a hand, wrapped around my throat.

The blistering and tearing hadn't helped make it look any more becoming, either. The burned flesh was red and swollen, and in several places, blood and other bodily fluids had dried and caked on my neck.

I cleaned it as carefully as I could, wrung out the towel and tossed it in the hamper.

I pulled my hair back in a loose ponytail, careful to not let it lay on the burn. Not being able to stand looking at the nasty burn any longer, I let my eyes wander to my face. To my eyes.

I could see it.

I *was* different.

And it wasn't just my eyes, which were no longer simply tawny yellow, but bright, burnished gold. My hair was different, too. It had always been a dusty auburn. Now it was vibrant red.

I guess magic likes to brighten everything up.

Well, not magic...my gift. Or whatever it was.

I let out an audible groan. It was too early to be trying to figure this all out.

Or too late.

Or something like that.

I took one last look at the new me, the A*wakened* me, switched off the light, and left the bathroom.

The sun was almost fully set when I walked out of my room.

The Kahl'Nar hummed around my neck as I made my way down the hall.

I stopped.

I had forgotten completely about the necklace. I lifted the pendant in the palm of my hand, sensing the pulse of power, of familiarity, in it. I was dimly aware that the delicate chain that slid around my neck and supported the weight of the pearl pendant. It caused no pain, even though it rested on the sensitive burn.

"I guess we're going to be working together for a while, huh?"

Quit talking to inanimate objects.

I felt the Kahl'Nar hum slightly before going silent again, almost as if it understood me.

This was going to take some getting used to.

Well, duh! What *wasn't* going to take getting used to here? Different realms, portals, people with *gifts*. Not to mention these Guardians, of which I was apparently one. And not just one, but one of the most powerful ones.

I didn't feel powerful.

I felt tired, more than a little confused and really, really hungry.

My feet led me to the dining room, almost of their own accord, while I pondered my new situation in life.

I opened the door and looked in.

Peach and Alex were the only ones left sitting around the table. A few dirty dishes and the remains of dinner still cluttered the table. I pulled up a chair without a word, sat down and piled food onto my plate.

I was aware of their eyes on me. Normally I don't like awkward silences, and go out of my way to be the first to break the ice.

Not this time.

I was ready to get into someone's face about it. I pointedly looked Peach and Alex in the eye without saying a word. I shoved forkful after forkful of whatever was on my plate into my mouth. I don't remember even tasting the food. I was too busy trying to win this staring contest.

Peach held my gaze for a brief moment before dropping her eyes to her already empty plate. She didn't look like the Peach I had first met; the Peach I thought I knew; the Peach I thought was my friend.

It occurred to me that she probably never would again.

The Peach I had first encountered, bouncing about the estate, was fake, a fraud, a mask.

This was the real Peach.

Oh, she still had the same features as the old Peach; only now everything was intensified. Her skin, which had always been pale, now appeared opalescent. Her laughing green eyes now took on liquid wisdom, like deep pools of a forest lake. Her body, which always moved with such grace and fluidity, now appeared alien, like one of those glass statues you might buy at a kiosk in the mall, all shimmering and weightless.

Alex, on the other hand, not only met my gaze, he held it.

He hadn't changed a bit. He looked the exact same; handsome face, gorgeous figure, perfect hair.

Yep, he was the exact same jerk who had played on my heartstrings, manipulating and tricking me into falling for him. Pretending to be my boyfriend.

Jerk.

Alex continued to stare at me with those perfect blue eyes of his.

I could feel my anger rising just by looking at him. The Kahl'Nar sensed my anger and reacted to it. I could feel its hum coursing through my veins.

Even though Alex maintained eye contact, I could tell he was sweating. It must have taken a toll on him to continue to keep my gaze.

My fork scraped the empty surface of the plate. I hadn't tasted a crumb.

"Well, I'm all done here," I said, forcing more anger into my words than was absolutely necessary.

I tossed my fork down and ignored it as it bounced and skidded across the table. I was out of my chair and stalking towards the exit before I heard Peach cry out,

"Lee, I'm still your friend!"

I paused at that and turned back toward her. I wanted to slap her face. I wanted to scream at her.

Still my friend? You were never my friend! Friends don't lie to you.

But the expression on Peach's face made it impossible to hold onto the rage. The anger that had been brewing inside me only a moment before melted like a snowcone on a hot, Jacksonville boardwalk.

"Cyle told us what happened to your mom," Alex said.

The anger was back, and this time it didn't need brewing. It was already full strength.

I spun on Alex, ready to blister his ears with a torrent of profanities that would do a sailor proud. But before I could utter a syllable, all the glass in the room - from windows to dishes - shattered as if burst from the inside, flinging shards of razor sharp blades flying across the room.

The Kahl'Nar around my neck was pulsing with power and a gossamer sheen of blue-white fire coated my body to match.

Startled by the sudden destruction, the anger that fueled my passion dried up like a faucet had been turned off and the fire covering my skin disappeared as rapidly as it had manifested.

Peach and Alex uncovered their faces; flecks of blood gave way to tiny rivulets of crimson on their exposed skin. They both stared at me, awe-struck; the kind of look usually reserved for explorers who stepped on the moon for the first time, or scientists who created a new virus that had the potential to wipe out civilization.

I suddenly didn't care that these people had lied to me. I didn't care about the reasons for their lies. I cared very much that I had hurt them.

And the fact that I had done it without even knowing how scared the living crap out of me.

"I'm so sorry," I said, tears brimming as I stepped toward my friends.

I struggled to think of something to do that might help. The look on their faces made me stop after just a few paces.

They are afraid of me. They are right to be afraid. What if I can't control this? What if I make things even worse?

"Peach, Alex. I'm so sorry."

Alex shook his head, sending sand-sized glass fragments scattering around him. Peach gently shook out her dress. The only sound in the room was that of clinking glass. After a few moments they both turned their attention back to me.

"I didn't mean to," I said lamely. "I never intended to hurt you."

"Neither did we," Alex said.

Peach slowly began to make her way around the table toward me, crunching glass under her feet as she came.

I stayed still, afraid if I moved I would cause some new catastrophe.

Once Peach got close, I could see the little cuts on her skin closing up, healing before my eyes, leaving only little trails of blood with no point of origin.

A week ago that would have seemed strange. Today, well... at least I didn't do permanent damage to my friends. Too bad the dining room didn't have the ability to reconstruct itself. I didn't know how I was going to explain this to Cyle...or worse yet, to Grandmother.

Peach locked eyes with me for a moment, then threw her arms around me, pulling me into a fierce hug.

I gasped as her arm squeezed the burn on my neck. Peach jumped back at the sound of pain in my voice and hissed at the sight of the burn on my neck, as if seeing it for the first time. I guess you don't notice a lot when you're busy trying to avoid someone's gaze - or exploding glass.

"Lee, what happened?"

Peach reached out tentatively and tenderly touched the burn.

"Does it hurt bad?" she asked, her eyes wide.

I winced but was able to keep from crying out.

"Have you ever heard of a burn hurting *good*?" I asked.

"Wait right here," she commanded. "I'll go get some burn cream and gauze."

She dashed from the room, her feet barely touched the ground, as if she only needed the smallest contact with the floor to propel her forward.

"Lee..." Alex said.

"You shut up," I snapped.

I could feel the beast called Rage waking inside of me again. I knew to expect it this time and I was able to keep it under control.

Alex stood looking at me with those perfect blue eyes. Hurt and confusion played across his face.

"Lee, please. Let me explain..."

"Explain what?" I interrupted. "That you toyed with my emotions?"

I tilted my head to get a better look at him.

"Or maybe you want to *explain* how you pretended to be interested in me so that you could get in good with the next Guardian?"

"It wasn't like that!" Alex protested.

"Really? Then what was it like, Alex? I'd love to know. Was I really so pretty, so graceful, so interesting that you would stop to give me the time of day? Tell me, would you have talked to me had I not been *this*?" I said, holding up the white pearl pendant.

Alex opened his mouth, apparently thought better of it, and then closed it again.

"Yeah, I didn't think so," I spat.

Rage growled inside of me, threatening to fully wake up and do some real damage.

"My world needs you so badly," Alex pleaded his case. "Lee, Earth doesn't have people with powers and gifts like the other realms do. They have no defense against what's coming. They can't protect themselves. I just wanted..."

I shook my head and closed my eyes. I didn't want to hear his excuses, no matter how much sense they made.

I just wanted...I just wanted...

What do I want?

"Leeowyn, I would like for you to come here," Rodrick said from doorway.

I wanted a distraction. And Rodrick would do nicely.

Chapter 40

I spared Alex one more angry glare to let him know he was not off the hook, then turned and followed Rodrick out of the dining room.

Something was different.

That disconcerted feeling I always had anytime I was around Rodrick was nowhere to be found. He no longer carried that familiar sense of unease that always set me on edge.

I wasn't sure how I felt about that. I was accustomed to viewing him as an enemy. With all that had transpired, I didn't feel like now was a good time to let my guard down.

Rodrick stopped in front of the library and held the door open for me.

"So, do you finally have something to teach me?" I joked.

Thoughts of high school, graduation, and college flitted across my mind like fireflies in the summer grass.

Were those things even factors in my life any more?

Rodrick didn't answer. He merely shut the door behind us and motioned for me to sit at the table.

I complied.

To my surprise - and trust me, after the events of the last forty-eight hours it took a lot to surprise me - he walked over to the bookcase, fished a key out of his pocket, and unlocked it.

He pulled the heavy glass door open, then ran his fingers along the leather bindings of the books within. His eyes closed. It was as if he was reading them with his fingertips.

Maybe he was. I wasn't sure I could put anything past this place.

Rodrick's fingers stopped on a particularly thick book. He pulled it out and set it aside, then repeated the process until he had a pile the size of a small toddler stacked in front of me.

"Looking to do some light reading?" I quipped, laughing slightly.

The laughter died in my throat when Rodrick turned his attention toward me. The look on his face stated clearly that he wasn't in the mood for jokes.

I was pretty sure Rodrick was *never* in the mood for jokes.

I coughed to cover up my nervousness, and nonchalantly reached for the top book on the stack. Before I could open it all the way, Rodrick's hand came down on the book, slamming it shut.

I pulled my fingers back just in time to prevent getting them smashed.

"You are The Guardian."

I wasn't sure if I should nod or answer, so I tilted my head in a sort of half nod and smiled weakly.

"In a week's time, perhaps less, the Council will want to meet with you. Each member will try and win you over; to convince you to choose their realm to aid."

I let out an exasperated sigh. I didn't think I was up to the task. I wasn't much of a leader. I tended to do more listening than talking. I made the tough decisions when I had to... but I hated having to.

"So what exactly is it that everyone needs my help to fight?" I asked.

Rodrick regarded me with the practiced eye of a master appraising a new student. I almost expected him to call me 'Grasshopper' or something. He lifted his hand off of the book he had just snapped shut, allowing his palm to hover a few inches above the stack of books.

"These books will provide the answer to that question," he snapped. "But they're not for reading. Not now."

I stared at him quizzically. How could books provide any answer if you weren't allowed to even open them?

"You have much to learn; but for now, I must teach you two things," Rodrick continued. "First, you must learn how to properly conduct yourself around the representatives from the Council. Second, you must learn how to control your powers."

I perked up at that last part. The Council meant next to nothing to me. But this power that was coursing through me; I wanted more than anything to learn to control it, to use it, and more importantly, to fight with it.

I had a man to kill – the man who killed my mother. I would never forget his face. I would hunt him to the end of time. And I *would* finish him.

The Kahl'Nar began to hum and glow as I pondered my revenge.

Rodrick noticed. He pushed the books to the far end of the table and sat down in the chair next to me.

"First things first," he said, pointing at the Kahl'Nar. "I'm going to teach you how to control that."

"My Kahl'Nar?" I asked, holding up the white pearl pendant.

"Where did you hear that name?" he asked, unable to conceal his shock.

"Um, a girl told me," I answered.

"What girl?"

"The girl who showed me how to get back home. It was the night I ran into the woods, after my...Awakening."

"Tell me," Rodrick commanded.

I swallowed hard. The story felt like a wild dream at best and I didn't want Rodrick to think I was some kind of lunatic. Still, his intense stare compelled me to continue.

"She was there with this big, white beast-thing that kept changing forms. Then it melted into a kind of puddle of sky and stars, and she told me I had to go down into it. She said I had to go quickly if I wanted...if I wanted to save my mother."

I said the last part softly, trying unsuccessfully to quell the bubble of grief that was climbing up inside of me, threatening another onslaught of tears.

Rodrick listened intently, but then just shook his head in denial.

"No. That is not possible. There is no way you could have ported from the woods. There is no portal in the woods."

"Oh, really?" I folded my arms and dared him with my eyes to contradict me. "Since you obviously already know the story so well, why don't you go ahead and explain to me how I got to Earth."

"I don't know, Leeowyn," he replied, his lips pursed. "But I do know that no one can just make a portal. They are anomalies of nature. Sometimes they open on their own, in unexpected places and at unexpected times. But no one has the power to open one up and decide where it will take them."

He locked his eyes on me as if that settled the matter; as if I was going to confess to making it all up.

I didn't want to fight with this guy. I figured I would probably lose. But I wasn't willing to deny my own experiences either.

"Look, I'm not saying I opened up any portal. I probably didn't. It was probably that girl who did it. She had a necklace just like this one. I guess maybe she was a Guardian, too."

"Wait," Rodrick acted as if he were hearing me for the first time. "What girl? Who are you talking about?"

An odd expression passed over his face, as if he knew who I was talking about, but couldn't believe it was true.

"The *girl!*" I shot back, throwing my hands in the air, getting just a tad bit irritated. "Hello. Have you heard a word I said?"

An amused smile creased Rodrick's face.

"Humor me and pretend I haven't."

"I don't know who she was," I confessed. "She was just some girl. The same girl who has been showing up in my dreams lately. I'm pretty sure she was dead; which I guess would technically make her a zombie. I would say 'ghost', but she could touch me and I didn't think ghosts were corporeal."

"Will you stop talking nonsense and say something that is actually helpful?" Rodrick snapped.

I looked at him with narrowed eyes. The Kahl'Nar was starting to pulse faster with my rising level of ire.

"I'm trying to be helpful, Rodrick," I shot back. "But we didn't exactly exchanged names and email addresses."

I paused for a moment to collect my thoughts.

"Alright, let's see," I said. "She appeared to be about my age. Blonde hair, down around her shoulders. Pretty. Red, full lips. Honey golden eyes. That is, until she started to fall apart in front of me. Literally."

Rodrick pulled something from his pocket and slid it across the table towards me. It was a photograph of the girl I had seen in the woods. The girl I had seen in my dreams. In this photo there were no blood stains, no ripped clothing. Her hands were normal; whole. She was looking over her shoulder and smiling, as if it were the most natural thing in the world for her to do.

"Is this her?" Rodrick asked.

I looked up at him.

The tone in his voice was so sad.

I nodded without saying a word.

He dropped his head and sighed. Retrieving the photograph, he tucked it back into his pocket.

"How many times have you seen her?"

"Um, I don't know." I said. "Three, maybe four times. I think four times."

Rodrick got up and crossed to me, grabbed my shoulders and pulled me out of my chair.

"Why haven't you told me this before," he demanded. "What did you talk about? Is she alive? Where is she?"

I jerked away from him.

"Stop playing good cop, bad cop with me and maybe I'll answer your questions," I told him.

The sudden movement tore open the wound on my neck. I hissed in pain and looked for a napkin or tissue or *something* to cover the seeping wound.

"Why didn't you have Alex heal that?" Rodrick asked, pulling my hand away from my neck so he could get a closer look at the burn.

"Why on Earth...or...wherever we are... would I ask Alex to heal my neck?"

Rodrick just sighed in my general direction and walked out of the library.

"I really *did* want an answer to that question," I called after him.

Left to my own devices in the suddenly too quiet library, I found a wadded up tissue in my pocket and stuck it to my neck. It didn't take away the sting, but at least it was kept whatever was oozing from the wound from staining my clothes.

I stood like that for a few minutes, wondering if I was supposed to follow Rodrick or what.

At least I had a moment to ponder my situation. People around here were finally starting to be honest with me, but it didn't seem to make a difference. I was still just as confused. I still had just as many questions. Only now my questions, if I asked them out loud, made me sound like a nut job.

Rodrick strode back into the library with Alex in tow. If Rodrick noticed the scathing look I directed toward Alex, he didn't show it. He just folded his arms and waited for, well, *something* to happen. When neither of us moved, Rodrick allowed a sigh of annoyance to escape his lips. He grabbed Alex's shoulder and shoved him toward me.

"Enough pettiness," he said. "We cannot have her presented to the Council with that welt on the side of her neck. Now, heal it."

I wasn't quite finished with my pettiness, however.

"Okay. A: he's not a doctor," I snapped. "And B: it's not that bad. All I need is some gauze and some burn ointment, and it's going to heal up fine on its own."

Rodrick pulled the now saturated tissue from my burn and showed it to me. The splotches of discharge that covered the tissue were a nasty mixture of blood laced with some kind of green ooze.

I gasped.

It hadn't looked like that earlier today.

"It's poisoned, Lee," Alex said softly.

I glanced up at Alex, letting the full weight of his words sink into my brain before looking back down at the soiled tissue in my hand.

Poisoned.

Great.

Rodrick nudged Alex's shoulder and indicated my neck. Alex sighed and took the final step toward me.

"Just...trust me, okay," he said.

I nodded. Trust wasn't one of my better qualities right then, particularly where Alex was concerned. But I felt like the alternative might just mean ending up like Zombie-girl.

Alex slowly, gently brought his hands up and placed them on either side of my neck, not quite touching the burn.

I tensed, expecting a sudden rush of pain at his touch.

Alex looked deeply into my eyes and said, "Trust me, Lee," one more time.

This time, I did trust him.

I smiled, nodded, closed my eyes and braced myself.

His hands closed together around my throat, covering the infected, poisoned burn. Instead of the expected searing pain, I felt a soothing cool rush flow out of his hands and into my neck.

My eyes flew open at this remarkable sensation. I had never felt anything like it.

Alex was completely focused on my neck. I watched the color of his eyes fade from a sky blue to a luminescent white. A sheen coated the surface of his skin. It was like when the Kahl'Nar coated my flesh, only with Alex it was a lesser light. It was like he had just walked out of the ocean and water was dripping off his body.

Alex shifted his focus slightly to meet my gaze. The intensity in his eyes caused me to catch my breath.

His gaze was much more intense than I had ever seen before. No longer boyish and charming, it was hard, commanding, powerful, masculine. It was almost like staring at a July sun in the middle of the afternoon. You could do it, but it would be painful and it leaves you reeling.

As suddenly as he started, Alex pulled his hands from my neck and stepped away.

I gingerly reached my hand to touch my neck. It was smooth to the touch.

No pain.

Somehow, I wasn't surprised. But I felt suddenly shy.

"Um, thanks," I said, avoiding his gaze.

Alex nodded, turned and walked out of the room.

"How exactly did that work?" I asked Rodrick.

"Alex is a Guardian, as you may have guessed," Rodrick answered. "One of the most powerful of all, although his powers pale in comparison to yours."

"Then, why couldn't I just heal myself?"

"Tell me, Leeowyn Blake, how would you have done that? Do you know how to knit muscle and sinew back together? Do you know how to burn poison out of the blood or make skin grow?"

I opened my mouth and then shut it.

Of course I didn't know how to do those things. But I was pretty sure Rodrick could have told me how to do it. I would have much preferred to have a crack at healing myself rather than letting Alex touch me.

I rubbed my neck one last time, remembering the cool fire of Alex's touch.

I noticed Rodrick noticing me, and I pulled my hand from my neck and sat down.

Rodrick sighed and ran his hands through his stark white hair. He looked at me like I was going to be a great deal of trouble.

"All right, let's begin again," he said. "You say you saw that girl in the photograph."

I nodded.

"And you say she was the one who told you about the Kahl'Nar?"

I nodded again.

"And you say she somehow showed you how to open a portal?"

He said the last part like he was talking to a toddler about a dream that they were convinced was reality.

"What I *said* was," I said, emphasizing 'said,' "I'm not sure. All I know is, there was this shining, white-fire, beast-thing. And it melted into a pool on the ground. I jumped in it and came out in the ocean near my house."

I shrugged my shoulders.

"Look, Rodrick. I wish I could be more help. I really do. Because then maybe then you would be the one answering some of my questions instead of the other way around. But I had no idea how I've done any of the things I've done since my birthday. Everything seems impossible, you know? But apparently *impossible* isn't a word that I need in my vocabulary any more."

Rodrick shook his head, a smile tugging at the corners of his mouth. He didn't look right smiling; I half expected to hear the muscles around his mouth creaking from lack of use.

"This is wonderful," he said, and this time he really did smile.

It was creepy.

I didn't like to see him so happy. He didn't seem the type who should have such an emotion.

"Do you know what this means?"

I shook my head.

"It means you are more powerful than we imagined. More powerful than we could even hope to imagine."

I was pretty sure he was talking to himself now and ignoring me completely.

"So," I injected myself back into the conversation, "if I'm so all-powerful, how come I couldn't heal myself?"

I forced my hand to stay away from my throat.

"Because while you are quite powerful, you are also completely untrained," Rodrick answered. "You're like a child with a chainsaw, extremely powerful and extremely dangerous."

"I'm pretty sure you're not from Earth. So, how do you know what a chainsaw is?" I asked.

Rodrick stopped smiling and gave me a look that shut me up.

"You're missing the point."

Rodrick sat down in front of me. He took my hands in his and held them gently, his eyes closed.

I couldn't help feeling a bit awkward and out of place.

Then I realized my hands were glowing. I could feel power flow into my hands, through my body, then back into my hands. Rodrick took his hands off of mine and the glow faded away.

"What was that?" I asked.

"I was trying to get a read on your powers," he replied.

He stood and crossed to the bookcase, removing a small, non-descript book from the shelf. He set it down at the opposite end of the table and stood behind it.

"Move this," he said, pointing at the book.

I started to get up and walk to the end of the table, but Rodrick stopped me with a stern command.

"Sit back down."

"How am I supposed to move the book if I'm sitting at this end of the table?" I asked.

Rodrick just looked at me until I let out an exasperated sigh and sat back down.

"Move the book while sitting down."

I reached my arm out and leaned as far as I could.

"I can't reach it."

"I didn't ask you to reach it. I asked you to move it."

I pulled my arm back and looked at him.

"You mean with this?" I asked, holding up the pearl necklace.

He nodded.

I leaned back and closed my eyes, trying to find the merest hint of a hum or the light that the Kahl'Nar emitted when I was angry or frightened.

Nada. Nothing. Zip.

It was useless, I didn't feel anything.

I opened my eyes and trained them on the tiny book at the far end of the table.

You can do this, Leeowyn. You are powerful. You are a Guardian. Move, move, move, move, move, move!

Nothing moved. And I almost passed out when I realized I was concentrating so hard I had forgot to breathe.

"I can't," I said.

"You can," Rodrick insisted. "Try again."

I stretched, rubbed my eyes and tried again.

And again.

For two hours I tried again and hadn't managed to so much as ruffle a page on the book.

How come I can make an entire roomful of glass shatter like a bomb, but I can't move a book that weighs less than a pound?

I was frustrated. I had a headache. And Rodrick was being no help, whatsoever. He never gave me any instructions, or critiques, or anything.

He just kept telling me to try again.

My back ached from sitting rigid for so long from *trying again*. My lungs were sore because I kept forgetting to breathe while I was *trying again*. My frustration was turning to anger because I was continually failing every time I *tried again*.

It was ridiculous. I was mad that I couldn't do this one, simple thing.

Really, Leeowyn? Moving a book with your mind is a simple thing?

I was mad at Rodrick because he was supposed to be my teacher, but he wasn't teaching me anything. I was especially mad at the stupid little leather-bound book that was sitting a mere five feet away from me. It was mocking me, sitting there all high and mighty.

My anger had reached the boiling point. I was hot with it.

A book flew off the shelf and slammed into the wall behind me.

I squeaked and ducked as five other books came soaring towards me, slamming into the wall and flopping open on the floor below it.

"That's it!" Rodrick shouted.

He rushed toward me and pulled me up from my hiding place under the table. More books shot across the room.

"Find it! Find the source of the power!" He said, locking eyes with me.

Sweat broke out on his face and his eyes kept a steely lock on my gaze.

"Find it!" he commanded.

I closed my eyes, looking inside for something; prepared to find nothing. But this time there was a sun burning inside of me. The light was so bright and hot that I felt like it would burn me alive and leave nothing behind.

"Find the core!" I vaguely heard Rodrick shouting at me.

I delved deeper into the light. It felt like being in the pool of sky and stars, the portal, moving rapidly, but not moving, not being able to tell what direction I was moving. Weightless, yet infinitely heavy. I couldn't hear Rodrick's voice any more, but I had the feeling that someone was holding me up, supporting me.

After an eternity, or a few moments, the blinding light that surrounded me began to dim. I had the sensation of moving toward... something. The light receded until I was surrounded by darkness. Only a single, tiny spark, perhaps the size of a mustard seed, was visible.

Was this the core Rodrick had shouted for me to find?

I tried to reach out for it, but was suddenly jerked backward. The next instant I was back in the library.

My legs had given out. Rodrick was holding me up.

Books flew around us in a literary tornado, banging into walls, slamming into chairs. I was surprised that none of them came close enough to hit either one of us.

"Focus on the core, and make this stop," Rodrick whispered into my ear.

I found the strength to nod and started to try and delve into myself again. That's when I noticed I didn't have to.

It was right there, like a tiny little road map leading to the core of me. I pinpointed the source of my power and focused on it.

Stop.

The books crashed to the ground.

Strength began to flow back into my limbs and I was able to stand on my own again. Rodrick slowly let me go, making sure I wasn't going to fall over.

I glanced at the table and was more than a little annoyed to find that stupid book still hadn't moved.

"You see what I mean about you being dangerous?" Rodrick asked, indicating the destruction all around us. "You are powerful,

Leeowyn. More powerful than any Guardian I have ever trained. Perhaps the most powerful Guardian in the last millennium. But you must learn control. Your powers are directly affected by your emotions. I thought it would be so. You're father was like that, too."

"You knew my father?" I asked.

I started gathering the books and cleaning up the mess that had resulted from the miniature cyclone I had created.

"I did," Rodrick said, his eyes seeing a different time and place. "He was a good man; and a good friend."

Rodrick shook his head and came back to the present.

"I started his training while he was still just a boy, so he didn't have it as hard as you."

Rodrick picked up three of the books he had pulled from bookcase and handed them to me.

"We're done for today, but I want you to keep practicing control," he said. "You can't rely on your emotions to fuel your powers. Now that you know where your core is, focus on that."

I nodded as I took the books from him.

"What am I supposed to do with these," I asked. "Practice tossing them around the room with my mind?"

Rodrick didn't even crack a smile at my attempted joke.

"Those are your homework," he replied. "Study them well."

I nodded and turned to exit the library. I paused in the doorway and cocked my head to take a final glance at the small book at the end of the table. A flick of my mind and it went flying through the air until it smacked the far wall with a satisfying splat.

Rodrick gave me a bemused look.

I just smiled at him.

"What? I couldn't let it beat me, could I?"

As I walked out of the library I couldn't help overhearing Rodrick.

"You are exactly like him."

And I smiled again.

Chapter 41

"You're sure?" Cyle asked.

He looked at Rodrick standing across from him in the courtyard. The moon was full, shedding enough light to see Rodrick nod his head.

Cyle felt his heart squeeze at the news.

Bethany.

Leeowyn had seen Bethany.

"Does this mean she's alive?" Cyle asked.

"Leeowyn doesn't seem to think so," Rodrick replied, fully aware of the impact of his words. But there was no choice but to impart the truth. "She thinks she's seen some kind of ghost. Or zombie."

Cyle took a step toward Rodrick. His face was white, whiter than it should have been, even in the pale light cast by the silver moon.

"But Rodrick...what if she's alive?" he whispered.

Rodrick grasped his friend's shoulder.

"Cyle, the Kahl'Nar would not have returned to us if Bethany still lived. We both know that."

"But Lee saw her! And she saw her *with* the Kahl'Nar. How do you explain that?"

"I don't," Rodrick replied as gently as he could. "There are more things in heaven and earth than are dreamt of in our philosophy, Cyle."

"Rodrick..."

"You didn't see Haven, Cyle. I did."

A haunted look clouded Rodrick's eyes as the memories rolled over his soul.

Perennial le Fay, the Guardian of Haven, had appeared on their doorstep, blood soaked and dying. Unconcerned with her own wounds, she had refused aid until she was allowed to speak to the Guardian of the Realms.

The Guardian had to come and protect her world, she begged.

They had all gathered and listened, troubled and dumbfounded, as Perennial told tales of men who were dead, yet refused to die; not-dead creatures who pillaged, ravaged, and destroyed their peaceful land.

"We weren't prepared for it," Perennial said, her eyes wide with terror. "How could we have been prepared for something that can't happen?"

Bethany healed Perennial's life-threatening wounds and was working on the smaller ones as she listened.

"They just kept coming, and coming; wave after wave of men, women and even children, with knives and swords, and weapons we've never encountered that threw death from a distance."

"Guns," Cyle said. "Whoever is doing this has had contact with Earth."

Perennial was completely healed, but her ordeal had taken its toll. She had been near death, and she required rest and food. She refused both until she accomplished her purpose.

"You must help," she begged, refusing to release Bethany's hand. "My people cannot protect themselves from this attack and my powers are not strong enough. You are the Guardian of the Realms. You must help us!"

Bethany nodded.

"I'll leave right away."

"I'll go with you," Perennial said. She stood to her feet, and immediately collapsed, unconscious.

Rodrick caught her and lowered her onto the sofa. Bethany placed her hand on Perennial's forehead, bent low and whispered in her ear.

"No, you've done your part." Bethany said, "Take your rest."

Bethany's hand glowed bright white briefly, and Perennial's ragged breathing slowed to the peaceful rhythm of sleep.

Bethany turned and started towards the library.

"Bethany, wait!" Cyle said, walking after her. "You don't know what you're up against."

He grabbed her shoulder and spun her around. "Let's get some more reports before you go barging in."

Bethany smiled and patted him on the cheek.

"Dad, they don't have time for us to wait. You know that as well as I do."

She cast a quick glance back at Perennial.

"Look at that girl. She was on the verge of death. She's a Fay, an Immortal. Death shouldn't even be possible for her. Haven needs my help. I am the Guardian of the Realms. I can't just ignore them."

"But..."

"I'll be careful. I promise. I'll gather as many Fay as I can and move them to a safe house, away from whoever is attacking them. Then I'll come back with a better idea of what we are up against. We'll take it from there. Okay? You have to stop worrying about me, Dad. I'm not a little girl anymore."

Bethany gently pulled away from Cyle's grasp, turned and walked into the library, heading towards the fireplace.

"Bethany, don't..."

She turned and gave him another smile.

"Cyle, let her go," Cecil said, placing his hand on Cyle's shoulder. "She's strong. She can take care of herself. And she has her duty."

"Thank you, Uncle Cecil, for having faith in me," Bethany said.

Cyle gave Cecil a chagrined look.

"Just wait until yours is old enough to go off making bad decisions," he whispered.

Cecil smiled.

"I think I'll trust Leeowyn a little more than you trust Bethany," he said. "Come on, Cyle. How bad can it be? The Fay have men who can fight along side Bethany. Not that she needs it. She's more powerful than you and me put together. She'll be fine."

The brothers turned and watched as Bethany Blake, the Guardian of the Realms, placed her hand on the mantel of the fireplace. The Kahl'Nar around her neck shone bright, bathing her body in white-blue light. The fireplace erupted in blue fire.

Bethany turned around to face her father and uncle. She stepped backward into the fireplace looking fondly at Cyle, her golden eyes shining with joy and anticipation.

"I'll be back before you know it."

That was the last time anyone saw her.

Bethany Blake had always been like that; running toward danger with a laugh and a smile.

She never showed fear.

"It's gone," Rodrick's voice was hoarse, choked with sadness. "It's...all gone; everything burned to the ground; the whole world in ruins. There is no way anyone escaped."

Silence reigned between the two men as a rogue cloud obscured the moon, as if even nature were in mourning.

Rodrick found his voice again. He had been preparing this speech ever since he first stepped foot on Haven and saw the wasteland that was left behind.

In slow and measured tones he said, "She's gone, Cyle. It's time to let her go."

Cyle nodded, pulling himself back to the present.

"And yet, somehow Bethany has managed to appear to Leeowyn, and is teaching her how to use the Kahl'Nar?"

"So it seems," Rodrick replied.

"I still don't understand how Leeowyn could have opened up a portal. No one has ever been able to do that," Cyle said. "Not even Bethany. And what is that beast she talked about?"

Rodrick shrugged, walked to a rosebush and pulled a vagabond leaf from it. He began absentmindedly shredding it, letting tiny, ripped up pieces fall to the ground.

"I don't know," he confessed. "This girl is changing everything that we thought we knew. Cyle, if the Council discovers Leeowyn's level of ability they would demand to conduct her training."

"Then we don't let the Council find out," Cyle snapped. "It's bad enough that Heril is in the Head Seat. We don't need anything else working against us."

They stood in silence for another moment. Rodrick ripped a few more leaves as Cyle contemplated the moon.

"We're just as lost as she feels right now, Cyle," Rodrick said.

Cyle nodded in agreement.

"I'll teach her everything I know, but she's going to have to learn the bulk of it by herself."

"I wish we had more time," Cyle sighed. "The Council will be breathing down our necks in just a few days. There will be representatives left and right, demanding she make a choice. She's not ready for that. She wouldn't be ready in a month. She's overloaded as it is. She'll make the wrong decision."

Rodrick held up his hands in agreement.

"You don't have to tell me. I'm on your side. Nevertheless, they will be coming, and we need to prepare her for it."

Rodrick gave Cyle an encouraging pat on the shoulder.

"If she's as much like her father as we think, she'll make the right decision."

"What is the right decision?" Cyle asked, looking at Rodrick with lost eyes.

Rodrick stood silent for a moment, listening to the quiet of the night.

"I don't know, Cyle," he said finally. "To have to pick one realm to save, and perhaps let the others fall to ruins..."

Rodrick shook his mane of white hair, like a lion in the moonlight. "It is a heavy decision. Not one that I envy."

Rodrick let the remaining shredded rose leaves fall from his hands and drift to the ground. He nodded once at Cyle, then walked towards the house.

Cyle stood for a moment longer, looking into the woods, wondering if he might see Bethany there.

Nothing.

He shook his head, turned and followed Rodrick into the house.

Chapter 42

I turned the page before realizing I couldn't remember a single word I had read on the previous page.

The books Rodrick had given me were full of *proceedings* and *traditions* and *the Council this* and *the Council that.* How to act, what to say, when to sit, even how you're supposed to drink around them.

Blah, blah, yada, yada.

It sounded to me like someone needed to be kicked off their high horse.

I sighed, closed the book and picked up a different one, hoping against hope that it would be more interesting.

I was curled up on my bed, surrounded by the books Rodrick had instructed me to study. And I was trying. I had a notebook, yellow highlighter and a few scattered ink pens. I thought I might take some notes. After all, you would think the history and cultural traditions of a whole a different set of universes would be interesting.

You would be wrong.

It was more like when they show "movies" during class in high school. They lure you in, make you think you're going to get to watch something cool and have a welcomed break from the same boring lectures that you are accustomed to.

Then, boom!

You're stuck with fifty minutes worth of the mating habits of South American primates.

Eww.

Even stuff that looked like it should be important was just...boring.

I tried to concentrate on things that had a direct affect on me, like the proper way to greet the Head Chair of the Council (whatever that was). I reached for a pen to make notes, but after a few moments of fumbling for it, I realized it had rolled to the edge of the bed, just out of my reach.

I started to lean forward to grab it when a thought crossed my mind. I sat back. I closed my eyes and focused.

There.

The core.

The Kahl'Nar hummed a greeting to me as I opened my eyes and focused on the pen. At first nothing happened. Then the pen began to quiver and shake, just slightly.

I smiled and continued to focus on it. Slowly the pen floated off the bed. I reached out my hand for it when my door suddenly slammed open. The pen shot across the room, embedding itself in the wall, not six inches from Peach's head.

She looked at the pen that was a breath away from having stabbed through her face, then back at me.

"You could have knocked!" I snapped.

I jumped from my bed and walked to where the pen was still quivering in the wall. I grabbed the end and tugged, trying to pull it out of the wall but, despite my best efforts, it refused to budge.

I gave up and turned toward Peach, who was leaning against the doorframe, her arms folded beneath her breasts, a cat-that-ate-the-canary smirk on her face.

"May I help you?" I asked.

"I just wanted to... you know... with everything that has happened..." she mumbled.

I rolled my eyes and walked back to my bed. I picked up one of the books and made a grand show of opening it.

"If you are not going to speak in complete sentences then please stop talking," I sniffed. "I have work to do."

My anger may have subsided a bit, but I was still licking my wounds. Peach *had* lied to me after all. And she was the one who kept erasing my memory every time Alex tried to tell me about all this.

Peach walked into my room, closed the door behind her and leaned back against it.

I looked at her; studying her features. She was hovering just off the floor, the tips of her toes not even touching the ground. She shimmered like gold in the sunlight.

This time I knew it wasn't my imagination.

"So, what are you?" I asked.

She gave me a confused look.

I gestured toward the space between her feet and the floor.

"Oh, yeah. What am I," Peach repeated. "I'm an Immortal; a Fay."

I nodded my head. On any other day this conversation might seem odd.

Peach walked toward me. Well, she didn't exactly...*walk*. She made all the motions like someone who was walking. But her feet were an inch above the floor.

"Are you the Guardian of whatever realm you're from? Are you here to plead with me, to try to win me over to your side, like I hear everyone else is going to do?" I asked as I flipped open the book and pointedly avoided looking at her.

"I was the Guardian of my realm," Peach answered, a poignant sadness tingeing her words. "But since my world and everyone in it was destroyed, it wouldn't make much sense to beg you to save it. No use in trying to save a graveyard, right?"

I shot my head up, horror playing across my eyes.

"Oh, Peach, I'm...so sorry. I didn't..."

I ended lamely. What could I say? When would I learn to keep my big mouth shut?

Stupid, stupid, stupid!

I bit my lip and looked back down at the book, unable to meet her eyes.

"Truce?" Peach asked, extending her hand.

I raised my eyes to look first at her hand, and then up at her face. She was smiling at me. I took her hand, so fragile and small, in mine, and shook it.

"Truce," I said.

All the anger I had harbored against her dissolved into nothingness. I thought I had suffered an unimaginable loss. But she had suffered even more. There was a sisterhood in our suffering.

"So...your world is gone? How is that even possible?" I asked, hoping it wasn't an insensitive question, but knowing it was.

I studied Peach's face for some sign of distress. She didn't seem too disturbed by the subject, though her eyes seemed to harbor an ocean of sadness.

"Haven is not gone," she said. "The realm is still there, but the land is dead. It used to be so beautiful. You would have loved it, Leeowyn."

She smiled inwardly, eyes seeing a different world.

"There was music every morning and dancing every night. The flowers woke you in the morning with their fragrance. The breeze blowing through the trees smelled of life. There was no war; no strife. Every creature lived in harmony with the world around them."

Her face turned dark and her mouth shut. I could almost see the nightmares playing across her face.

"But then, *they* came."

She shuddered softly and turned to look at me. The darkness was gone from her face, replaced by a lively smile and bright eyes.

"But that's another story for another time."

I marveled at her ability to shift moods so quickly.

"So, why did you fling that pen at me?" Peach asked.

"I wasn't...I mean, I didn't...fling the pen at you. At least I didn't mean to. I was trying to float it towards me and things kind of got out of hand," I said, laughing a little.

I desperately wanted to know more about what had transpired that could bring about the end her world. But I had also had my fill of heartache for a while, and wasn't exactly eager to invite more of it into my life.

"So, whatcha reading?" Peach indicated the book in my lap.

I looked down and groaned.

"Homework. There's just so much everyone expects me to know, and I don't feel like I'm at all up to it."

I gave Peach a sideways grin.

"I can't even make a pen float towards me. How am I supposed to protect an entire realm?"

Peach threw her arms around me and gave me a reassuring hug. I felt static energy pop and sizzle off of her when her body came in contact with mine.

"Aren't you supposed to be telling me that everything will be alright?" I asked.

Peach just smiled and shrugged her shoulders.

"I wish I could, Lee. But then I would be lying, and as you already know, I never lie."

We shared a rueful laugh over that whopper. Peach got suddenly very serious.

"I don't know that anything will ever be alright again," she said. "And I'm afraid there is a very strong possibility that everything will turn to dust and crumble away."

The blood drained from my face at her words. She turned and looked at me with her sparkling green eyes; so wise; so sad.

"That's why we need you so badly."

"Wow...great pep talk..." I said. "Can you at least tell me what it is that's making everyone want me so badly? No one has really explained to me what's going on. I know that there's a rogue Guardian and he's doing some crazy damage or something, but no one's really explained what."

"Well, that's mostly because none of us really know anything about Ruok."

That got my attention.

"Wait. Did you say, Ruok? Cyle mentioned that name before when he was talking about the man who killed my mother; the man who tried to kill me."

I rubbed the smooth, hand-shaped scar on my neck at the memory of his hands around my throat.

Peach's eyes widened, in shock or disbelief, I couldn't tell which.

"You met Ruok? And he didn't kill you?" She gasped.

I nodded. I could feel the dull ache of grief that was hiding just below the surface trying to force its way out. I pushed the ache away, refusing to let my mind wonder to images of flames and smoke devouring my house. My Mom's house.

I shook my head, shaking away the images.

"Tell me about him," I demanded.

I wanted to learn as much as I could about this man. I wasn't expecting her to tell me weaknesses or his secret lair or anything, but any information I could get would be helpful.

"No one knows that much about Ruok," Peach confessed. "We can't even pinpoint which realm he was the Guardian of."

"Wouldn't you just look for the realm that no longer had a Guardian?" I asked.

"It's not that easy, Lee," Peach started lecturing like I was a kindergarten kid that needed to have the obvious spelled out. "Guardians don't die like humans. Their lifespan is; well, it's hard to explain. But, after a while, a Guardian just *knows* that it is time to step down and make way for a new Guardian. The old Guardian fades into the background. Nobody really knows who they are. Each realm my have dozens, even hundreds, of old Guardians still living among their people. And Guardians don't lose their powers."

"So this killer could be a what? A *retired* Guardian?"

She nodded.

"Very few people have met him and lived. It sounds like you are one of the few."

"And this guy is basically just going around and…"

"Murdering people by the thousands," Peach finished my thought.

I held the book Rodrick had given me to my chest as if it were plate armor. How was I supposed to protect anyone from a man who obviously had so much power? I suddenly very much wished I was holding a trig book and studying for mid-terms. High school was starting to look so much more inviting than my real life.

"Does anybody know why?" I asked.

Peach shook her head.

"Like I said, not many people have met him and lived. I'm not sure anyone has had an in-depth conversation with him."

A sudden knock at my door startled us both. Our collective gasps were followed by an uncontrollable burst of giggles as Alex cracked open the door and peeked in.

"Cyle needs to see you," he said to me.

Peach giggled again, stood up and exited the room, patting Alex on the cheek as she left, a gesture that caused a look of complete confusion to wash over his face.

I set my own book aside and stood up as well.

"Lee…"

"Don't," I said, cutting him off with a speak-to-the-hand gesture.

He grabbed my hand and pulled it down.

"No," he demanded. "It's not fair. You've forgiven everyone else but me. I don't get it. I didn't do anything they didn't do."

"Really?" I spat. "Everyone else kissed me?"

He stopped; dumbfounded for a moment, his hands balled into fists, trying to contain his anger. Or anguish.

"Lee, I don't want you to hate me. I *do* care about you."

I walked past him and out of the room without bothering to respond.

Yeah, sure he cares about me. He cares that I can help save Earth.

I was halfway down the hallway when I stopped. I turned and strode back toward my room. Alex was just shutting the door behind him as I rounded the corner. I stormed up to him, stopping only a few inches away, invading his personal space the way he used to invade mine back on the boardwalk in Jacksonville, a lifetime ago.

Alex stood stock still, unsure of what was coming next.

"I don't hate you," I said.

I turned to walk away, thought twice about it, then turned and slapped him as hard as I could across the face.

The look of shock on his face was worth the pain that shot through my hand and up my arm. It took everything in me not to cradle my hand and cry out in pain. I was pretty sure I had done more damage to my hand than I had to his face.

"You may be a liar and a jerk," I said as I tried to shake some feeling back into my hand. "But you *were* the only person here who tried to be honest with me...so, thank you."

Alex hadn't moved during the entire ordeal, including when I slapped him. He just stood there, staring at me like I had turned green or sprouted wings or something.

I finally turned and walked away.

I hadn't really intended to say any of those things to Alex, though I really did want to slap him. But something inside reminded me that my powers were linked to my emotions; and negative emotions could be the most devastating of all. A small voice inside my head said that revenge was a negative emotion that I couldn't afford to hold on to.

I quelled that voice and pretended I had never heard it. Besides, what I planned to do to this Ruok wasn't revenge; it was justice. There was a difference.

Cyle was waiting for me at the bottom of the stairs. His normally emotionless face wore a mask of exasperation, and it didn't look like it was directed at me for a change.

"Cyle, what's wrong?" I asked.

He handed me a letter that was written on some strange kind of paper, all brown and thin, the type you see used on letters in museums.

"What's this?" I asked.

"It's for you," Cyle replied.

He just nodded toward the letter. The red wax seal was already broken. I unfolded the paper and quickly scanned the ornate script.

Guardian,

We have been informed of your Awakening.

Expect a Representative soon.

- Jezreel Heril

Head Chair

The Council of the Seven Realms

Chapter 43

I read over the letter three times. I flipped the single page over a couple of times looking for more information. Finding none, I held the letter out to Cyle.

"I don't understand," I said. "What does this mean?"

"It means the Council has learned of you," Cyle replied, his lips tight. "We thought we would have more time to prepare you, but apparently your impromptu trip to Earth tipped them off. So now, instead of having at least a few weeks to train you...well, they'll be arriving at any time."

"Oh," was all I could think of to say.

"Cyle, I had to go. My Mom..."

Cyle took my face in his hands and shushed me with fatherly gentleness.

"No one's blaming you. You did what you had to do. But Leeowyn, you have to be very careful around these people. They will study every word you say; every move you make. Be especially wary of Heril. He comes from a realm that values women as little more than possessions. He would deem you unfit simply because of your sex. As Head Chair, his opinion carries a certain weight. He could persuade the Council to strip you of your position."

"Wait. How could they take my position away from me? I thought this was a *birth right* kind of thing? Not that I asked for it in the first place."

"They would kill you," Alex stated.

I turned to see him walking down the stairs behind me.

"Kill me?"

"Lee, there is a rogue Guardian out there; one with extraordinary power, creating chaos and threatening the very fabric of our existence. Do you really think they would take the chance of allowing an untried, untrained *girl* to protect their realms? If they think there's the slightest chance you're not up to the task, they'll simply kill you, and wait for the next Guardian of the Realms to emerge."

I was dumbfounded. I'm sure my jaw was on the floor. Up to this point nobody had said anything about dying as part the job description for this Guardian position. I shot a look at Cyle, pleading for him to deny Alex's claim.

Cyle lowered his gaze to the floor and merely nodded in agreement.

I looked back at Alex, who was leaning up against the door frame, his arms folded across his chest. His impossibly blue eyes flashed, but there was simply no expression on his face.

I noticed, with just a guilty hint of self-satisfaction, that there was a red welt in the shape of a hand on his left cheek.

I took a deep, cleansing breath and blew it out.

"Then I just won't give them a reason to doubt me. It'll be easy."

I smiled.

I'm doomed.

Chapter 44

I spent most of the rest of that night with Rodrick and Cyle, pouring over ancient books and obscure documents in Cyle's study.

There was so much I needed to learn about the stupid proceedings of the stupid Council; and I just couldn't make myself care. I mean, yeah sure, the thought that these people might want to kill me provided a certain amount of motivation. But I just felt so detached from it all.

I curled up in one of Cyle's overstuffed chairs, my eyes glazing over as I tried to concentrate on a page from some dusty old tome. It was hard to concentrate while Cyle and Rodrick debated loudly about the best way to deal with the representatives of the Council.

They were obviously most worried about Heril, so they spent a good deal of time discussing how I should dress, and how I should talk, and blah, blah, blah.

Since I was retaining nothing from the old book I was reading, I set it down and reached for another, smaller book. I smiled slightly when I noticed it was the same leather bound book that Rodrick had used when teaching me to control my powers.

I flipped it open, looking for a title along the lines of *The Council of Guardians: A History* or *Rules and Proceedings*. But the book had no title. Instead it was filled with hand written pages. Intrigued, I flipped forward to a random page and began reading.

It's my birthday tomorrow. No one has said anything to me yet, but I think they suspect me to be The Guardian of the Realms. I've seen Rodrick roaming about the house like some kind of ghost. It is strange, because I have no powers and no one will speak of it.

But I'm not stupid. I've seen my eyes.

I've read the logs of all the previous Guardians of the Realms. More than half of them have come from our family line.

On a happier note, Uncle Cecil is ecstatic these days. There is a sparkle in his eyes whenever he looks at Aunt Karen's belly swelling. I overheard him say if the baby was a girl they would name her, Leeowyn.

I think that is a lovely name. In the Old Language it means, Little Bird.

I slammed the book shut as hard as you can slam shut a small, leather bound book.

A quick glance at Rodrick and Cyle proved they weren't paying attention to me. I stood up quietly, walked to the side-table where my book bag rested, gently opened it and slipped the diary inside.

I didn't know how they would feel about me reading this diary. But I wasn't taking any chances.

"So, any guesses about who will be the first to arrive?" I asked.

I crossed to Cyle's desk and started fiddling with a small carving of some strange creature that had surely never existed on Earth. It had a long neck, and a head like an ostrich, but it walked on four legs like a leopard.

"There's really no way to tell," Cyle answered, taking the little statue from my hands and placing it back on the desk. "But we're convinced Heril will be the last to arrive. He always did like to make a grand entrance. So perhaps we'll have a little more time to prepare, after all."

"We suspect it'll either be the representatives from Goham or Piir to arrive first," Rodrick added.

Goham or Piir. The names were not as strange to me as I might have imagined. Along with the books Rodrick had given me about how one conducted one's self in the presence of the Council, he also include selected readings on the nature of the other realms.

There was Earth, of course, which was technically referred to as The Third Realm; don't ask me why.

The First Realm was known as Archend. They got to be first because they were apparently the first realm to discover the existence of another realm.

Goham was the Second Realm and Piir was the Fifth. I didn't know much about Goham, and I knew even less about Piir. From what I could gather, Goham was a tropical world, covered in jungles and forests. It was supposed to be populated by primitive, tribal cultures. Neither Rodrick nor Cyle had said much about Goham, so I assumed I didn't need to worry about their representative.

But when I mentioned Piir, Cyle let slip a grimace.

"What's with the face?" I asked.

Cyle and Rodrick exchanged looks before Cyle shrugged.

"Piir is closely allied with Archend. Those two realms thought they had a divine right to rule over all the known realms, back before the time of the

Council. None of the other realms have quite forgotten... nor forgiven."

"So is Piir governed by a bunch of chauvinistic pigs, too?" I asked, my feminine dander getting totally up.

"Funny you should ask," Cyle rubbed his chin. "For the most part Piirish society is matriarchal in nature. Women occupy most of the governmental offices, serve as heads of families, and make most of the decisions. I have no idea why those two realms get along so well, but they do. Which only serves to make me distrust them all the more."

I walked away from Cyle's desk to stretch my legs. I had been reading for so long that my eyes were stinging and I was beginning to get a headache. I reached my arms above my head and heard my back pop. Instinctively, I raised my left leg, placed my foot on Cyle's desk and bent over to stretch out in a smooth, ballet posture.

"So, what should I expect from these representatives?" I asked.

I didn't hear Cyle say anything, so I glanced up. There was a bemused look on his face.

"Leeowyn. Really?" he said, pointing at my foot on his desk.

Embarrassed, I pulled my leg back down to the floor. I hadn't even realized what I was doing.

"Sorry. Mom always tried to make me less clumsy by putting me in endless dance classes, which I flopped at. I guess I've just never forgotten the stretches." I smiled briefly at the memory, before my heart squeezed at the thought of my mom. I swallowed hard against the hot lump forming in my throat.

Cyle leaned back in his chair, a look of deep exhaustion creasing his face. I guess he was having just as a hard time with this as I was.

"The representatives from Goham are twin sisters. At first the Council refused Goham's request to have them both serve as representatives. Then the Council discovered that when these twins were together they had the unique ability to see into the future. At least sometimes. The Council saw the wisdom of having the sisters share Goham's Council seat.

"Ku'it is the representative from Piir. He's a sniveling little rat, but he is the Queen's favorite, so everyone tolerates him."

Rodrick let out a rich, baritone laugh. I cast a sideways look at Rodrick, shocked. Laughing just did not suit that man.

"I don't remember the last time I heard you talk politics, Cyle. I forgot how much it entertains me."

Rodrick walked over and clapped Cyle on the shoulder. Cyle permitted himself a wry smile.

"I'm glad my distrust and treasonous lack of respect for the Council amuses you," Cyle said. "In some circles, this kind of talk could cost a man his head."

"Fortunately, we are not in those circles," Rodrick replied. "At least, not right now."

Cyle stood and the two men turned to look out the window while they continued discussing which representative supported which policy, and which realm was in most danger, and who they didn't trust and blah, blah, blah.

I collapsed into a comfy, overstuffed chair and tuned them out. I didn't even notice when my eyes closed.

"Kathryn!" I heard Cecilia calling my name.

I balled up my fists, trying to hide my frustration from the ladies-in-waiting that were surrounding me. We were seated in the garden, watching the sunset. My ladies were working on needlepoint or knitting while I sat sewing a doll.

I yelped as I stabbed myself with the needle. I swore under my breath and stuck my finger in my mouth, sucking on the wound.

Cecilia came striding towards me. Her raven black hair curled about her face in perfect ringlets held back by the silver crown that my mother had worn before she died.

She was dressed for court, wearing a flowing silver dress with purple and gold scrollwork lining the edges. A gold, braided belt encircled her slim waist. The coloring suited her wintery pale skin and highlighted her bright gold eyes. She smiled and it was like heaven lighting up.

I hated her.

"Did you not hear me calling, Kathryn?" She said, holding out her hand toward me.

I frowned up at her, my finger still in my mouth.

"Oh, no, did you hurt yourself, dear girl? There's blood on your doll," she said.

I looked down at my doll and sure enough, some of my blood had dropped onto the doll's face.

"Here, give it to me and I'll have one of the maids wash it," she said, reaching out towards it.

"No!" I snapped, holding the doll away from her, staring holes into her. "I like it this way."

Standing up, I tucking the doll in my belt; defiant.

Cecilia sighed and knelt down in front of me.

"Kathryn, please. Must you act thus?"

She placed her hand on my face.

I grimaced at her touch.

"Can we not be friends?" She continued. "I know I could never replace your mother, but I would like to..."

I slapped her hand away, rage boiling inside of me. How dare this whore even speak of my mother?

"You may have fooled my father, but you won't fool me," I said, spitting at her feet before I stormed off.

My ladies-in-waiting, who had been intently ignoring the interchange between Cecilia and myself stood and began to follow me.

"Leave me!" I shouted over my shoulder.

I began to run.

Cecilia would tell my father about my outburst, but I didn't care. He had lost interest in me on the day I was born with green eyes.

Why would the King of Reneath, the most gifted of all the realms, care about a daughter who was born without any gift? And if that wasn't enough to make him hate me, my birth had killed my mother.

I hopped on the fence that surrounded the garden. The fence was overgrown with thorny vines, but I ignored them as they cut into my skin, tearing and ripping at my hands and feet. My dress caught and tore on the grasping thorns.

I ignored that too.

I had been using this wall to escape ever since my father married that woman. When they discovered my escape route, they had the thorn vines planted, hoping they would deter me.

They didn't.

I jumped down the last couple of feet and then took off at a run toward town. I didn't have to worry *about anyone hurting me. The whole town knew who I was.*

Who wouldn't know the only daughter of the King of Reneath?

I could hear the villagers whisper behind their hands as I passed, calling me "the Empty Princess."

Empty.

That's what people called someone who was born without a gift.

Someone like me.

I shivered as I walked through the town. It was close to winter and I had left my cloak sitting in the garden.

Of course, I could go into any shop I wanted and they would give me a cloak. I was, after all, the princess; empty or not.

Rage swelled inside of me.

They were all just like Cecilia and my father. They didn't care about me. They just pitied me. I was a burden to them. As the first born I was destined to rule this land, and how could an Empty Princess ever hope to rule?

"I know you're there," I said, stopping in the middle of the road.

It was the supper hour, and the streets were nearly empty. I could pick out the sound of his footfalls on the cobblestone streets easily enough.

Besides, he was always following me.

After my first few escapes, my father had ordered him to follow me everywhere.

"You always were observant," he said, stepping out of an alley.

He was dressed in a nondescript, dark colored suit and cloak. He could have been anybody, but the sword on his belt identified him as a trusted guard of the royal family.

"Hello, Ruok," I said.

Chapter 45

"Leeowyn, wake up."

Rodrick was shaking my shoulder.

I gasped and sat up, my eyes wide at the dream, or vision, or whatever it was I had just experienced. My grief was obviously playing itself out in my subconscious.

My mind was still a little fuzzy. I rubbed my eyes, which felt assaulted by the sudden light. The sun had risen while I slept in Cyle's office. My back and legs were sore from having slept all cramped up.

"It's time for your lesson."

Rodrick didn't wait for a reply as he walked out of Cyle's office.

I stood up and stretched, groaning as my muscles grumbled at me. I reached down and touched my toes to stretch the kinks out of my back, then grabbed my book bag that contained the diary I had filched. I slung the bag over my shoulder and hurried after Rodrick.

"Hey, Rodrick?" I asked once I caught up to him.

He looked at me questioningly, but didn't slow his pace.

"Who was the Guardian of the Realms before me?"

Rodrick stopped dead in his tracks. I walked a step or two past him before I could recover.

"I mean, Peach said the Guardians in her realm could sort of retire, and make room for the next Guardian. I assume the last Guardian of the Realms retired to make room for me. If there's this big decision to be made, shouldn't I at least be able to consult with the previous Guardian? That's not too much to ask, is it?"

Rodrick stared at me for a long moment, then just started to walk away without saying a word.

"Hey!" I said, hurrying to keep up with him. "That's not an answer, and it's rude to ignore people."

Rodrick ignored me and continued into the library.

I stopped in the doorway, folded my arms across my chest and stared at him.

"I'm not going to practice anything until you answer my question," I said.

Rodrick regarded me with a curious mix of frustration and sadness on his usually expressionless face. He ran his fingers through his white hair, blew out a deep breath and sat down.

"That girl you saw, the one that taught you about the Kahl'Nar?" Rodrick's voice was barely above a whisper. "*She* was the last Guardian."

My arms unfolded of their own accord and dropped to my sides.

"The girl with the flesh missing from one hand?" I asked, subconsciously rubbing my own hand.

Rodrick nodded.

"The last time anyone saw her was when she went to Haven. That was more than fourteen years ago."

"But Haven is dead, right?"

I was confused. Peach told me that she had been the Guardian of Haven, but that the entire world had been burned; ravaged; everyone on it killed. She had escaped to seek help, but no one else had survived.

Rodrick nodded.

I stood there, a dark chill running over my soul. I had suspected the girl who visited me was a phantom of some kind. But I had never really believed she was dead.

So, I wasn't just making her up, and the last place she had been was a world that got torn to pieces by the man I was supposed to stop.

Great. Now I could add *I see dead people* to the list of things I'm now capable of doing.

"Wait," I held up a hand as some unsettling truth started settling on me. "Fourteen years ago? But Peach was the Guardian of Haven. She came to get help from the last Guardian of the Realms...fourteen years ago? That's not possible. Peach is my age."

"Peach is a Fay, Leeowyn," Rodrick said. "They don't age the way humans do. Peach served as the Guardian of Haven for two hundred and thirty years, the way Earth counts years."

There I was, doing my best codfish impersonation again.

"Who was she, Rodrick? The last Guardian. Please?"

"Her name was Bethany," Rodrick whispered. "You knew her, though you were too young to remember. She was Cyle's daughter."

"She didn't come back from Haven," the words trickled from my mouth. "Fourteen years ago. My mom stole me away and returned to earth when I was still only..."

Rodrick waited quietly as I did the math.

"Leeowyn, your mother loved your father deeply. But she knew the potential in you. When

Bethany failed to return; well, you can imagine your mother's dilemma. But this is not something you should discuss with Cyle."

He walked over and took my hands in his. He squeezed them hard and looked at me so intently that all I could do was nod.

"Good," he said. "Cyle knows his duty and will do it, I believe. But he is fragile right now. He has already lost his daughter, his wife and his brother. Much more hangs in the balance than any single life. Do you understand?"

I didn't understand, but I nodded just the same.

Rodrick released my hands, turned and crossed to the bookcase.

I shook myself, trying desperately to clear my mind; to focus on the here and now. I glanced at my book bag and paused.

Her diary was in there...the diary of a dead girl. The diary of my cousin. Bethany.

I shivered at the thought.

Quit that! Clear your mind.

Rodrick pulled two books from the bookcase. He placed a large ornate book on the table next to a much smaller, duller looking one.

"Place your hands on the books," he said.

I stood across the table from Rodrick, and did as he instructed.

"Now, switch them."

I started to move the books when he slapped the table, making me jump.

"Not with your hands; switch them with your Kahl'Nar."

"Alright, look," I said. "I'm not a Jedi, and you're not Yoda, so you don't get the right to talk to me in nonsensical sentences. If you want me to do something that involves using my *powers* or *abilities* or whatever, you're going to have to be a little more specific. Okay?"

Folding my arms over my chest, I gave him my best death glare.

"What's a Yoda?" Rodrick asked.

I hung my head and sighed.

"Pop culture references are lost on you," I mumbled before looking back up at him.

"Remember how you moved the books into a whirlwind, and then made them stop?"

He took my hands and placed them back on the books.

"This seems a little more difficult than just thinking *move*," I said.

"Why?" Rodrick asked, taking his hands off mine and crossing them behind his back.

He reminded me of a general in some army, watching his soldiers practicing maneuvers.

Maybe he was a general. But was I a soldier?

These thoughts swirled through my mind while the possibility that there really was a war going on right now; that thousands were dying; had already died.

Including my mom.

And I would have to be a part of it.

Could I kill if I had to?

One thing at a time, Lee.

"Alright," I said taking a deep breath. "I'll try."

"There is no try," Rodrick snapped. "Do. Or do not."

I looked at his face, searching for some trace of a smile.

I didn't find one.

I stared at him for another second before I looked back at the books and closed my eyes, glad to see the proverbial road to the core of my powers was still there. I tapped into it and opened my eyes, focusing on the books in front of me.

As I watched, the leather binding began to disappear on the book under my left hand, and it started to appear on the book under my right hand. The books began to change sizes, either growing or shrinking. I could feel the changes happening under my hands; hands that were now glowing with the power of the Kahl'Nar.

In just a matter of moments, the two books were completely switched.

I laughed and clapped my hands, looking at Rodrick with a triumphant smile.

Rodrick didn't smile back. He picked up the larger book that was under my right hand, the one that had been small and plain. He opened it to a random page, flipped it over and showed it to me.

My smile faded.

The printing was limited to a square the size of the old book in the middle of the page.

I opened the smaller book to see words filling the page, top to bottom; sentences tumbling off the edges of the page, as if someone had just taken a cookie cutter to a larger book and pasted the pages inside.

"It didn't work." I said, dejected, tossing the book back down on the table. "How come I can make random things happen without even trying, but when I try to do something specific I fail miserably?" I sniveled.

"I would call this far from a miserable failure," Rodrick replied. "Your powers are intensified when you are under emotional strain. I'm assuming that every big thing you've done has been when your emotions were intensely engaged?"

I nodded.

"Now you need to learn to tap into that kind of power when you are not under emotional duress," he said.

"I thought that's what the whole whirlwind thing was about," I said.

"No, you merely discovered the source of your powers. Now you must learn to access it at will."

I stayed in the library with Rodrick for the rest of the day, changing books into other books. After a while, I was able to even get the font and typeface the correct size without even looking inside the book.

After a couple of hours of shifting books, Rodrick showed me how to change disparate objects. Chairs became candles at will; the grandfather clock appeared to be the statue of an old Chinese guy.

Rodrick worked me like a red-headed stepchild for the rest of the day. I was tired and cranky and more than a little hungry when Peach came rushing into the library, her eyes wide.

"Rodrick, Lehann and Chee are coming, now!" she said. "And they are bringing Ferren."

"What?" Rodrick fumed. "Why is he here? Why did Cyle allow it?"

"Who are these people?" I asked, standing up and dusting off my hands.

"They are the representatives from Goham," Peach said. "And their Guardian."

Rodrick stormed out of the room, spewing a string of profanities that I was glad I didn't quite understand. My heart was pounding and all the blood drained from my face.

"Peach, I'm not ready."

I was trembling, the Kahl'Nar pulsing in time with my heartbeat.

"You'll be fine." Peach said as she took my hand. "You just need to calm down."

Before I could think, I grabbed her other hand in mine and closed my eyes.

"Hey, what are you doing?" Peach said; then I heard her gasp.

I opened my eyes and it was like looking into a mirror. I was looking at myself; and myself had a confused look on my face; and myself's mouth was hanging open.

"Lee, what did you do?" myself asked.

This was confusing.

I looked down at my hands.

They were Peach's hands.

I looked down at my feet; and they were floating an inch or two above the ground.

Peach, the Me-Peach, grabbed my hands and shook me.

"Change us back," she demanded. I had talked to myself before, but this experience took it to a whole other level.

"Peach, please," I said, weirded out just a bit to hear Peach's voice coming out of my mouth. "I'm not ready to have a bunch of people I don't even know looking at me like I'm some kind of teenaged messiah. I need you to do this for me; just for a little while. I'll be in there, I promise, but I need to be able to just watch; to just listen. I can think so much better if the attention isn't on me."

Me-Peach frowned, but, after a moment, she dropped my hands; her hands...*wow, confusing*...and motioned me back into the library.

She pointed to the fireplace and I turned in time to see it light up with the same white-blue fire I was coming to know as the Kahl'Nar.

I gasped, and Me-Peach nudged me in the ribs.

"Stop looking so shocked," she whispered. "I'm used to this stuff, remember?"

I closed my mouth and nodded, putting what I hoped was a normal expression on my face.

Three outlines appeared in the flames, then solidified into human forms. Rodrick and Cyle walked into the room as the three forms stepped out of the fireplace.

The first one out was a young woman, about my height, but with a more muscular build. One side of her head was covered in hair that was a dark brown and braided, with beads and feathers falling off the tips. The other half of her head was shaved bald.

Her skin was tanned a dark brown, and her eyes matched her skin. Those eyes were piercing and sharp, like a hawk's eyes. She had unusual markings, kind of like a birth mark, underneath each eye, whether a tattoo or natural, I couldn't tell.

She had similar markings across her shoulders and arms, some stretching across her chest and up her neck.

If there had ever been such a thing as an Amazon, I think she would have looked like one. She looked primitive and fierce, with a staff in her hands that looked more utilitarian than ornamental, and a pair of daggers on her hip.

The second person through was the mirror image of the first; the same build, the exact same face, everything. Except this one wore her dark brown hair in a Mohawk.

The markings under her eyes were different, too. But the staff and daggers were identical.

Both women approached Cyle, who introduced them to the Me-Peach. Peach did a great job of looking nervous and confused, just what I figured I would look like.

My eyes trailed away from the two women and settled on the third form that had exited the fireplace; a young man who had moved to the side and was standing in the background, studiously paying no attention to me at all.

He was tall, almost as tall as Rodrick. His hair was dark brown and close-cropped. There were no markings under his eyes, or anywhere else that I could see.

He was dressed to blend in on his world, I surmised, in a dark, nondescript shirt that looked to be well worn. His pants appeared to be leather, and his soft, sole-less boots laced up to his knees.

A white ivory ring pierced his left eyebrow. Unlike his companions, his eyes weren't dark brown, but bright golden.

He carried neither staff nor daggers, but he was powerful. Far more powerful than either of his companions. I could tell in an instant. And he was glowing with the light of the Kahl'Nar, though no one but me appeared to notice.

Smoke-like tendrils emerged from the white glowing light that surrounded him and began wafting around the room, as if searching for something.

The tendrils wrapped around Me-Peach, then lifted and turned toward me. The closer they came, the closer I came to losing it.

What are those things; and what would they do if they touch me?

"Hey!" I shouted.

Everyone turned to look at me. The glow of power around the young man, along with the searching smoke-tendrils, disappeared.

"Yes, Peach?" Cyle asked.

"Why don't we go somewhere more comfortable?" I asked.

I rubbed my arms as a strange prickly feeling washed over me. I hoped and prayed that didn't mean the effect between Peach and me was wearing off.

"That's a fine idea," Cyle said, turning his attention back to the women. "Lehann, Chee, why don't you follow me into the living room?"

He and Rodrick led the way, followed by the two girls and the Me-Peach who gave me one more *save me* look before exiting the room.

The young man followed a few steps behind them to the doorway. To my dismay he just shut the door, turned and looked at me. His expression was unreadable.

"Did you honestly think you could fool me with such a simple trick, Guardian?" he asked.

Chapter 47

"I'm sorry?"

I did a creditable job of keeping my voice from shaking too much.

The young man took a step toward me, his hawk-like eyes piercing; his hands glowing bright.

"You heard me, Guardian," he said, taking another step closer.

"The Guardian left with the others," I said, "and we should join them."

I sidestepping him and headed toward the door, but as I passed him, he grabbed my arm, pulling me to a stop. Something shifted; a kind of *snap*; and I knew without looking that the illusion I had created was gone.

I was me again.

Somewhere in the back of my mind I wondered if Peach was Peach again. If she was, things were about to get really awkward.

"I could sense your power the moment we stepped into the room," he said, "as I am sure you could sense mine."

His voice was deep, powerful and as firm as his grip on my arm. I tried to pull away but he held me fast.

"Why would you want to hide from us?"

I thought about denial again, but realized that was a lost cause. Instead I decided on a new tactic – arrogance.

"You may release me now, Guardian of Goham," I said in my most commanding voice.

If he was impressed, he didn't show it. He let go of my arm, but he continued to hold my gaze. He tilted his head, a smile pulling at one corner of his mouth. He was enjoying my unease.

"I ask again, why were you hiding from us? It is rude to play tricks on someone you haven't even met."

I lowered my eyes and stepped around him. My hand was on the doorknob when he made one more verbal jab.

"It's even ruder to ignore someone who is directly addressing you."

There was a laugh behind his words and I got the feeling he was mocking me, or testing me, or something. Whatever it was he was doing, it was infuriating me.

I turned on him.

"Why are you even here?" I demanded.

Newfound courage bubbled up inside me. Nothing made me brave enough to stare down complete strangers quite like ridicule.

"I thought only representatives were important enough to be invited to this meeting."

"It is a time of war, Guardian," he answered smoothly enough. "How would it reflect on me if the representatives from my world were ambushed and killed while on a meeting of the Council?"

"Probably as bad as it would look for you if your world was ambushed and destroyed while you were where you're not needed. Or wanted," Alex said, pushing the door open.

"You okay, Lee?" he asked without taking his eyes off the Guardian of Goham.

I nodded.

"Are you sure? Because everyone in the study is wondering why you suddenly turned into Peach."

"Oh," I responded. Yes, it was definitely going to get awkward.

"Hello, Alex," the Guardian of Goham said. His voice was sharp and held a slight tinge of disdain.

"Ferren," Alex said.

Alex held the door open for me to step through, but never took his eyes off of Ferren.

"I wasn't aware that the representatives for Earth were here," Ferren said, narrowing his bright eyes.

"They're not," Alex replied, smiling smugly, like a child who had just won a stupid bet. "I'm here with Lee."

"Not any more, you're not," I said. "Look, I don't know what kind of little turf war you boys are having, but I am not going to step into the middle of it."

Ferren didn't bother to try to hide the smile that darted across his face. He motioned for me to go ahead of him.

"After you, Guardian," he said, tilting his head in a slight bow.

"My name is Leeowyn," I said as I marched out of the library. "Use it."

I didn't give him, or Alex, a second look.

The pair of them fell into step behind me, whispering like schoolboys. I couldn't quite make out what they were saying.

Not that I cared...sort of.

I spared a quick glance over my shoulder to see Alex giving Ferren a death glare, which Ferren ignored. He walked as calmly as if he were in his own house.

The arrogance!

I didn't have time for this nonsense. I needed to focus. If I could just get through this first meeting, perhaps then I would at least have some idea as to what to expect from the other meetings.

I turned the corner into the study before remembering that I needed to have some excuse for why I had traded identities with Peach. I mean an excuse other than, "I was scared."

"Is this the real one?" The girl with the half shaved head asked. She stared me up and down, sizing me up.

I wondered if I passed whatever test she was mentally putting me through.

"Um, yeah. I mean, yes. Yes, I'm Leeowyn. Or just Lee. I prefer just Lee. It's easier to say than *Leeowyn*. Well, obviously not, *Just Lee*, but...just...*Lee*."

I ended my discourse with a nervous laugh.

The girl with the half shaved head looked at the girl with the Mohawk.

"*This* ...is the Guardian of the Realms?" she asked.

Cyle and Rodrick looked at me with an expression that could only be classified as horrified.

I guess I would be looking at me like that, too, if I were in their shoes. If there was a bigger way to make a complete fool out of myself, I couldn't imagine what it would be.

Peach stood next to Cyle, shaking with what I knew to be a silent case of the giggles.

At least someone is finding this ordeal to be entertaining.

I desperately needed a moment, but since there was no pause button on life, and I didn't have a KitKat Bar, I rubbed my hands together and dove in head first.

"Yes, I am the Guardian of the Realms."

The title tasted strange on my tongue. I was pretty sure I would never get used to it.

"I am called Lehann, and this is my sister Chee. We are of the Fyr Clan," Lehann, the girl with the Mohawk, said holding out her hand towards me.

I reached out to shake her hand, but instead she gripped my wrist. I copied her action, hoping it wasn't too obviously awkward.

Chee stepped forward and greeted me in the same fashion.

"This is Ferren, the Guardian of our realm," Chee said.

"We've met," I said.

Ferren tipped his head in recognition. He merely stood against a window, melting into the background. He could have been carved out of stone for all he moved.

"Why did you bring your Guardian along with you?" Rodrick asked, not even attempting to hide the displeasure in his voice.

"We saw it," Chee replied, as if that settled the matter.

"What exactly did you see?" Peach asked.

"Exactly what we see is for our Clan to know," Lehann answered, narrowing her eyes.

Oh great, they are easily offended and I have no idea how not to offend them.

I wished suddenly that I had paid more attention to the little bits I had read about the realm of Goham.

"You saw it?" I asked, confused.

"Yes, we saw it." Chee answered, as if that cleared anything up.

I managed a weak smile.

"I'm sorry. I don't understand," I said.

Now it was Chee and Lehann's turn to be confused.

"What is there not to understand?" Lehann asked, those hawk eyes of hers trying to pierce down into my soul.

"Lee," Peach said softly, "they *see* the future."

My eyes widened.

These are the ones Cyle was telling me about! I remember, now. The light shines in the darkness.

"Oh," I said. "Of course. You...*saw*...this guy, um, Ferren, here today; so you just assumed that meant you had to bring him."

I cast a death glare towards Ferren, who still hadn't moved that I could tell. He could have told me that when I asked him why he was here.

He smiled and winked at me.

Anger began to churn inside of me.

Don't let it get to you. Control it.

It was as if Rodrick was inside my head.

"You'll have to excuse me," I addressed the sisters from Goham. "I'm not really used to any of this. I don't know all the protocols, so I hope I do not offend by my actions."

I smiled in what I hoped was a reassuring manner.

Lehann leaned towards Chee and whispered something in her ear. Chee nodded then walked towards me.

"Guardian, if you would permit me."

I glanced over at Cyle and Rodrick. Their faces were blank. Neither of them nodded or shook their heads.

No help there.

"Um...sure?" I said.

Chee placed her hands on either side of my face and looked in my eyes.

"See," she whispered.

Chapter 48

Children ran before me, laughing. Their dark hair waved behind them, feathers and beads, entwined in braids and wrapped around ribbons, trailing in their hair. I turned to see huts made out of stretched animal skin and clay bricks with wooden doors.

Older children were preoccupied with tending fires or washing clothes in a stream that was just behind me.

I looked down at myself. I was the same me. I stuck out like a sore thumb with my bright red hair, and my jeans and t-shirt.

No one seemed to notice. No one even turned my way.

I walked a few steps - tentatively at first - and when I saw that still no one noticed, I began to explore the village.

It was as if I had walked into an early Native American village. At least what I imagined such a village would look like.

Men and women worked side by side; repairing houses, tending the chaotic herd of children that were running everywhere, or even skinning and butchering animals.

I gagged and quickly looked away from that last sight. I never had a very strong stomach.

A group rode into the camp on horses. Each member of this group had the curious tribal tattoos I had noticed on Lehann and Chee. Everyone in the village treated the newcomers with great respect, and spoke in hushed tone around them.

The newcomers looked war-hardened, prepared for battle. They did not look like someone you would want to meet in a dark alley.

One of them was Ferren.

A few of the children ran up to him, laughing and clapping to be picked up.

Ferren smiled, leaned down and scooped up a little girl whose hair was cropped short, except for one long braid next to each ear that trailed down below her chin. A feather adorned the tips of each braid.

Ferren ruffled the hair of a boy at his feet, then walked away.

An older woman with silvery hair walked up, stretching out her arms to him. The resemblance between the old woman and the young man was too striking to be coincidence.

Ferren smiled as he gave her a sideways hug while listening to the child in his arms chatter on. They all disappeared into a hut.

I followed them.

"Ruki, run along now and leave Ferren alone. We need to speak in peace," the old woman said to the little girl. She pouted and Ferren knelt down, pulling her into a quick hug.

"I'll come find you when I'm done with all this boring big people talk," he whispered.

She giggled and shot out of the room, squealing and laughing as she joined another group of shouting, playing children.

The smile slid from Ferren's face as soon as Ruki had left the hut.

The woman had her back turned, tending a cookpot that hung in the fireplace at the edge of the hut.

"What news, son?"

Ferren paused until his mother turned to look at him.

"It's getting worse," he said, settling into an ornately carved wooden chair.

The woman let her head fall forward as she let out a soft sigh. But she straightened her shoulders again, her face set in a hard expression that I doubted ever really left her face.

"Then we will fight. As we have always fought," she stated simply.

"It is no longer that simple. There are not enough of us. And the few times we have encountered the enemy, they have," Ferren ran his fingers through his hair and blew out a deep breath, "...refused to die."

Ferren closed his eyes and shuddered. I would have missed the weakened look in his face had I not been studying it so intently. The woman came around and took his face in her hands.

"Hush, son. Hush."

She met his bright, golden eyes with her own dark brown ones.

"We have faced trials before, and we have always come out the other side."

She let her hands drop from his face before walking to the door of the hut. I followed her just in time to hear her say, "The Guardian of the Realms awakens. Chee and Lehann have seen it."

I paused in the doorway, a little startled to hear them talking about me.

I heard a chair creak and turned to see what Ferren was doing, but the scene had shifted.

I was no longer in the hut, but in a dark room. Herbs and dried plants hung from hooks in the ceiling, and the walls were lined with shelves that housed books. Tables held jars and bottles that contained body parts, whole animals, and even what appeared to be an unborn human baby.

There was a small fire crackling in the corner, but it gave neither light nor heat to the room. A woman was seated in front of the fire, and I could barely hear her whispering something.

I drew closer.

I could see legs stretched out on the floor in front of the woman.

Another step and the smell of death hit me like an avalanche.

I gasped and coughed as the smell invaded my lungs and eyes, but I still continued forward.

"I...can't," I heard a girl's voice crying.

"You must. You wish greatness, do you not?"

The voice came from the woman in front of the fire.

I took another step, trying to see the little girl who was crying. Suddenly the old woman stood and spun around on me.

Her hair was black as night and straggling in every direction, as if her own hair wanted to get away from her face. Wrinkles and scars drew deep lines around her colorless blind eyes and toothless mouth.

She grabbed my wrist, her sharp nails piercing into my skin. I opened my mouth to cry out, but I choked on the ever-thickening odor of death and decay.

"Do it now!" the woman screamed.

I caught a glimpse of pale, silver-blonde hair on a frightened little girl. Anger mingled with fear burst through my subconscious. I balled up my fist and struck the woman in the face, sending her reeling back.

Chapter 49

"Leeowyn!" Cyle shouted, dragging me away from Chee.

The representative from Goham was lying on the floor, holding her cheek and giving me a stricken look.

I shouted, struggling against Cyle's embrace, straining to get away from the old blind woman.

"It's alright. You're safe," Cyle's calm voice soothed me.

I was back in the study, breathing in air that didn't reek of death. I looked down at my wrist; there was no blood on it.

"I..." I said, trembling. What could I say that wouldn't sound insane?

"What did you show her?" Alex snapped, walking forward and towering over Chee.

Lehann was already at her sister's side, helping Chee stand. Ferren was suddenly just there, between the sisters and Alex.

"I only showed her our village; I give you my word," Chee said, taking her hand away from her now red cheek and staring at me.

"I was showing her our way of life, and what we have to lose, if..." She trailed off.

Lehann turned to face me.

"You saw more," Lehann stated.

I nodded, still shivering uncontrollably. I kept looking around the room, expecting to see that horrid old woman come running after me.

"You saw the one who threatens us," Chee said, walking toward me. Ferren placed a hand in front of her, but she pushed him aside and continued walking.

"N-no. I didn't see that man, whoever is doing this...I saw..." I couldn't finish. I wasn't sure exactly what I saw. And I wasn't sure if I really wanted to tell anybody about it.

"Guardian," Lehann said, stepping forward and taking her sister's hand, "we need your help. You saw our land, you saw our people. We are warriors. We do not give up without a fight. We do not give up even *with* a fight. Our people will die defending their lands against this Ruok. Help us, help them."

I stood there, staring at the two sisters, then glanced back at Ferren. An image of him smiling and holding little Ruki flickered in my mind's eye.

"You ask for help from the Guardian of the Realms." Cyle asked. "Does that mean you approve?"

I looked at Cyle, confused.

Approve of what? Of me?

Lehann and Chee nodded.

"She has passed our test." Lehann stated, giving me the kind of smile you normally reserve for a dear friend you haven't seen in months.

"Test?" I mouthed to Peach.

She shrugged and motioned for me to look back at Cyle.

Lehann and Chee were giving him what looked like a gold coin, about twice the size of a silver dollar, with holes pierced through it.

Cyle nodded his head toward them, closed his hand over the gold disc and put it in his pocket.

With that, Lehann and Chee both turned and walked out of the room.

"Wait, was that it?" I asked, before quickly walking out of the room and following the sisters.

They were fast and moving with determination towards the library. I skidded around the corner in the hallway, all but running to the library.

"Wait," I called out. "The things you made me see? Was it real? Did it happen? Will it happen?"

Lehann and Chee stepped into the fireplace.

Lehann just smiled.

"You will find out," Chee said.

I stood there, utterly confused. Ferren was suddenly standing beside me, gazing down at me.

"Come to Goham, Guardian," he said, taking my small hand in his big, rough hand.

The darkness of his skin made mine look even paler by comparison. Why did I always notice the oddest of things at the worst moments?

Suddenly he pulled me forward and wrapped an arm around my back, giving me a weird hug, although my arms were pulled up in front of me, trying to push against him.

"Until we meet again," he whispered before pulling back and laughing.

He walked to the fireplace and placed his hand on the mantel. The fireplace began to glow and he stepped in just as bright white flames suddenly consumed the three of them.

They were gone.

Just like that.

No goodbyes; no explanations.

Just gone.

Confusion was making a home for itself in my head.

Cyle and Rodrick walked up behind me.

I took a deep breath.

"Was anyone going to tell me there would be a test?" I asked. "Follow-up question: what was the test? I don't remember taking any test."

I looked at the empty fireplace, as if it was going to suddenly start talking and give me some answers, because nobody else was.

"Get some rest, Lee." Cyle said as he turned to walk back to his office. "We'll talk about it in the morning."

"No," I said.

"Come on, Lee. It's been a long, eventful day. You're tired and need to get some..."

"No!" I shouted, my voice echoing down the halls.

Cyle stopped, turned and looked at me. I'm pretty sure I had never shouted at him like that before.

"Cyle, this is my *life*. You brought me here, forced this huge responsibility of saving the universe on me, and now you're thrusting me into it completely blind. And let's face it - you haven't been completely honest with me up to this point. Today would sure be a great day to start." I swallowed and lowered my voice.

"Cyle, how can I protect anybody if I don't know what's going on?"

Cyle leaned against the door, a crooked smile tugging at his mouth.

"You've never looked more like your father than you do now, standing up to me like he always did," he said.

"Does that mean you're going to answer me?" I asked.

Cyle paused, considering for a moment, before he pulled the weird looking disc out of his pocket.

"Remember how we said that the Council could decide you're not good enough to be Guardian of the Realms?" he asked.

"Yeah, you don't exactly forget when someone tells you that a group of random people can decide if you get to live or not," I said.

Cyle held the disc out to me.

"Each realm, when they meet you, will not only be lobbying for your help, but they will also be running a series of tests on you. It is their way of determining whether they think you can properly protect them. The tests are also designed to find out if you will go insane and start killing people; like Ruok."

Cyle dropped the disc in my hand and I examined it; flipping it over to look at both sides.

"This is Goham's emblem. It is their way of saying that you passed their test. They approve of you. You need to get the approval of at least half the realms before they'll let you continue as the Guardian."

"Great, and here I thought tests were behind me with the rest of high school," I quipped, trying to joke and failing.

Cyle smiled and put his hands on my shoulders.

"You will be fine, Lee. You impressed Lehann and Chee, and they don't impress easily."

I smiled faintly and nodded. I thought having this first meeting under my belt would make me feel better about all this, maybe even make things easier.

I thought wrong.

Chapter 50

I excused myself shortly after Cyle dropped the disc into my hand. Cyle tried to get me to eat something, but I wasn't hungry.

I probably should have been hungry since I really hadn't eaten anything all day, but my stomach was knotted up. I wasn't sure if I could keep anything down, even if I managed to eat.

I climbed the stairs slowly, one plodding step after the other. I was beyond tired.

Maybe I'll fall sleep tonight and wake up in my room in Jacksonville, and it will be four years ago, and this will all be a dream.

My heart squeezed at the thought of my home; my Mom. Tears sprang to my eyes and I stopped walking. I gripped the banister hard; so hard it hurt.

I couldn't afford to break down right now, not in front of everyone. I swallowed hard and made myself sprint the rest of the way up the stairs. Tears escaped my eyes and left telltale streaks down my cheeks.

I careened through the hallway and was almost safe inside my room when I stopped.

Alex was there, leaning against the door to my bedroom, effectively blocking my way.

I turned my face away so he wouldn't see, wiped my eyes as nonchalantly as I could, sniffled once, then looked at him.

"Yes?" I asked, covering the crack in my voice with a fake cough.

"Are you crying?" he asked, walking forward, concern in his eyes.

I couldn't take concern right now. I didn't want to be comforted by anyone. I just wanted to be left alone.

"I'm just tired," I said.

Which was the truth, albeit maybe not the whole truth and nothing but the truth.

The whole truth was, I was exhausted. I was also afraid I wouldn't be able to sleep. And I was afraid, if I did sleep, of the dreams I was sure would follow.

Alex stopped within inches of invading my personal space. A series of emotions played across his beautiful face. Those blue eyes of his...

It took some effort, but I was able to put a look of annoyance on my face.

"Look," I snapped, "if you don't have anything super important to say, could you please just move? I have an important date with my mattress and I really could use the sleep."

I gestured to my door behind him.

He didn't move.

He didn't speak either.

Instead he took another step forward and wrapped his arms around me.

Now he was definitely invading my personal space.

"What do you think you are you doing?" I demanded. "Let me go!"

I tried to pull away, but more I struggled, the stronger he held me.

"It's okay to be weak," he whispered softly in my ears.

I froze at his words. My eyes flew open wide and I stopped struggling against his embrace.

A thunderstorm of emotions had been building behind the wall I had constructed. It was ready to break the second I let the wall crumble.

But I couldn't let that wall crumble. I knew the destruction that could ensue when my emotions fueled the Kahl'Nar.

"Lee...it's okay," Alex whispered again. "I'm here. Let yourself grieve."

A trickle of my emotions dribbled down the wall of my resolved and sparked the Kahl'Nar. I don't know if I pushed with my mind or with my hands, but Alex flew backward until he crashed against my bedroom door, stunned.

"If I wanted comfort from someone, it wouldn't be you," I spat.

I stalked past him like an alley cat defending her territory. I slammed the door behind me and locked it. Safely inside my room I leaned my forehead against the cool wood of the door. I could still feel his arms wrapped around me; safe, warm, protective. I could still smell the rich, earthy scent of him.

Stop thinking like that!

Think of something else; anything else.

I tried to think of all the reasons I hated Alex; reasons not to trust him. But all I could remember was his arms around me.

He's put some kind of spell on me to make me think this way.

I knew that was wrong. Cyle told me that Guardians didn't use spells or magic.

But did that mean they couldn't change the way someone thought, the way someone felt?

I sighed and held my head with my hands. I had a headache twisting right behind my eyes, which I attributed to lack of sleep. I stumbled into my most comfortable pair of tattered old sweats and an oversized t-shirt, then switched off the lights and crawled into bed.

Not that I expected sleep to come. I felt too tired to sleep.

But the darkness was kinder to my eyes than the light had been. I snuggled under the covers, wrapping them closer around me like a cocoon.

I glanced out of my window and allowed myself a childlike smile.

It was starting to snow.

I continued to watch the small white puffs float down from the sky, mesmerized by them, until I began to drift with the snow.

Chapter 51

I shivered as I walked through the town. It was close to winter and I had left my cloak sitting in the garden.

Of course, I could go into any shop I wanted and they would give me a cloak. I was, after all, the princess; empty or not.

Rage swelled inside of me.

They were all just like Cecilia and my father. They didn't care about me. They just pitied me. I was a burden to them. As the first born I was destined to rule this land, and how could an Empty Princess ever hope to rule?

"I know you're there," I said, stopping in the middle of the road.

It was the supper hour, and the streets were nearly empty. I could pick out the sound of his footfalls on the cobblestone streets easily enough.

Besides, he was always following me.

After my first few escapes, my father had ordered him to follow me everywhere.

"You always were observant," he said, stepping out of an alley.

He was dressed in a nondescript, dark colored suit and cloak. He could have been anybody, but the sword on his belt identified him as a trusted guard of the royal family.

"Hello, Ruok," I said.

Ruok smiled as he stepped out of the shadows.

He was at least a foot taller than me, with dark, shiny hair and bright, yellow eyes that darted around the street, searching for potential danger.

Not that anyone would harm me. No one would dare. It may be publicly known that my father cared nothing for me, but his anger was also publicly known. I was still his daughter, after all. Punishment for harming me would be excruciating and death would be slow.

"And what compelled you to wander these dangerous streets unescorted at this time of day, my Princess?" Ruok asked, falling into step a pace behind me as I continued to walk down the road.

"The same thing that always compels me," I grumbled.

"Ah. Her Majesty," Ruok mused.

I stopped and turned to him.

"You don't have to follow me, Ruok. I tell you that every time."

It was obvious that Ruok didn't hate Cecilia, and I was in no mood to be accompanied by anyone who did not share my hate.

Ruok stepped around me, halting my progress. He took my hand, tighter than was absolutely necessary, bowed over it, and brought it to his lips, where it remained for longer than was absolutely necessary.

"I would follow you anywhere, my Princess, even without your father's royal command," he whispered in a tone usually reserved for the bedroom.

A smiled wriggled its way across my mouth before I finally pulled my hand away and continued walking.

"Would you truly follow my anywhere, Ruok? Fine; then today you can meet Abbek."

Ruok kept a close pace with me as I turned down an alley and walked into the poorest part of town. Here decent citizens feared to tread, while beggars and thieves, peasants and paupers called this district home.

A one-legged man who sat at the entrance to the alley held out his palm to me, spewing out some story about a horse crushing his foot.

I ignored him.

The filth here was always vomiting forth some lie or another to try and win a few coins from their betters.

Vermin. They made me sick.

Ruok aimed a kick at the man's head when he got too close to me. The wretch yelped in pain and scurried back into the darkness that had spawned him.

I smiled. Ruok always looked out for me.

"I wasn't aware that your friend lived in such a dangerous part of the city," Ruok mused.

As good as Ruok was at following me, I was even better at avoiding him when I really wanted to. The dark underbelly of the town was my solitude. On one such day I had met Abbek, my mentor, my saving grace from this world.

Another turn down another empty alley brought us to a dead end, a box canyon of fired-brick buildings.

I grabbed Ruok's dagger and pulled it from his belt before he could react.

"Highness, what are you doing?" he asked, his voice spiking.

While he was still speaking I gripped the blade with one hand and jerked it free with the other. I hissing in pain as the razor sharp blade cut deeply into the soft flesh on my palm.

Ruok made a grab for the dagger, but I held it away from him.

"If you do not start conducting yourself properly I will order you to leave me," I said coolly.

Ruok just looked at me in confusion for a moment, then nodded and stood at attention.

I smiled and handed the bloodied dagger back to him. I turned back to the wall, tracing my uninjured hand over the bricks until I found just the right place. I set my bleeding palm against it. I felt the blood being pulled out of me, and glanced over my shoulder to watch Ruok's expression.

His eyebrows shot up in surprise as a door appear, a handle forming beneath my hand. I turned the handle, opened the door and called out.

"Bekky, I've brought a friend."

Chapter 52

The light was bright in my bedroom when I finally opened my eyes. I must have fallen asleep while watching the snow fall.

I blinked rapidly, working some moisture back into my eyes while they adjusted to the light. I looked out my window to find the entire world blanketed in snow.

Somehow the trees in the distance looked less foreboding when they were wrapped in fluffy, white snow. I drew my hand over my eyes to rub the last vestiges of sleep from them, then jerked it away.

You'll get blood on your face if you use that hand.

...wait.

I looked down at my hand; my perfectly fine, uninjured hand.

Why had I thought there was blood on it?

A flicker of a memory flew like a raven through my mind; something about a dagger and a dull, throbbing in my palm.

I looked back down at my hand again, flexing my fingers. It looked just the same.

I shrugged and got out of bed. No sense in trying to force the issue. If it was anything important I would remember it later. If not, then it was just another goofy dream that was not worth wasting energy on.

I showered and dressed, pulling my hair back in a braid while it dried. I decided that I was going to pay extra special attention to the book today. I didn't want a repeat performance of being caught off guard by the next representative.

Rodrick seemed to have the same idea. By the time I walked into the library, sitting on the table there was a stack of books and documents that would choke a mule.

That metaphor made no sense to me. Why would a mule be eating books in the first place?

And why wouldn't it stop eating before it choked itself?

But I digress.

I spent the next few hours studying up on the court proceedings of the Rethean realm. It was actually kind of interesting.

Then Rodrick came in and pulled the book out of my hands.

"Lesson time?" I asked.

I stretched lazily, twisted in my chair to pop my back. When I turned back something hit me; hard. The next think I knew I on the floor against the far wall.

"What the...?" was as much as I could manage to shout as Rodrick strode toward me; deadly purpose reflected in his eyes.

He held his hands out and I was once again smacked by an invisible wrecking ball. This time, instead of falling to the ground, I was pinned against the wall, dangling with my feet off the floor.

The weight pressing against my chest made it impossible to breathe. Lights popped in front of my eyes as I started to pass out.

Not going down without a fight!

Somehow I managed to bring my hands up and placed them between my chest and whatever force was pressing against me. I pushed; at first just physically, then with the weight of my Kahl'Nar.

Inch by inch, Rodrick's feet slipped backward. I swear I saw a hint of a smile flash behind his eyes before he forced his hand forward again, shoving the invisible wall against me.

I didn't bother to shout this time. Instead, I poured my anger, frustration, pain, and confusion into the Kahl'Nar and pushed forward with all my strength.

Rodrick flew backwards, smashing into the far wall.

I landed in a crouch this time, instead of on my face. My arms were shining bright blue-white with power. I formed my hand as if I were holding a ball and threw it at Rodrick, sending white fire flying towards him.

Rodrick batted it away, but I already had another one flying at him.

He managed to swat away everything I threw at him, but I could tell I was besting him. He was getting tired. He stumbled once and I threw a ball of fire at him before he could regain his balance. He fell on his back, and without thinking I jumped on top of him, my hands going for his throat.

And he was smiling at me. Actually smiling!

Alright, this must be some kind of test.

I pushed myself off of him and took a step back. My arms were still afire and I was ready to resume my attack if need be. But Rodrick just laughed.

"Rodrick, what in the name of the happy cows from California was that?" I shouted, punching him in the chest as hard as I could, and only succeeded in hurting my own fist.

"The happy what?" Rodrick asked between fits of laughter.

"Pop culture; ignore it. Answer the more important question," I snapped, anger swirling inside of me. My Kahl'Nar pulsed around my neck, waiting for me to make a move.

"I needed to test your instincts; which are apparently as sharp as a knife," he said as if that explained everything.

He stood, offering me his hand. I just stared at him with a dumb look on my face.

"Leeowyn," he continued, "when the representatives from Goham arrived yesterday, you panicked. I believe that emotion created energy that you used to change your image and Peach's as well. That's extremely advanced, and quite frankly, unexpected. I decided to put my theory that you work better under pressure, to the test. It would appear that I am correct."

I still stood there, breathing heavily and just looking up at him.

"So you decided throwing me against the wall was the best way to test that theory?" I asked. "How am I supposed to trust you now? Now I'm afraid that I'm going to get something thrown at me every time you want to teach me a new lesson."

Suddenly a book was flying at my head. I held up my hand to bat it away, but before it could reach me the book smacked against an invisible wall and dropped to the ground.

I glared at Rodrick.

"That's not funny," I said.

The white-blue fire was fading and my arms stared to resume their normal skin tone. I still felt an odd prickling sensation as if they were asleep and blood was rushing back into them.

"I do not have the luxury of time, Leeowyn," Rodrick replied. "I know these methods are extreme, but I have no choice. You remember how you traded places with Peach? Do you think you are the only one who knows how to do that? What if Ruok shows up wearing my face? You must be ready to face anything; to fight anyone. Even someone who looks like someone you care about; someone you trust."

The glare slid from my eyes. That thought had never crossed my mind.

We continued to practice the rest of the day and, not for the first time, I was shocked to find that I understood things that shouldn't have made sense to me; as if I had learned them a long time ago and I was just now remembering them.

I learned how to form an invisible shield around me, and to keep it up while things were being tossed at me. I had already done it instinctively when Rodrick threw that book at me. Now I knew *how* I did it.

Rodrick showed me how to use that shield as a weapon. It was actually pretty cool, not that I had time to think about it in terms of its coolness.

A thought tickled the back of my mind.

"Rodrick, everyone, including you and Cyle, was fooled when I changed places with Peach. Everyone except Ferren. How did he know who I was?"

"Ferren is a Guardian. He could sense the power of your Kahl'Nar as easily as you could sense his," Rodrick replied. "You *could* sense his Kahl'Nar, couldn't you?"

I thought back to our first meeting and how I knew he was the most powerful of the three visitors from Goham.

I nodded.

"Ferren knew the same way Ruok recognized you on Earth the night he killed your mother, even though he had never seen you before."

A pensive look clouded Rodrick's eyes.

"I must teach you how to hide your Kahl'Nar," Rodrick said, nodding toward the white-blue glow that surrounded me. "There may come a time when you need to be invisible to those who seek you."

Then he added, "But this is not that day. Today we are finished."

Chapter 53

I took advantage of Rodrick's decision to cut our lesson short and walked outside to spend a little time in the snow.

Being a Jacksonville girl, snow was not something that I grew up with. I had come to love the way it muted everything; colors, sounds, emotions.

The snowfall was so peaceful, and I desperately needed peace right now.

I snuggled deep into my thick winter coat and pulled the hood up over my head as I strolled aimlessly around the yard. I walked over to a little snowdrift where I knew a garden bench should be. A little digging into the snow proved me right.

I dusting it off and sat down.

I took a deep breath and gave a cursory look around to make sure I was completely alone, then I pulled the little brown diary from my pocket.

I flipped it open to the beginning and began to read.

It was pretty boring at first. Nothing out of the ordinary; just the normal, random scribblings of a normal teenage girl. She mentioned my father's name a few times, but not mine. I was about to close the diary and go back into the house when an entry caught my eye.

Everyone expects me to know what to do.

Ruok is growing in power. He's gathering more and more followers. People are beginning to panic and everyone keeps looking to me for answers.

I know they expect me to find Ruok, confront him and defeat him. I am, after all, the Guardian of the Realms. But, as strange as it sounds, I don't think Ruok is the one behind all of this.

I keep having these dreams about a girl - almost like I'm her; like I'm seeing through her eyes. And the more I dream about her the more I realize that she's-

"Whatcha reading?" Peach asked.

I jumped like a scalded cat, dropped the diary in the snow and cursed a blue streak at the same time. I scooped the diary up and shoved it in my pocket.

"Jiminy Christmas, don't you ever make any noise," I exclaimed, trying to catch my breath.

"Not usually," Peach laughed, "but this time I made enough noise stomping through the snow to wake the dead. So, what had you so enthralled that you didn't hear me coming?"

"Um, nothing," I stuttered. "Just a book about...you know...stuff."

Because that doesn't sound like a lie.

Peach raised an eyebrow at me, but didn't pursue it. The look on her face said there were important matters afoot. I could feel what it was before she said it.

"Lee...they're here."

I sighed inwardly and nodded.

More representatives.

More tests.

More of the unknown that I didn't want to have to face.

I stood up, dusted the snow off my backside, and accompanied Peach back toward the house. Nothing interrupted us but the sound of snow crunching under our feet. I glanced at her and noticed her feet actually touching the ground. She caught my gaze and smiled.

"I like the sound snow makes when you step on it, so I walk on it when I can."

"Oh," I said, logging away more information about Peach in my mind.

"Who is it this time?"

"Ku'it from Piir and William Hayford from Rethean."

I pulled up short and stared at her.

"Two? At the same time?"

Peach gave me a comforting hug, and I felt power seeping into me from her. I don't know what she did or how she did it, but suddenly I didn't feel as lost or exhausted as I had.

She pulled back, smiling sadly at me for the ordeal she knew waited for me, and we continued inside.

Chapter 54

I shed my coat and hung it on the peg next to the door. I stamped my feet, knocking the snow off my boots, before following Peach into the study where we had met with Lehann and Chee.

I prepared myself mentally, as best I could, to meet with the representatives from two realms. But all preparations fled when I opened the door to the study and saw not two strangers, but five.

I paled and froze in the doorway.

Cyle turned to face me. He didn't have to say a word. I could see he was furious and his anger was not directed at me.

Rodrick was nowhere to be seen.

Neither was Alex.

Cyle quickly walked forward and grabbed my hand and dragged me to his side.

"Is this her?" A man asked.

I know it is rude to stare, but I couldn't help myself. The man was tall and impossibly thin. He held himself like a circus contortionist. His eyes were so dark they were almost black, as was his thick, shaggy hair.

I could have handled all of that without batting an eye. But the fact that his skin was sea green, with random patches of shining scales, unnerved me. It didn't help that, when he spoke, I could see fangs.

"Yes," Cyle answered curtly.

I looked at Cyle bewildered, mouthing, "Who are all these people?"

He gave me a tiny shake of his head and a brief look of sympathy before anger once again fixed the set of his jaw. He stepped between me and the visitors.

"This is a complete breach of protocol," he seethed. "Representatives are to come one at a time and they are to provide advanced notice before hand. You all know the standards."

"These are new times Cyle," an old man with salt and pepper hair said. "They demand new protocols."

His eyes were a dull yellow and his face was grim. He wore a business suit that would not be out of place on Earth. Well, except for the sword that hung from a belt about his waist.

A boy standing behind him looked directly at Cyle, as if trying to see through him to me. The old man could have been the boy's father, they looked so much alike. Their eyes were the same muted yellow; their faces carried the same grim expression. They even wore their swords alike.

"I wasn't aware that changing times permitted the Council to break its own rules, Heril," Cyle countered.

Heril.

That was the name that Rodrick and Cyle used for the Head Chair of The Council. Which means that boy behind him must be his son, Roger.

I had read about him in the books Rodrick had forced on me. Roger was the Guardian of Archend.

I studied his face as he continued to look at Cyle. He was the only one in the room who didn't appear to be looking at me.

I instantly hated him. I can't tell you why.

"We do not have time to sit and wait," the green man said. His accent was thick and rough, like a mummy from an old B movie. "Ruok has an ever growing army. There is no time!"

He looked at me like I was prey and he was about to strike out. I briefly wondered if he would lunge at me like a snake.

"Ku'it speaks truth."

The words came from a man who looked human, sitting next to the green man. He was also dressed in a crisp, Earth-style business suit.

His sandy brown hair was combed neatly back and his eyes were a normal shade of blue. He looked in every way...normal.

He had an open notebook in front of him and a ballpoint pen rested on top of it, as if he were preparing to take notes.

I assumed he was from Earth – and yes, I know what happens when you 'assume' - since he was the only completely normal looking one in the bunch. He said his name was Jonathan Freeman.

"My realm cannot protect itself from the constant portal openings that we know are caused by Ruok," Jonathan said, addressing me directly, as if Cyle were not there. "You know Earth, Guardian. We have no weapons to fight what's coming."

"Don't appeal to her like that!" another man snapped, glaring at Jonathan from across the room with bright, green eyes. The man was dressed in attire that wouldn't be out of place in Colonial Williamsburg. His hair was graying and longer than the other men's, hanging down to his shoulders.

"William, be silent," Heril snapped.

William balked for only a moment before continuing his tirade.

"I will not be silent! It is not fair for Jonathan to use these tactics with her. None of the rest of us have the advantage of claiming her home is in our realm," he roared.

"I use no tactics on her!" Jonathan shouted back. "I am merely pointing out that our planet is not fit to stand against Ruok in battle. It's not my fault that her mother lives in my realm."

"She doesn't," I said quietly.

William stood up, ignoring me as if I didn't exist.

"You leave her mother out of this!" He snapped.

"William, sit down!" Heril shouted.

"Her mother is a resident of the realm I represent," Jonathan stood and took a step toward William, pointing a finger at his chest. "I can and will bring her into this if it'll help me provide the aid that my realm requires."

"Jonathan, will you sit down?" Heril shouted.

"Everyone just shut up!" I shouted.

I pulled away from Cyle, who was looking at me wide-eyed. For a moment you could have heard a pin drop. The attention of everyone in the room was suddenly on me.

Fine. I'll deal with it.

"My mother doesn't reside on Earth anymore, Jonathan. She's dead."

My voice shook slightly as I struggled to quell the waves of grief that suddenly welled up inside of me.

No one spoke.

Jonathan and William both sat back down. But Heril looked at me as if I were road kill.

"It is not polite to speak unless spoken to, young lady," he said curtly.

But he, too, sat back down.

I could feel the Kahl'Nar hummed against my chest as fury grew inside of me.

Control it.

I took a few deep breaths to calm myself down before I accidentally lashed out and burned that cretin to a cinder, no matter how much I may want to.

"Let's get this over with," I said between clinched teeth.

Cyle tried to grab my arm, but I pulled away from him.

"No, Cyle, I don't care that they're all here. I don't care that they don't have the guts to play by their own rules."

I hoped that dig hit home in at least some of the representatives.

"In fact, I prefer it. Now they can all run their little tests and have their little say; and then leave me be."

Cyle frowned, but he nodded nonetheless, and stepped back to join the assembled Council.

"Very well, Guardian," Heril said, leaning back in his chair and looking me up and down.

"Let the testing begin."

Chapter 55

I sat in the dark study alone for what seemed forever, but was probably only a few minutes.

After Heril's command to *Let the testing begin,* everyone had gotten up and left. Cyle had grabbed my hand and squeezed it before exiting. Roger was the last to leave. He stopped on his way out and stared at me for a long moment; just stared, then he gave me a wicked smile and left.

I stood there awkwardly by myself in the empty room, unsure of what to do next.

Was someone going to come in and administer the test?

Was someone going to come in and give me a clue about what to expect; or was I just going to stand here for the rest of the night.

Lehann and Chee had apparently performed some kind of test on me that I passed. I still wasn't sure what the test was or how I had passed it.

I was pretty sure the ACT was going to be a piece of cake after this.

Questions spun like a whirlwind in my mind. Of course, no one was there to provide any answers. You'd think I would be used to that by now.

I sat down. No sense wearing myself out, right?

Then I got bored sitting down.

I paced for a few minutes.

Looked out the window.

Sat back down.

Twiddled my thumbs.

Alright, this is just ridiculous. Test or no test, I'm not just going to sit around in here by myself all night while everyone else is enjoying themselves at my expense.

I stood and stomped to the door. I grabbed the doorknob, turned and yanked.

Nothing happened.

I pulled at the doorknob again, but it wouldn't open. The knob was twisting just fine. I could hear the tumblers turning inside, releasing the latch, but the door wouldn't budge.

I grabbed the doorknob with both hands and braced one foot against the wall like I'd seen in some B movie back in Jacksonville.

It didn't help. The door didn't move an inch.

Frustrated, I let go of the doorknob and backed up.

Okay, so I'm locked in. No need to panic.

I was on the ground floor. I could easily climb out of the window. I opened the curtains, unlocked the window and gave it a tug.

It wouldn't budge.

Surprise, surprise.

I grabbed a chair and hurled it at the window as hard as I could, surprised at my sudden strength.

The wooden chair legs splintered and broke, but the glass in window didn't even crack.

My heart sped up and my breathing was coming in quick gasps.

Okay; might be time to start panicking.

I didn't like enclosed spaces. I certainly didn't like being locked inside enclosed spaces.

I was starting to freak out a bit; pacing the room like a half-crazed tiger in a cage.

Slow down. Take a deep breath. Think this through.

I stopped pacing, closed my eyes and willed my breathing to slow; in through the nose, out through the mouth. Going crazy was not going to help me get out of the room.

I opened my eyes and walked back to the door. I grabbed the handle and, as I twisted it, I added a trickle of power from my Kahl'Nar.

The latch clicked, the bolt drew back and the door swung open.

I allowed myself a brief victory smile, but somewhere deep inside I knew this was too easy to be the real test.

When I stepped into the pitch-black hallway, the smile slid off my face.

Someone had pulled the curtains over the windows, cutting out any source of light. I looked left and right, but could see nothing and no one.

I knew the hallways of the house like the back of my hand. Not that I could really tell you what the back of my hand looks like, but Mrs. Keen, my 8th grade English teacher, would be proud of my use of simile.

Okay, focus.

I turned to the right and began to slowly creep down the hallway towards the front door, allowing my right hand to trail along the wall for support.

"Cyle?" I whispered.

My voice floated through the house like a ghost and faded like a phantom, but no one answered.

I spun around at a sudden creak behind me.

The hallway was still empty, but the door to the study was closed, even though I had intentionally left it open. The Kahl'Nar began to throb at my throat as I resumed walking toward the front door.

My right hand encountered a light switch. That meant the next door would open into the dining room. I flicked the switch a couple of times without really believing it would work.

It didn't.

But there were candles in the dining room. Reynolds liked to use them for formal occasions. He kept them in the sideboard.

Find candles, and then find Cyle.

The doorknob that granted entrance into the dining room turned easily enough and the door creaked inward. I started to go in, but paused.

The dining room had no windows whatsoever. The only available light in that room came from the antique chandelier that hung over the dining room table. Or the massive fireplace on the opposite side of the room.

Or the candles.

I tried to blink vision into my eyes, but I wasn't a cat. No amount of 'want-to' was going to help me see better in the dark than I did at that moment.

If I was going to get those candles, I was going to have to go in blind.

No problem, I've been in this dining room hundreds of times. I know where things are.

Taking one slow step at a time I left the relative security of the hallway and ventured toward the center of the pitch black dining room.

My heart was pounding into my ears. Every instinct in me yelled for me to retreat; make a run for it.

Can't give into fear; not right now. Right now I needed candles.

I bumped into something and let out an undignified squeak, then laughed when I recognized the edge of the dining table.

I used the edge of the table as a guide and fumbled around to the far side. The sideboard should be...right...there.

With one hand on the table I stretched out the other as far as it would go.

Nothing.

I knew the dining room wasn't that big. The sideboard had to be there. I stretched farther, but was loath to take my hand of the sold comfort of the table.

Then I heard the creak again.

I whipped my head around in a useless attempt to see what was behind me.

All I could make out was the outline of the dining room doorway, which seemed impossibly far away. While I watched, the door slowly began to shut.

My heart rate peaked and I started to run for it. I stumbled in the darkness; regained my footing and sprinted the last few steps.

I was too slow. I heard the lock slam into place just as I reached the door.

Now the darkness was complete.

Don't freak out, don't freak out, don't freak out, don't freak out!

I kept repeating that to myself as I slowly turned around, my unseeing eyes casting about for a glimmer or sheen of some kind of light source.

Don't freak out, don't freak out, don't freak out.

I heard the creak again.

It was inside the room with me. I could hear it breathing.

I covered my mouth, trying to muffle any sound I might make.

Creak.

It took a step.

Creak, creak, creak.

It was moving toward me.

Creak, creak, creak, CREAK!

Something or someone touched me.

Okay, freak out!

I screamed and lunged out, grabbing the wrist of whoever or whatever touched me. I'm not sure where the strength came from, but I managed to shove it, him, whatever to the side and ran.

It must have been a *him*, because I heard him swear as he struggled to regain his feet.

I slammed into the table, knocking the wind out of my lungs. I wheezed, desperately trying to draw a breath.

Anger suddenly flared up to mingle with fear. With a clarity of mind I hadn't experienced since Rodrick's faux-attack, I realized I didn't need candles.

I turned in what I hoped was the direction of the fireplace, thrust out my hand and sent out a stream of white-blue fire that flowed from my hand like a fountain of water.

My aim was true and the white-blue fire of the Kahl'Nar ignited the wood laid in the fireplace. The familiar orange glow of natural fire filled the room and I released the flow of power from my hand.

The sudden illumination left me just as blind as the total darkness. I closed my eyes for a moment to regain my sight, but stretched out with senses that were accentuated by the Kahl'Nar to find my stalker.

Nothing.

My vision return. I spun around, quickly scanning the room.

No one was there.

I looked again; under the table. There was no place in this room to hide.

There was no one in the room but me. I was alone.

The dining room was just as it had always been. Except there was no candelabra on the table. And no candles in the sideboard.

I didn't fancy stumbling around in the dark anymore. Neither was I interested in using my hand as a human torch. I figured I might need it for other purposes, like beating someone to death if I could ever get my hands on whoever was behind this.

I grabbed a chair and banged it against the table until a leg broke free. I ripped the tablecloth into long strips and wrapped them around one end of the chair leg.

My grandmother always kept a bowl of perfumed oil on the mantel. At least it was still there. I poured the oil onto the make-shift torch, giving the fabric enough time to soak up all the oil it could hold.

Then I stuck the torch into the fireplace and watched as the flames licked at the oil soaked cloth.

Funny how light can help to dispel fear.

Holding the torch in front of me, I turned toward the dining room door, and froze.

The door was standing open.

I swallowed the bile of fear that crawled up my throat and forced myself forward. I needed to find Cyle.

Now that I had a light source, I moved much more swiftly.

I can't say I was completely comforted by the light. The torch made it possible to see, but it also cast weird shadows on the wall, and I found myself jumping at the slightest flicker.

Pull yourself together, Lee. Shadows can't hurt you.

I did a quick sweep of the rooms on the bottom floor.

No Cyle.

No anybody else, for that matter.

I made my way back into the foyer and pondered the grand staircase in front on me.

My heart had taken up permanent residence in my throat; I'm sure of it.

Come on, Lee. Time to put on your Big Girl pants.

I blew out a deep breath and started up the stairs. My ears strained for the slightest sound, but the only thing making any noise was me.

As my foot hit the top step I heard it; muffled shouting.

I ran down the hallway toward the sound. I opened each door I came to. Every room was empty.

One door at the end of the hall refused to open. The muffled shouts were coming from inside.

Gathering all the courage I could muster, I added the force of the Kahl'Nar to my hand, twisted the doorknob and burst through the door.

I expected to be plunged back into darkness, but was startled by the warmly crackling fire in the fireplace that cheerfully lit the room.

My Grandmother's room.

It was just as she always kept it; neat as a pin. But there was no one inside; no evidence of the muffle shouts I had heard only seconds before.

The adjacent bathroom and closet were both empty. I even looked under the bed. No monsters hiding there.

The torch seemed superfluous in this well-lit room, and I didn't want to take a chance on setting the house on fire, so I added the still burning torch to the wood in the fireplace. The flames licked it eagerly

Frustrated, I sat on the edge of the bed to ponder my next move. A reflection on my Grandmother's bedside table caught my attention.

It came from a picture frame. I reached for it.

A smile crept across my face.

It was a photograph of my father and Cyle as boys. They looked so much alike, but there was no doubt which one was Cecil, my father. I really did look like him.

I trailed my finger over the picture and froze.

In the reflection from the glass on the picture frame I could see someone. On the ceiling.

I shot to my feet and looked up.

There, secured to ceiling, my grandmother was wrapped in a black spider web, her long, silvery hair trailing around her. Her eyes were wide in terror, her mouth bound with a thick black cord.

"Grandmother!"

I looked around for anything that would help me reach her. I shoved her chest of drawers to the foot of her bed and climbed up on it.

It was too short. I couldn't reach her. The ceilings in this house were at least twelve feet high.

Surely there was something I could use to cut her down.

Then I heard it; a low rumbling growl.

Please, don't be a giant spider.

I whirled around.

Nothing.

I looked into my Grandmother's eyes.

"Don't worry," I said. "I'm not going to leave you. I'm getting you down!"

I jumped off the chest and searched the room for anything that might extend my reach.

The fireplace.

Maybe one of the pokers.

Maybe I could use a poker to cut through the web.

I grabbed a poker, then turned around and stared into the eyes of darkness.

Chapter 56

My breath caught in my throat and the poker dropped from my hands.

The thing growled and clicked as it shuffled with liquid grace toward me. I blinked, trying to get a better look at it, but it kept shifting forms whenever the light struck it a different way, shifting from insect to predator with an oily fluidity. It was like shadow incarnate.

Why am I not moving?

I tried to make my hand reach for the poker, but my hand wouldn't respond to my mind's command. I was immobile.

The thing laughed; a gristly, grating sound that offended my ears.

Foolish girl.

Its voice was inside my head, taunting me.

You looked into my eyes; now you're mine.

I kept trying to move; my hand, my finger, anything. But I was unable to so much as blink.

The thing just kept laughing as it crawled up the wall toward my Grandmother.

No!

Grandmother began to squirm and strain against the web that bound her. Struggle as I might, I couldn't loosen the invisible cords that were wrapped around me.

The laughter grew louder, not only offending, but hurting my ears. I felt a trickle of blood seep from my ears, run down my neck, and onto my shoulders.

My ears were my last concern. I was focused solely on the thing that was inching its way towards my grandmother. It shifted with the flickering light, from a black ameba-like blob to a slithering worm to something like a cross between a spider and a praying mantis.

Watch, little girl. Its voice rang inside my head. *Watch while I consume your Grandmother.*

I wanted to scream, to cry out, to burn it to a crisp. But I couldn't move anything other than my eyes. I tore them from the horror that crept towards my Grandmother, desperate to find something, anything that might help.

That's when I felt it. The fire burning brightly behind me, casting flickering shadows across the floor, the walls, the ceiling, it was the only source of light in the room.

Shadows need light in order to exist. This creature *was* a shadow.

I heard my Grandmother's muffled scream and looked back at the ceiling. The creature was on top of her now, its black jaws opened over her neck.

I closed my eyes and focused on the fire behind me. A gust of wind whipped past me, forming a vortex. There was a pressure in the room, like an impending thunderstorm as the air surrounding the fire was sucked up the chimney, strangling the fire.

The room was plunged into complete blackness.

The thing's taunting laughter morphed into an agonized banshee scream; then it was gone. My body was free, and I fell down on my hands and knees, grateful to still be alive.

I heard a sickening thud that could only be my Grandmother dropping from the ceiling to the floor.

A fall like that could kill a person. No! I won't let her be dead. Not after all this.

I crawled on my hands and knees to where I heard the sound, and found my Grandmother's limp body. I cradled her head in my lap, rocking back and forth, like a mother with a sick infant.

No, no, no, no, no...

I cast a quick glance in the direction of the fireplace, and decided to risk it. I was prepared now. I knew how to fight it, if it returned.

In an instant the wood was blazing and light filled the room.

"Grandmother, are you all right?"

There was no one on the floor. No one's head lay in my lap.

She was gone.

Had she ever been there?

Was I losing my mind?

I stood and walked back to the fireplace that continued to burn cheerfully, crackling and laughing like it was all a big joke.

I picked up the poker I had dropped. This time I was taking a weapon with me. I would have taken the make-shift torch, but it was already burned down to coals.

Laughter rang out from the hall.

I ran to the doorway and threw open the door in time to see a dark figure running down the hall. Without thinking I shot out after it, plunging into the darkness of the hallway headfirst.

The Kahl'Nar throbbed and hummed louder with my heightened emotion. I pulled up short. I could have slapped myself. Why had I even bothered searching for candles or making that torch? I could make my own light.

I held my arms out in front of me and closed my eyes, tapping into the core of me. My arms flared up, piercing the darkness with the white fire of the Kahl'Nar.

I took off again at a trot, determined to find whoever was toying with me and give them *what for*, as my mom always said.

I was so intent on the chase that I almost didn't realize that where the hallway came to an end, there was nothing.

No floor.

No walls.

No nothing.

Just darkness as far as I could see.

I skidded to a halt at the very edge of the pit, cycling my arms back and forth to keep my balance.

Just as I was safe and turned to step back, a raven flew straight at my face. I threw up my hands to shield my face and tipped over backward, falling down into the darkness.

I reached out desperately, trying to find something to hold onto. With my concentration shattered, the light from the Kahl'Nar flickered and went out. I was picking up speed; falling faster and faster. I was growing cold; so cold; my body was growing numb. My mind was growing numb.

A distant part of my brain - the part that always seemed to maintain a dispassionate sanity in the face of insanity - whispered that this felt exactly like the time I had jumped into a portal and gone to Earth.

It might have been a comforting thought, if it hadn't been interrupted by me crashed into something hard and losing consciousness.

Chapter 57

I awoke to the smell of bacon frying, and the feeling on sunshine streaming across my face. I pulled the blanket over my head, cocoon-like.

I didn't want to wake up, even for bacon.

It was my birthday and I could sleep in as long as I wanted. So what if it was a school day. It was my birthday; Mom would let me skip.

I opened my eyes and threw the covers back.

Mom?

Mom is dead.

I shot up and looked around me. I was in my room.

Not my room at Cyle's, but *my* room. My room on Earth.

I kicked the covers off, stumbled out of bed and I took off running out of my room and down the hallway.

I stopped when I heard a woman humming.

Not just a woman; my mother; my Mom.

My Mom was humming.

I turned the corner from the hallway into the tiny kitchen.

And I saw her.

She was standing at the stove, turning the bacon with a fork, just like she always did. She was wearing her favorite, comfy, faded blue nightgown and her fuzzy, pink slippers. Her hair was thrown up in a messy bun, just like she did every morning.

"Mom?" I whispered.

She turned and beamed a glorious smile at me.

"Leeowyn. You're awake."

"What?"

"Well, hey, birthday girl," she said, pulling a slice of bacon from the frying pan and setting it on a plate. "I thought you would be asleep for another couple hours at least. Or were you just too excited to be turning fifteen?"

I frowned at her and then turned to look at the calendar hanging on the wall. The date was right, but the year was wrong. It was my birthday, but three years ago.

"Mom," I said. "I'm not turning fifteen. I'm eighteen."

She laughed her beautiful, tinkling laugh as she set a plateful of bacon on the table.

"Don't try to grow up too fast, Lee," she said.

I opened my mouth to reply but stopped when I noticed that the table was piled high with towers of pancakes and waffles, plates full of fried eggs and biscuits. Crystal pitchers of orange juice lined the table.

This was wrong. This was so wrong.

This was not my home.

And that was not my mother.

Was it?

"Sit down, sweetie, have something to eat," the woman who looked like my mother said, pulling out a chair for me.

I slowly walked over, never once taking my eyes off of her. She continued to smile, but now the smile looked wrong. It was too big, as if it was stretching her skin too tight. And her eyes were too bright, almost feverish. Her hands gripped my chair too tightly; her knuckles turning white under the strain.

You are dreaming. This has to be a dream.

I sat down, but I turned so I could watch her as she grabbed a plate and started piling it with breakfast foods. She slathered butter and syrup over everything, including the eggs.

Her hands were shaking.

Her whole body was shaking.

"Now I know your friends are coming over later today, but what did you want to do until then? Maybe we could go to the mall and I could buy you a new outfit that you could wear tonight and *run* we could get some coffee. Oh...or I know, you wanted *run* to get that new book in that series *run* you've been reading."

"Mom..." I said softly as she continued to stack more and more food onto my plate.

"Would you like to go to the beach? *Run.* We could just walk around. *Run.*"

"Mom, what are you talking about?" I asked. If I hadn't been freaked out before, I was getting seriously freaked out now.

The woman who looked like my Mom started shaking violently as she grabbed the crystal pitcher and poured orange juice all over my plate.

"The weather is so nice today. *Run.* Lee, why don't we *run* go for a walk? *Run. Run.* Run, Lee, Run, LEE RUN!"

She screamed, throwing the crystal pitcher across the room where it crashed into the wall.

"LEE, RUN! RUN! RUN!"

As the pitcher shattered, the wall splintered, cracked and started to disintegrate. The lights started flickering and grew dim as the world around us began to fade.

"RUN! RUN! RUN! LEE, RUN!

"Mom, I won't leave you!" I shouted to be heard above the roar of destruction.

The woman who looked like my mother stepped forward and took my face between her hands, forcing me to look into her eyes.

Flames tore through the house. I could feel the heat on my back. My mom's eyes were wide with horror, courage, and resolve.

"Fight them, child. I never taught you to be a quitter, and you have your father's blood in your veins. Use it. Fight them. Fight them!" she commanded as the flames climbed the walls and licked the ceiling like dragons.

Tears poured from my eyes.

"Mom, I don't know how to fight." I shouted, my voice cracking. "I don't know what to do!"

I began to cough as thick black smoke poured into my lungs. My mom leaned forward and kissed my forehead. Despite the flames raging around her, her lips were ice cold.

"Yes, you do. You are Leeowyn Blake. You are your father's daughter. And mine!" she whispered fiercely. "You know what to do, sweetheart. Now, run. Run!"

Then I was running.

The house caved in around me, flames eating at the walls and floors. I leapt to the side as the roof crumble down, blocking off the front door. I turned and ran at the window, blocking my face with my arms as I leaped through it.

I landed on the sand and rolled, glass shards embedded in the exposed skin of my arms and face. I retched the contents of my stomach onto the ground, gasping for breath as fresh air replaced the smoke in my lungs.

I stood up to watch my house burning down, but darkness enveloped the flames until all was black.

I turned to look around me and all I saw was darkness. Except for a tiny flicker of light in the distance

I began to walk toward the pinprick of light, and the closer I got, the brighter the light grew. I began to trot, then to run, desperate for the light.

The light expanded, intensified; grew bigger, brighter. It surrounded me, enveloped me.

I was in my room.

My room in Cyle's house.

But it wasn't my room. It was someone else's room. At least the room was the same, but someone else's stuff was in it.

"Hello, Leeowyn," a familiar voice said.

I turned toward the sound of the voice.

Bethany was standing against the window. Outside was completely dark, as if nothing outside this room existed at all.

"You're supposed to be dead," I said.

Bethany just looked at me, waiting for the questions she knew I must have.

"What is going on?" I asked.

Dead or not, I was thankful that this time she appeared to be alive and normal; not the bloodied, half-crazed dead looking version I had first encountered.

"This is a test," she answered.

She walked to the bed and sat down, gesturing for me to do the same. Reluctantly, I obeyed.

"This is all a test?" I repeated, frowning.

"Well, no. Not this part," she said. "I initiated this part. Falling down the pit, that was Heril's test.

It's supposed to test your sanity level, I believe. Stupid test, if you ask my opinion."

She frowned, anger obvious on her lovely face.

"You do not have time for these tests," she declared.

"No time," I sighed. "That's what everyone keeps saying. No time. I have to make a decision of cosmic proportions, yet there is no time."

I looked down at my arms and hands that were still leaking blood where I had been cut while jumping through the window.

"My mother? The fire? Was that a test too?"

"It was supposed to be. Yes. But you didn't enter his test. It was almost as if you created one of your own."

Bethany turned her bright yellow eyes to me.

"The test was another one of Heril's. He wanted to convince you that you were back on Earth. He wanted to prove that you would rather stay on Earth than be the Guardian of the Realms."

"I would," I answered without hesitation.

"Then why didn't you stay?"

"It was all wrong," I sighed. "For one thing, my mother is a lousy cook..."

My voice trailed off, my heart aching at the thought of my mother.

"In the end though, maybe she was my Mom. She tried to warn me. Was that part of the test, too?"

I wanted her to tell me that it wasn't real; that none of this was real; that my mother was still alive and waiting for me at home in Jacksonville and that when the summer came we would be together.

She didn't.

Bethany tilted her head to one side, as if listening to someone, and a slight smile curved her ruby lips.

"Well?" I asked, gripping the bedcovers hard.

She turned her attention back to me, startled as if she had forgotten I was there. Blood started to seep through the fabric of her clothes.

"Leeowyn, my time is almost done," she said, placing her hands on either side of my face, exactly as my mother had done.

I shivered at the touch of the bones that replaced the flesh of her hand.

"There are things I learned that you must know. I have kept my spirit alive long enough to be able to tell you. Now listen, and listen well..."

Chapter 58

What do you mean she's gone?"

"I don't know, Cyle," Heril snapped back, His eyes were closed and his hands rested on top of a faded sheet of paper. He opened his eyes and looked at the men surrounding him. "She was fine when she entered the test, but then she was just...gone."

Cyle jabbed his finger into Heril's chest.

"If that girl has been harmed in anyway..."

"Peace!" Jonathan demanded.

They were all seated in Cyle's office, waiting for Lee to finish the tests.

She had passed the problem solving tests that both William and Jonathan had set up. She had passed the protection test against the shadow creature that Ku'it had summoned. But when she left to follow the illusion created by Heril to test her will and sanity, she had simply disappeared.

"It's all your faults for insisting she go through this series of asinine tests in the first place," Alex snapped.

Jonathan gave him a dangerous look and Alex clamped his mouth shut, biting back the comment sitting on his tongue.

"Would you have us give ultimate power to someone who isn't mentally capable of standing up to it?" William asked, glaring at both Jonathan and Alex.

"What? You think it is your power to give?" Cyle snapped back. "You didn't give her any power, she was born with it."

He rubbed his hands over his eyes.

"That girl is the only hope in the Seven Realms, and now she's gone," he said. "And it's your fault," he pointed at Heril.

If Cyle's outburst offended the Head Seat of the Council, Heril didn't show it. He continued to roam his hands over the piece of paper in front of him. He said nothing, but the frown on his face deepened.

"What do we do now?" Ku'it hissed.

"We prepare our lands for battle," Heril answered. "And apparently we do it without aid from the Guardian of the Realms."

He opened his eyes, folded the paper and placed it back into his coat pocket.

"No, no, no!" Alex snapped.

Fury masked his face as he leaped across the room and grabbed the front of Heril's shirt. He pulled the man to his feet and shook him like a cat with a mole, shouting "You inserted her into that test; now you go in and find her!"

"Get your hands off my father!" Roger grabbed for Alex's arm. Alex turned and landed a roundhouse punch square into the middle of Roger's face, sending him reeling backward.

White-blue fire rolled over Alex's body; matched in turn by a red-hued aurora around Roger.

"Back off, Roger," Alex spat.

"Alex, sit down!" Jonathan snapped, standing and grabbing his shoulder.

"Is no one going to try and find her?" Alex shouted, looking from one person to another. His eyes stopped on Cyle, who shook his head and sighed.

"Alex, we have no way of knowing where she is," he whispered. "All we can do now is wait."

"No, Cyle," Alex snapped, his eyes growing brighter as he grew angrier. "That is *not* all we can do. We can start searching the different realms for her presence."

"We would feel her on our land," William said, sitting back in his chair and taking a sip out of a teacup. "And we don't. Do you?"

Alex looked around again, opening and closing his mouth in a vain attempt to speak.

"Sit down, Alex," Jonathan ordered in a quiet, but firm whisper.

Alex's shoulders sagged. Defeated, he sank into his chair.

"As I was saying, before I was so rudely interrupted," Heril began, when the door burst open.

Every man in the room rose to his feet as Leeowyn Blake, the Guardian of the Realms, entered the room.

Chapter 59

"Lee!" Cyle shouted.

He rushed forward and pulled me into a tight bear hug. I returned the hug, smiling and wincing at the same time.

"You're hurt!" he said, as the blood from the cuts on my exposed skin stained his hands.

"Yes," I said simply.

I walked to the peg where I had left the coat I had been wearing earlier. I reached into the pocket, pulled out Bethany's diary and set it on Cyle's desk.

"What happened to you?" Heril asked.

I turned and gave him a blank stare. It was all I could do to not strike out at him. Instead I ignored his question and turned my attention back to Cyle.

"According to the rules of the Council, I must decide which realm I will help preserve against this unspeakable evil," I said, my hand covering the book on the desk.

Cyle nodded.

"I've made my decision."

Heril scoffed.

"You don't even know if you passed our tests you impetuous little child."

I held my hand out toward him and a wall of air slammed him against the bookshelf, sending books scattering to the ground.

My arms were burning with Kahl'Nar as I walked toward Heril, holding him hard against the bookshelf.

I bent low until my eyes were level with his.

"I don't care," I spat.

The white pearl necklace at my throat hummed with glee as I spoke.

"I am the Guardian of the Realms, whether you acknowledge me or not. And you need my help, whether you want it or not. You put me through these little tests to make yourselves feel better; to make you believe you had control; to make yourself feel like you had any power at all."

I straightened in front of Heril, watching with satisfaction as he squirmed like the rat he was, trying to get free of me.

"How dare you pull my mother's spirit into your sick little game, you weasel," I bit off each word with barely controlled rage.

I sensed Roger dash toward me from behind, but a flick of my wrist and a wall of wind hurled him across the room. I never once took my eyes off Heril.

"If you ever attempt to do something like that again, to me or anyone, I will find you. And you will regret the day your mother first kissed your father. Do we have an understanding?"

The room rang with the echoes of my words. No one spoke.

Heril nodded, wide-eyed.

Cyle crossed his arms and smiled slightly. Alex made no attempt to hide his smile. Jonathan and William both looked torn between the loyalty of helping Heril and the fear of invoking my wrath if they did.

Ku'it was the first to find his tongue.

"Which realm do you chose? You said you had decided. Who will you aid in the fight against Ruok?"

The room grew deathly still as everyone leaned forward, waiting for my reply.

"No one," I answered.

Open mouthed silence greeted my words, followed by a burst of outraged chaos. Heril opened his mouth to protest, but quickly swallowed whatever retort he had planned. I let the Council members stew for a moment, then held up my hand for silence.

"Are you meaning to tell us that after all your self-proclamation of being the Guardian of the Realms, you intend to shirk your responsibilities and help no one?" William asked.

"I did not say that," I responded. "You asked who I was going to help fight Ruok. That answer is, no one. Because Ruok is not the sickness. He is only the symptom."

Confused silence reigned, and before the inevitable questions could start, I flipped open the diary and pointed to a page.

"This is the diary of the last Guardian of the Realms," I said, my eyes fixed on Cyle. "The diary of Bethany Blake. Your daughter."

Cyle's face was unreadable, but I could tell there was mingled pride and anguish behind his eyes.

"Bethany had dreams; dreams that she was someone else; dreams that she experienced through someone else's eyes. She doesn't think...she *didn't* think they were dreams. She thought she was experiencing the thoughts and actions of the person who is really behind all of this."

All eyes were on me now. I could almost hear the heartbeats of everyone in the room.

"I've been having those exact same dreams," I confessed. "Someone, or something, was trying to warn Bethany. And someone, or something, is now trying to warn me. Things are about to get much worse that you imagined."

I walked from the desk to a shelf of books removing a thick volume of genealogies of the rulers of the Seven Realms. I flipped through the pages until I found the right one, then laid the open book on Cyle's desk.

"Kathryn Rethean?" William's paled and he began to shake his head.

"The Empty Princess?"

"Who is she?" Heril asked, looking from me to William.

"She was the princess of Rethean, until she went insane and killed both her step-mother and father," William said. "She disappeared. Everyone assumed she killed herself as well since she was never seen again."

"But she didn't kill herself," I add. "And Ruok isn't a rogue Guardian. He was, in fact, never a Guardian, though he was a man of great power. He was Kathryn's personal guard. He helped her murder the royal family, and now he's helping her destroy worlds."

Everyone looked to William to confirm this, but he was just stared blankly at the book on the desk.

"According to one of the last entries in Bethany's diary, she believed the reason Ruok was so successful in his destruction was his ability to travel between realms through the portals."

I looked up at Cyle and Alex, and then every other man sitting in the room around me.

"Of course, everyone travels using the portals," Heril snapped.

I fixed him with an even look.

"Exactly," I said, and closed the diary.

"So who are you helping protect against this *Kathryn*?" Ku'it asked. "Which realm do you choose?"

"All of them," I said.

Once again chaos ensued. I let it go on for a few moments to allow the shock to pass, then held up both hands to quiet them.

"Lee, you can't help them all. It's too much," Cyle whispered.

"Oh, I'm not going to help anyone fight," I answered for everyone to hear. "I'm not strong enough to defeat her. Not by myself. Not even if I was joined by the other Guardians. Bethany tried to defeat Kathryn, and was killed. Bethany was more experienced, and more fully trained than I."

Cyle stared at me as if seeing me for the first time. I think for a moment he was seeing a girl with curly blond locks and a ruby red smile.

"Kathryn can't destroy a realm that she can't reach," I said.

I walked forward and took Alex by the hand.

"You're helping me, and Peach, too," I said. "I need people I can trust."

Alex's eyes widened at my statement; then he smiled that radiant smile that had caused me to swoon when I was still a schoolgirl on the boardwalk in Jacksonville.

Cyle wore a mixture of deep-rooted sorrow mingled with pride on his face.

"Just what is it you intend to do, Guardian," Heril asked, and I could tell it grated for him to address me so.

"We are going to shut down the portals," I replied. "All of them."

Epilogue

I ignored any other outburst that followed as I walked out of the room.

I pulled Alex behind me. The Kahl'Nar, my Kahl'Nar, hummed a victory song as we continued down the hall and out the door.

Peach turned to look at us, a mask of worry breaking off of her face as she saw me emerge mostly unscathed.

"Lee! You're alright!" she shouted as she wrapped me in an energetic hug.

I looked from Alex to Peach to the bright moon casting light over the white field of fluffy snow. I glanced up at the window of my room, and thought I caught the eyes of a curly headed blonde girl who had once been in the same position as me.

The girl in the window raised her hand. A glowing, white pearl pendant hung around her throat. I think she nodded at me, and smiled.

A cloud passed over the moon, bathing my window in darkness; and she was gone.

Thoughts of impending war drifted away with the swirling snow that wafted around me.

I turned my attention to Perenniel le Fay, the last Guardian of Haven.

"Yeah, Peach, I am all right," I said.

I took her hand in my free one and smiled, really smiled, for the first time in a long, long time.